(Louis Weber)
Publisher Chicago

The Holocaust Chronicle

From

The Women's Press Ltd (Manufactured in China)
34 Great Sutton Street, London EC1V 0DX

Gave
Book to
every single person
250-3? a cut

Introduction —

Wants to give away to people
teaching the Holocaust

Well layed out
Large print

The Shoah Foundation Grants
Holly Jacobsen — Reviews
Spielberg's Promise   grant
4.5.y.   proposals

Rosemary Jackson was born in Yorkshire in 1951. She read English and European Literature at the University of Warwick and in 1978 completed a doctorate for the University of York. After various lectureships in literature and cultural studies, including five years at the University of East Anglia and six years at Bristol Polytechnic, with teaching visits to West Germany, Holland and the United States, she left academia in 1988 to devote her time to more creative activities. Her critical study *Fantasy: The Literature of Subversion* was published in 1981.

Fascinated by unconscious processes, and familiar with a wide range of theory, she has experienced a number of 'alternative' therapies in Britain and abroad, and has spent some time training and practising in analytic psychotherapy.

She now writes full-time and lives in the West Country.

ROSEMARY JACKSON

The Eye of the Buddha

and Other Therapeutic Tales

 The Women's Press

Many thanks to Sarah Lefanu for her insight
and support.

First published by The Women's Press Ltd 1991
A member of the Namara Group
34 Great Sutton Street, London EC1V ODX

British Library Cataloguing in Publication Data
Jackson, Rosemary
  The Eye of the Buddha
  I. Title
  823.914 [F]

  ISBN 0–7043–4255–3

Typeset in 10½ pt Bembo by Input Typesetting Ltd,
London
Printed and bound in Great Britain by
Cox & Wyman Ltd, Reading

For John Harlow

Grateful acknowledgment is made for permission to quote from the following:

Excerpts from *Anna Freud* by Elisabeth Young-Bruehl. Reprinted by permission of Macmillan.

Excerpt from *The Life and Work of Sigmund Freud* by Ernest Jones. Reprinted by permission of Chatto and Windus.

Lines from 'In Memory of Sigmund Freud' by W. H. Auden. Reprinted from *Collected Poems* by W. H. Auden by permission of Faber and Faber Ltd.

The last sentence of the story 'The New Jerusalem' is a quotation from Ode 23 of Jelaluddin Rumi's *These Branching Moments*, translated by John Moyne and Coleman Barks, © 1988, and is used by permission of Copper Beech Press.

Excerpt from Melanie Klein, *Love, Guilt and Reparation and Other Works 1921–1945*. Reprinted by permission of The Hogarth Press.

Excerpts from W. R. Bion, *Learning from Experience*. Reprinted by permission of Mark Paterson and Associates for the Estate of W. R. Bion and by permission of H. Karnac Books Ltd.

In 'Hideous Progeny', the lines on pp. 174–5, 'She knew the grief . . . ' and 'The mother . . . ', are from 'Cassandra (Un)Bound: An Examination of the Fiction of Mary Shelley', by Barbara Couchman, an unpublished thesis (University of York, 1989), with thanks to Barbara. On p. 178 the lines beginning 'Demeter, wandering through many lives . . . ' are adapted from 'To Demeter' in *Fausta* by Anna Taylor, Rivelin Grapheme Press, 1984. The original reads: 'I have wandered/through so many lives/Now with Demeter/a mother, turned from the sun/black-grained shadow/shrinking.' This adapation is made by permission of the author. The quotes on p. 181 beginning: 'Things as they are', 'The earth is not earth', and 'That I may reduce the monster', are short extracts from 'The Man with the Blue Guitar' by Wallace Stevens and are reprinted by permission of Faber and Faber Ltd from *Collected Poems* by Wallace Stevens.

The other day while we were talking, Papa
and I agreed that analysis is not a business for
mere humans, but that one needs to be
something much better – who knows what!
It is not the analytical work that is so difficult,
for one can accomplish that with some human
reason, it is the everlasting dealing with human
fates. That comes even more to the fore if one
is not dealing with real pathology.

Anna Freud to Lou Andreas-Salomé,
19 August 1926

The unworthiness of human beings, even of
analysts, has always made a deep impression
on me, but why should analysed people be
altogether better than others? Analysis makes
for *unity*, but not necessarily for *goodness*.

Sigmund Freud

I am so glad that you have begun to be a bit
of a psychoanalyst. There is no time or age
limit to the pleasure and benefit ones gains
from looking at oneself and at other people
that way. So far it is the only thing I know
which makes this difficult life easy.

Anna Freud to Max Schiller,
18 February 1946

He wasn't clever at all: he merely told
the unhappy Present to recite the Past
    like a poetry lesson till sooner
  or later it faltered at the line where

long ago the accusations had begun,
and suddenly knew by whom it had been judged,
    how rich life had been and how silly,
  and was life-forgiven and more humble,

able to approach the Future as a friend
without a wardrobe of excuses, without
    a set mask of rectitude or an
  embarrassing over-familiar gesture.

W. H. Auden, from 'In Memory of Sigmund Freud'

Contents

Learning the Signs of the Zodiac

Driving home in the rain, reflections from the day moving from side to side with the rhythm of the windscreen wipers. It was all about boundaries, she thought, boundaries that wouldn't fail. Everyone in search of a safe container, a cot that wouldn't fall when the wind blew, indefinite holding, endless love. Yet hating the need, fighting it, stabbing you in the arm as you reached out a hand. Such a feat, to hold the attack as well as the longing, she wondered if she'd ever manage it, as she manoeuvred the car into its narrow parking space between the patio and outside walls, forced to squeeze past profligate honeysuckle with all her packages, like an overladen mountain goat. It must be possible.

Tired from the long day and drive, she dumped bags and files on the kitchen table, relieved to notice the smell of cooking and the clean room. Frankie was stretched out on the lounge floor, arms clasped behind her head, listening to what sounded like Joan Armatrading.

'I've not heard that before, have I?'

'Shouldn't think so, it's just come out – I treated myself to it today.'

'Did you go into Wells, then?'

'Yep. Painted all morning, then I got bored, so I drove around, did some shopping and things, bought this and some cigarettes . . . '

'Oh, Frankie, I thought you'd stick to your resolution this time.'

'. . . and cooked a delicious vegetarian bake.'

'Yes I noticed, it smells wonderful.' Was she imagining guilt and anger in Frankie's cursory replies? 'Any post?'

'Just a couple of letters for you – they're on your desk.'

The way Frankie reached for a cigarette made it clear she was more interested in a solitary time with Armatrading's *Secret Secrets* than desultory talk, and Harriet knew better than to push beyond the curtness into confrontation.

'I'll go and shower before supper, then.'

'Fine.'

She could see Frankie watching slow spirals of smoke rising towards the ceiling where it might reach her. Why was she doing it? Frankie knew she hated having smoke in the house, but whenever there was any conflict, there would be this defiant return to the weed, as if exhaling black rage here would successfully pollute her white-lunged nuclear family. It was almost a year now since Frankie had moved in, still waiting for some viable sponsorship or grant aid for her painting, and the more obvious her need for support, the more anger came between them.

'Don't you see, Harriet, I need to be independent. Time's running out and here I am, far from my blue Californian skies, sinking into rural anonymity like some West Country idiot.'

No matter what techniques of persuasion Harriet had tried, she'd not been able to convince her of the need for more patience or a merely temporary dependence.

'Any phone calls, Frank?' She put her head around the door as the music faded between tracks.

'No, there weren't, though I have to admit I forgot to put the answer machine on when I went out.'

'Bloody hell, Frankie, you *know* how important it is. I was expecting a client to ring about a session tomorrow, to let me know if they could make it.'

'Well, why don't you phone them?'

'You know that's not on. This one's someone I never phone at home. Anyway, I think they're still away, that's why they were going to let me know.'

Frankie's shrug suggested a hopeless horizon, beyond caring for the intricacies of therapeutic borderlines, but Harriet was too tired with her own anger, or angry with her own tiredness, to call up mother courage yet again.

'OK Francesca, so you're pissed off at being doorkeeper round here. I get the message.'

And the evening meal, whether seasoned with simple love or guilt, remained untouched.

Ben hadn't told anyone he was in therapy. He had convinced himself that by keeping Sheila in the dark he was protecting her from his ambivalence towards their marriage, similarly shielding himself from what he feared would be hostile incomprehension and attack should he tell any of his colleagues in the media. Their left-wing allegiances made them suspicious of anything as individualistic and introverted as psychotherapy, whatever the variety. It was all lumped together in a sack labelled 'ideologically unsound', its perpetrators 'rip-off merchants', its victims as 'duped' as Marx's masses by religion, so he'd become quite practised at dissimulation. Evading their questions, he suspected they had come to read his intermittent Friday absences as symptoms of a juicy affair, and he was quite happy to collude with that: there were *some* responses to feeling wrecked inside that were not only allowed, but attractive, even on the left.

This week he'd managed to compress his London business into two days instead of three, and so could afford a morning out of the cutting room. Thank God the weather was good, it made the drive a pleasure, especially on his first visit to the new venue. He flipped over the cassette – Brahms felt more suitable for these country lanes than Kurt Weil – and drove appreciatively, his arm draped over the open window. Yes, it was a lovely part of the world, verdant, secluded, she had good taste, no wonder she was moving her practice down here. There was that delicious little Norman church, which she had said was almost opposite her entrance, yes this must be the driveway, mind the honeysuckle. And splendid hanging baskets, dripping with bright blue lobelias, tobacco plants, petunias, huge pots of scarlet geraniums, the patio studded with colour and perfume. He wondered vaguely if her other clients could be as flexible as him with their time, but he never wanted to dwell too much on admitting she *had* other clients. Irrational though it was, he wanted her to himself. For that hour she was his, that was what mattered, for himself alone, and in that time no one else had any claims on her. Meanwhile, just sit in the car and wait, mustn't be too early, that was even more invidious than being late, as if you were asking for too much again, being impatient, greedy: he knew how all the bad symptoms were read.

The church bell was chiming in unison as he rang the old-fashioned door-pull – exactly eleven, good timing – and imagined it echoing through the house. Rather disconcerted when there was no reply, for Harriet usually answered immediately, he wondered if he did have the right time after all. Yes, he was sure they'd agreed eleven for the whole of that month whilst he was editing the documentary, despite the change of place, he remembered that. Surely she'd not forgotten? She couldn't be ill, Harriet didn't get ill, but maybe she'd broken her leg or her back in there and was lying in the house, just beyond those walls somewhere, dying. Harriet was dying . . . Hang on Ben, hold it, save all that infantile stuff a little longer, you're not in the session yet, and when he rang the bell again a few minutes later, he could hear it resounding, like an Indian gong in an empty room.

'Oh.'

A young woman was suddenly in front of him, evidently annoyed, with streaks of paint up her arms, a hammer in one hand while the other held tacks that had been in her mouth. Angry at being interrupted, her eyes were distracted, focused elsewhere and her abrupt 'What do you want?' was more of an impatient reprimand than a question.

'Oh, sorry, I'm . . . I seem to have disturbed you.'

'You sure have, I was just in the middle of stretching a canvas and it's difficult enough without interruptions, holding it with one hand and pulling it with the other.'

Without thinking what he was saying, his automatic response, 'Could I help you?' provoked another irate dismissal. He'd obviously got the wrong house.

'God, here's this guy I don't know from Adam, he rings the bell and asks to come in, in broad daylight. You think I was born yesterday? Miss Naïve's my middle name? Come *on*, now.'

It was a West Coast accent, used to standing up to men, how different from Sheila.

'Well, I'm sorry it seems like that. I offered because I made canvases up myself, years back, when I was at art school, and I know how tricky it is, especially with large sizes.'

'You can say that again, I'm trying an eight by twelve, feet that is, and it's puckering all over the goddam place.'

She was actually looking him in the face, a smile at last. Beautiful eyes, long auburn hair tied up untidily in a pony tail with what looked like a broken shoe lace. Skimpily dressed in shorts and a tiny black T-shirt, a staple gun lodged in her pocket, here was someone who didn't mind mess. Mess, that reminded him. 'I'm sorry I disturbed you, anyway. I'm looking for Whitney House, I thought this was it, but I must have got it wrong.'

'No, you've not got it wrong, this *is* Whitney House. You haven't come about landscaping the garden, have you? I thought that was going to be on Friday.'

'No, no, I've come to see a Dr Weaver.'

'Not for therapy?'

'Er, yes,' hesitating at the unprecedented admission, 'yes, for therapy.'

'Oh my God, you're not one of her *patients* are you?'

'Well, I prefer to use the word *client*, but yes, I am.'

'Oh my God, and here I am chatting away to you. God, I'm sorry. But she doesn't work here at the moment, she's still working in the city, in Exeter. She's there today. Are you a new . . . client?'

'No, no. I'm an old hand, but I understood she was moving her practice down here.'

'She is, but not just yet, we've got to get the extension and garden finished so she can see people separately from the house. *Boundaries*, you know,' they shared a grimace and half-laugh at the word, 'and it'll be another month probably before it's finished. Then she'll be working here.'

'Jesus, I got it all wrong, I can't have been listening right.'

'That's usually the therapist's problem!'

Their mutual laughter surprised him, shouldn't he be feeling more disappointed?

'That's right.' A pause, then, 'Oh well, these things happen. It's an hour wasted, but I can't get back to Exeter in time for the session now. I did try to phone yesterday lunchtime to check, but there was no answer.'

'Hey, I'm sorry, that's my fault. I forgot to put the machine on.'

There was a suggestive silence. Neither seemed ready to terminate the encounter nor did they know how to proceed.

'I think you'd better phone Harriet to let her know you're not coming. She hates sitting there for an hour waiting.'

'Yes, I should. Is there a phone box nearby?'

'In *this* backwater? You must be joking. Come in and use ours.'

'Are you sure?'

'Sure, come on in. I'm Frances, by the way.'

'Well thank you very much. Ben . . .' they mock-formally shook hands, '. . . and, Frances, I know I shouldn't offer this, really, but I would be more than happy to give you a hand with that canvas.'

'Well, it is *highly* improper, in the light of the *boundaries*' – was that look seductive or sardonic? – 'but OK thanks, I think it would be prudent not to mention this to Harriet, though.'

'Of course not. Mum's the word,' entering the house as the church clock chimed the quarter.

'Hi, Harriet,' Frankie's voice was cheerful, excited, 'I'll be down in a minute, just priming a couple of canvases.'

'No hurry.' Despite inner resolutions not to over-react, Harriet still found it an inordinate relief when Frankie gave her a positive welcome. Lifted her heart. Must be to do with Mother's unpredictable moods when she got in from school, she told herself, uncorking some wine, emptying large black olives into a dish.

'Hi, Harriet, how was your day, honey?'

'Frustrating. Four heavy sessions and two clients who failed to turn up. Drives me crazy, that.'

'Well, they pay you anyway, don't they?'

'Oh, yes, they pay all right, but that's not the point. You're all geared up to attend to their misery or joy or dreams or whatever and then all you get is this inscrutable silence that you can't actually *interpret* till the next session: you don't know if it's unforeseen circumstances, illness, resistance, anger, or what. Everything goes on hold, and you're left on your own, struggling with an intractable unconscious for an hour, not even knowing who or what the enemy is. It's bloody tedious.'

'Why don't you just have fun, read a book or something, play the radio? Maybe they're just having time out, enjoying themselves.'

'But that's not what they *pay* me for. I'm the one who has to be there in readiness for the bad times. And they have the right, theoretically at least, to come along for the last five minutes or even for one minute. It's their time. This morning, twenty minutes into the session, one phoned to say he'd got held up with his film editing work, and that surprised me – he's always worked to deadlines, but never actually cancelled before. Something else is going on there, I suspect

Seeing at last what he can get away with. But anyway, enough of me moaning. How's your day been?'

'Do I get a hug first?'

'Sure, come here.' It was a relief to hold and be held again after last night's freezing.

'Sorry about yesterday, Harry.'

'It's OK, I understand. I'm sorry too.' Enjoying the smell of turps and paint, she leant back her head against that warm stomach as Frankie stood behind her chair. 'So what did you get up to today?'

'Stretched some canvases . . .'

'Oh, *damn*, I meant to help you with those last night.'

'No, don't worry, I managed all right, then I reworked some of the abstract painting. It's almost done now. Do you want to see?'

The canvas picked up the last evening light in the studio, violent streaks of geranium pink searing the sky like slashings in a blue garment.

'Fantastic colours, Frankie' – abstract splashes of magenta and orange, rich and heavy – 'it reminds me of a Helen Frankenthaler.'

'It's meant to.'

'Superb. How about a kiss as well?'

'That depends on how your nicotine tolerance is today!'

'Why, how many have you had?'

'Only three.'

'Well, I reckon I can stretch to kissing a threesome mouth!'

'What about supper?'

'Oh, that too, everything. I could do with some simultaneous gratification around here, it's been a hard week.'

'No holds barred?'

'No holds barred! No boundaries!'

She felt pleased as she wrote up her characteristically cryptic notes after the session. Good, she couldn't help feeling jubilant, good, maybe Ben is progressing at last into adult sexuality. I even feel a little jealous, so if I'm picking up the countertransference correctly, this means he is wanting me to envy his sexual encounter with another woman. It feels it might happen for real at last, maybe he'll be able to leave that stifling marriage after all. Not that I should want that, of course, you're not responsible for client *progress*, Harriet, only for therapeutic *process*. 'Remember, my child, should you lose your head, The first golden rule of Bion, Wilfred: When time with your client sets your heart on fire, Relinquish your own memory – and desire.' Still, he was the only male client she'd ever *really* fancied, the only one she'd been seriously tempted to break the boundaries for and fall into his bloody arms in week three or four. The only one who corresponded to *her* phantasies. But she'd controlled that impossibility, trying harder than ever to undo her compulsory heterosexuality, and had committed herself to relationships with women much more deeply than before, which was when she'd decided to live with Frances.

What punishment though, she thought, throwing a cushion back on to the couch, what masochism, to *really* desire someone, and have to tell them that their desire is mother transference and your own that it's merely countertransference, and ne'er the twain shall meet. *Great*! What would poor Tristan and Iseult have done if they'd met in therapy? No moonlit lovings there, my friend, only analysis, only the *understanding* of desire, damn it, only some bloody omniscient Frenchman like Jacques Lacan telling you that desire and love are nothing but projective mechanisms, seeking to fill the gap, therefore replaceable by any other. Love objects, interchangeable. She understood it, yes she understood the theory, and understanding was some consolation when all around was chaos and hardly anyone understood why they did anything, but her heart felt as if it didn't believe any of it, not a word.

She looked at the clock, only a few minutes left before the next hour, and hurriedly jotted down a few words. Ben P, session 123, battles with guilt at transferring sexual desire from mother and me to young woman artist he met through friend. Scared it will kill me, destroy my care for him. Sweating badly on palms of his hands. Nervousness. Fear. Something unsaid? Note my jealousy. This is a real challenge for me. If I can transcend the countertransference here and *not* want him any more, let him go, I'll be freeing him and myself. My loss his gain. Await the next episode without desire or suspense. Think on Bion: want nothing, want nothing, want nothing.

'Harriet, I shall be away for five days at the end of the month. I'm going to London to have an interview with one of these grant bodies, and I'll try a few galleries.'

'That's fantastic, Frankie, I do hope you get something, you deserve it. It looks like there's going to be a mass exodus that week though, two clients are going to be away then too. Time on my hands.'

'You can cope with it, Harry, you're a tough old boot.'

'Yes I can cope with it, being on my own. But is survival enough I ask myself,' stroking Frankie's long hair ruminatively. 'I guess I can cope with anything, with all the work I've done on loss, but,' twisting Frankie's locks around her fingers like cats' cradles, '*grant not nature more than nature needs . . .* '

'What's the matter?'

'Oh, nothing, I'm just a bit morose at the moment, PMT, I expect. Don't take any notice.'

'You shouldn't be such a workaholic. How about a drink?'

Something was amiss, but she couldn't put her finger on it. Frankie was moving away from her, subtly excluding, yet her latest paintings were brighter than usual, her brush strokes larger. She'd reverted to acrylics for speed, yet Harriet had a sense of something having died, of the sun being made of gold foil. All the difficult hesitancy which had been there in the canvases she did last autumn was missing from these louder statements, yet Frankie flared up when she questioned her, as if she were trying to deny her something.

'You know, Harriet, sometimes I almost believe you *want*

people to be miserable to keep you in business. There's not enough *joy* in you, not enough *fun*. What's wrong with being happy?'

'Nothing, sweetie, nothing when it's for real.' But at the same time a look crossed Frankie's face which traced in the very world which she was missing. It was whatever she had first loved in her, something so hard to give a name to, around listening, not-knowing, truth. It was that sudden willingness to stop time for half a day to paint a tangerine, but then it was gone, and Harriet was left holding an image of possibility she wondered if she'd dreamed.

The phone call, when it came, was anonymous, left on the answering machine during her last Friday morning in the Exeter premises. It simply stated the facts: that Frances and Ben had been seen in London at a party with people who knew Harriet, and that in view of the professional repercussions, the caller thought it better she should be told the raw truth. That was all. She almost jotted down the details and time of the call along with other messages about sessions and meetings, so automatically did the heart try to defend itself with indifference when it sensed life at stake. Businesslike, she cleared the room, depositing on the rear seat of the car her leaving present of tall evergreen shrubs, their proud endurance utterly at odds with the defeat she now felt in the ending, and drove back to the cottage. Indifferent now to scratching the bodywork and angry at the display of needs by wilting plants, she slammed the door of the unloaded car behind her.

Searching through Frankie's room, newly unmindful at invading that sacrosanct space, she took some untipped cigarettes, and lay on the lounge floor, her feet on an antique armchair, inhaling the poisonous heat. The house was quiet, it was early evening, darkness slowly descending. So, she thought, so. This is how Troilus felt, this is what betrayal truly tastes like. So, so. A double betrayal. Frances and Ben. Sister and brother, mother and father, daughter and son, lover and beloved both. So, so. You set yourself up to contain difficulty, but then it's assumed you're immune to the ordinary blows of life, you can take anything. She can cope, Harriet can manage. 'She's a tough old boot.' Would it always be a case of having to mother kids catching up on their delinquency? What was it all about? What was it *for*?

She stared at the cushions she could hurl at the wall, bumper packs of tissues that could soak her tears, simulated artifacts she could stab. Oh, she knew how to rage, to weep, to kill, the options stood in front of her like cardboard cut-outs, which to choose, which self to be. She could hunt the two of them down, denounce them in their act, show valid feelings, exemplify the perfect confrontation. *When the wind blows, the cradle will fall, down will come cradle, baby and . . .* But the training was about not falling. The training was about being buffeted by the wind and not a leaf being lost, it was about being Lear in the midst of the storm and not going mad. Not the formal training, no, but the inner training, the path that had brought her to this spot: it was about not breaking, not collapsing, enduring rough edges.

She imagined being the perfect therapist. She could envisage the whole scenario, saying nothing, withholding, waiting, containing. She would be omniscient, pretending ignorance, letting their drama unfold as it had to, as they tested out their good mother to see if she would break, and she had no choice but to be strong. For they were attacking her to see if she could tolerate their mess. Ben would tell her about his affair, and she would listen, non-judgmentally. He would feel guilty, ashamed, and disappointed, without knowing exactly why, for he still hadn't got what he wanted, and would feel he had lost the right to her love. Meantime, Frankie's anger at what she thought was Harriet's ability to unstick herself, to keep away from the glue of ordinary needs, would be thrown back at her with a vengeance, and she would tell her she wondered if she was not *really* heterosexual after all, and make excuses to leave. She too would be confused, guilty in her defiance, unable fully to mourn what she was losing with Harriet for in a way she had never fully *had* it. Too hard to stay with the slow unfolding, she had rushed and grabbed at life like a glossy technicolour soap opera and it could not but taste synthetic, garish.

So there we are, Harriet thought, another shooting star burns out. Time after time, this incredible playing out, this interminable acting out of compulsive patterns in the striving towards intimacy. See how deeply embedded our unconscious stencils go. Even now, they are repeating one variant amongst many, 'naughty' children having sex whilst mother's not looking, gambling with the chance of being caught and reprimanded. But how weary she was of it all, these patterns, compulsions, repetitions, how she wished they *would* confine themselves to normal working hours. For meantime, what about *her*, where did it leave her, hanging in the dark? Knife us, do we not wound? Did not healers bleed?

It was late now, but she couldn't sustain all this understanding alone. She phoned her supervisor, knowing she would be compassionate, even at that hour.

'My goodness,' her voice was warm, no she didn't mind being interrupted, 'that's a heavy one. Very painful for you at present, very painful. What acting out there, what acting out. He wants you, but he cannot have you, so he sleeps with your lover, the one who does not respect the same boundaries. You are not there when he goes to your house for his hour so he is lost, he has to find another there in your place. It is classic, see how he phones you on a Friday morning, the same time as his usual session, to make confession, so intense is his guilt. Classic, my dear, it could have been invented by Freud himself.'

'Well,' Harriet retorted, 'I wish Sigmund Freud would keep himself out of my private affairs. It's quite bad enough having him scripting things *inside* sessions, let alone outside.'

'But my dear,' Martha's Polish accent intoned the obvious, 'the unconscious does not work by rote. It is far too crafty for that. It wants to get everywhere, to take over. Now here we see that it has slipped out, it has escaped the chain and gone on the loose, and we must learn to tie it up again before it does more harm.'

'I know, I know,' Harriet groaned, 'don't say it. Don't say it, "It's all to do with boundaries. Your boundaries slipped." '

They shared a laugh of familiarity.

'There you are, you see, you know what it's about, you take the very words out of my mouth. Now, you go to bed, perhaps with some brandy and sugar, and tomorrow maybe you will be able to see the amusing side of things, too! You come and have an hour with me on Sunday and we talk about this further, yes?'

'OK, Martha, I'll see you on Sunday.'

'Don't forget, Harriet, everything has a meaning, if you look far enough, everything has a meaning. This has happened to make us alert to some meaning, for you, for them. Do not despair. We will find the meaning.'

There was still some residual bitterness lurking in the room as she threw the cigarettes in the bin, poured a large brandy and soda, played some well-worn baroque concertos. Everything has a meaning, damn it, everything has a goddam meaning, you can't even despair when you're a therapist, you have to understand, the catch just slipped and introduced stinking foxes of pain and loss, you have to *understand*. But by the time she'd watered the window-boxes and rescued the shrubs from the car, at two or three a.m., some irrepressible hunger and acceptance of life, with all its dark alleys, was resurfacing.

Martha was right, it *was* a bit of a farce, after all, this tragic to-ing and fro-ing, this movement in and out of bodies and hearts in the frenzied attempt to find a love that holds. Meeting, love, desire, deception, betrayal, loss, healing, tragedy, farce, it all came round again and again, there was no end to it. Perhaps that's what Martha had meant, that she would see the funny side to it, absurdity, no one's immune. What else could you expect, being alive and human? It was all par for the course. You had to go on. Not with that inexorable determination that was the tight-lipped grip of so many who had suffered, no, that grim-faced stoicism of surviving for survival's sake was almost as destructive as not going on at all. But a way that was lighter, that cared for quality, that knew about mistakes.

There was no point trying to evade, transcend. Life at its best had no short-circuits, didn't cheat. You had to live. You had to be involved. Maybe celibacy *would* be better than this mess, but who would trust you if you were ice not fire, if you were *outside* the human? You had to let the bough bend, to be touched by the storm yet not disturbed. It was what had to be done, the real work, for the wind in the world was blowing strong.

All therapy offered was a holding still in the midst of all that chaotic movement in and out and to and from – self, mother, other, object, me, not-me, in here, out there, and back again and out again – the endless play. It was just an answer to the search for something that contains, that holds, somewhere for hate and love to come to know themselves, to balance out, and so, eventually, be still. But that came afterwards, the stillness. For now, there was just endless movement around, towards.

Brandy in hand, leaning out of the open bedroom window and watching a horseshoe bat skid past, she stared at the clear night sky, with the church clock chiming the quarter hours. How little she knew, she thought. Who was it wrote the bigger boundaries? Who held the firmament? Who dreamed this dream that we're compelled to act, bringing unconsciousness to life? Was Freud's phrase more true than he knew, his *future of an illusion*, was that what all time was, a dream? The very boundary of the universe a whim? 'Maybe tomorrow you'll see the joke, Harriet.' 'Don't take it so seriously, you need more fun.' Maybe that *was* the joke, the illusion that they read so earnestly, the waking dream they acted out as unconsciously as all their half-known deeds. Who would draw out the meaning of *this* dream?

But it was tomorrow now, dawn filtering through black beeches behind the church and brandy sending her to sleep. That's quite enough drunken philosophy from a woman disappointed in love, she insisted, shaking her head ironically as she closed the latch. Get thee to bed, Harriet Weaver, get thee to bed: you don't even know the names of the bloody stars.

Rough Edges

Bruce tilted backwards in the leather chair, sucking his Parker pen. He liked Fridays, he saw only three patients before lunch, made a few notes on the week's sessions, then spent the afternoon with Dick, a colleague, swimming and doing some weekend shopping. This half-hour before anyone arrived was his equivalent of meditation, a time to compose himself, to take a step back from identification and involvement. He looked around his consulting room, light and spacious, the couch under the window, his swivel chair half-facing the walnut tree in the courtyard, neatly tucked away from the chaotic traffic of Wimpole Street at the front. It was a comfortable, neutral space, protected but alert, able to deal with any spillage, any psychic tempest that might blow through.

His Friday sessions concentrated on patients with food issues. There were three at present: 'anorexic' Nina, a hollow-eyed twenty-year-old; Michelle, a high-powered business woman in her early forties, whose 'bulimia' was disclosed to him alone; and Sally, one of his few working-class cases, unemployed and tormented by what she described as 'a syndrome of compulsive overeating'. Despite their specific qualities and differences, he enjoyed associating them together, for he had not yet entirely rid himself of an old tendency to classify and identify *symptoms*, though it was precisely such a narrow focus which had squeezed him out of the psychiatric wing of the National Health Service into private practice. Now he convinced himself that the pleasure he took in comparing and contrasting these women was one of understanding the relationship between their social backgrounds and inner turmoil. The wider canvas that came from exploring external as well as internal conditions fitted his radicalism nicely and supported his sense of justification in accusing many analysts and therapy practitioners of being insufficiently political, even reactionary, in their stance.

Not that this position kept him out of trouble. On the contrary, even on the home front, he and Marilya still had frequent differences of opinion about the consequences of his political convictions, especially financial ones.

'Look, Bruce, you're a very experienced doctor, offering professional treatment. I don't see why you should put yourself on a par with these wet-behind-the-ears therapists that are burgeoning all over the place, even charging less than them in some cases and selling yourself short, just because you object to the politics of the system.'

She still hadn't quite forgiven him for refusing a major consultancy in one of the central London hospitals and opting instead for this bizarre autonomy of unpredictable private practice. He could understand her feeling cheated, after her years of supporting him through the mazes of medical hierarchy and promotion, only to see him refuse the last hurdle like some thoroughbred bucking the final post at the National. But it was a strain, nevertheless, withstanding all her recriminations.

'I don't sell myself short, Marilya. I feel we have an ample income from my work. I just choose to see some people for a reduced fee.'

'Why? They could go to cheaper therapists. You get what you pay for, you know. I really don't see why you have to subsidise people on the dole. You're just like some overgrown schoolkid, playing Robin Hood, stealing from the rich to give the poor.'

'But it's only us I'm stealing from.'

'Exactly.'

'But it's on such a small scale, Marilya: I only have half a dozen lesser fee spaces, you know that.'

'That half a dozen makes the difference of several hundred pounds a month, though.'

'And it makes the difference of more than that for the patients, you know.'

'Why can't they see someone on the NHS?'

'Marilya, we've been here before. You know how I feel about NHS practice. I wouldn't wish it on my worst enemy. The waiting, the condescension, the short-term treatment, the medical model, behaviourism, you know my objections. Let's not go over it all again, *please*.'

And they would be left with a characteristic stalemate: the compromise of a resentful, resigned silence.

Such debates usually happened around summer holiday times, when vacation trips had to be more modest than before, or like now, in the depths of winter, when many of Marilya's female friends were bribing themselves through marital boredom with expensive new clothes or cars. But he wanted to believe that Marilya was above those mercenary inducements. He understood her yearning for wealth and streamline security, for she had come from a lower middle-class home, her once working-class parents weakened by the fear of recurring poverty, and by a kind of emotional and social bewilderment. All the opulence in the world would never completely repair for her that inner sense of vacancy, that fear of falling back to not having enough, panic at the prospect of sinking into the gutter. Even their empty wine bottles she would jokingly refer to as the empties. 'See how far we've come,' she'd say, their status measured now not in the number of milk bottles outside the house, but in the rows of green and clear glass that had carried Claret and scented Muscadet. He couldn't ascribe blame. He knew he would find some means of pacifying her, for despite their increasingly frequent disagreements, neither of them could afford to look at them too closely. Over a decade and a half they had constructed a pleasant, solid life together and they didn't want it keeling over in its very ripeness.

This morning's session with Nina left him feeling big and loud, brash at being alive and at having had those wonderful peaches and fresh croissants for breakfast. He saw her as quite mythical, conjuring up snow queens, white horses, polar coldness, for she had this extraordinary facility to avoid all food that was not white. At first, he'd been dumbfounded at how she survived, were there really that many white foodstuffs? But her ingenuity had enlightened him: measured amounts of white rice, white bread, white fish, potatoes, cottage cheese, mooli, egg-whites, and for 'pudding' yoghurt, semolina, cream, milk, meringues, coconut, ice-cream, bananas, peeled apples, sugar mice, mints, icing sugar, bars of white chocolate. Her inventiveness astounded him. She had lived on this diet of purity for five years, with all the social repercussions it caused, and he often tried to imagine what it must be like, a planet of winter. No colour. Little change of texture. No crunchy carrots, no juicy green salad, no red tomatoes, no peppers, strawberries, mangoes, papaya, oranges, lemons, no blue cheese, red claret, let alone a bleeding steak. It was an anaemic regime, like eating snow, sweet and sour snow, as if she wanted her veins to reveal only the finest white liquor.

With her, progress was slow. For eighteen months now they had been unpicking the tapestry which her childhood and adolescence had stitched into such agonising patterns. Her exuberant, domineering mother, so replete with ideas and confidence, so sure for herself and her children that doubts and fears had no recognition. Timidity was weakness, forebodings indulgence, holding back a sin. 'You must live, Nina, live, you only live once, look at all these opportunities, make the most of them.' But Nina, instead of catching the leather gauntlet before it hit the dust, as her brothers and elder sister had done, looked at the glove lying there in the dirt as if it were a dead rat. Like the Lady of Shalott she had retreated more and more into a half-life, finding a world of reflections and mirrors more satisfactory than a solar system orbiting around mother and her copious certainties.

First, meat had gone, then dark fish, cooked vegetables, coloured drinks, tea, coffee, all dark foods, heavily textured grains, and anything difficult to digest. She couldn't cope with any overload, all intake had to be gradual, minimal, so Bruce measured out his interpretations accordingly: tentatively, in teaspoon size, he offered her suggestions of the meaning of what had happened to her and what was happening now, teaspoons which she could taste and select before swallowing. He had learnt that by doing it this way, she didn't mind some of the bitter truths, in fact she seemed to prefer them as being closer to her reality than the cheating stuffing of 'goodness' which she suspected was a betrayal. Slowly, week by week, hour by hour, Nina allowed in a little more and let filter out some of the 'blackness' with which she said she was possessed.

But it was slow, painfully slow, laborious, with as many steps backwards as forwards, weight losses as well as ounce-by-ounce gains. Some weeks, the understanding and merging had become so acute that Bruce had picked up her symptoms. He too had been unable to eat 'normally', refusing Marilya's coq-au-vin, embarrassed at the gorging of their weekend dinner parties and pleading headaches or allergies against their friends' rich duck and orange feasts. Other times, as he knew was so common in reactions to anorexics, he'd become impatient with her, wanting to shake her awake from her reverie of half-life, her death-in-life condition, to tell her to snap out of it, stop being so silly, grow up, just *eat*, as her previous psychiatrist had done, the one Nina had tricked with stones in her pockets to convince him of a steady weight gain, and so contrived her release from hospital. Just in time, his own impatience would be caught as counter-transference: mother's intolerance acted out again through him. His own repulsion from food he managed to interpret as guilt at leaving Nina starving whilst he could enjoy, again picking up her accusation against mother indulging in life whilst she was left dying. So the identifications eventually passed and he became the therapist again, the one who was normal, the one who lived and functioned and ate *normally*, the measuring rod against which her deviancy could be read.

Michelle was due at ten, but she always arrived exactly seven minutes late. At first, he had found empathy or engagement with her much more difficult, for bulimia was so much more complicated. It smacked of something hypocritical, wasteful, so much more so than other eating disorders, even though his rational mind told him they were all parallel, different symptoms but with the same aetiology. What he baulked at with bulimia, at least he had done with Michelle, was the expense and concealment. She would spend over a hundred pounds a week on food – the best quality – smoked meats, caviare, olives, cheeses, cakes, wines, liqueurs, the most specialised gourmet foods, only to be rid of them as soon as possible with a variety of methods, from 'innocently' giving them away to people, discarding them in dustbins, or actually eating – as she had to on conferences and business lunches – with the inevitable disgorging which would follow, or chasing down the food with packet after packet of laxatives, so the food would leave no trace, for the body must not be soiled.

He'd heard about it of course, 'evacuation of the bad object' it was termed in psychoanalytic parlance, but he'd never encountered it at close quarters before, and the reality of it had amazed and appalled him. He found it hard to believe the statistics when he heard of the thousands of bulimics in the country, for it was such a Jekyll and Hyde phenomenon. There was such a discrepancy between this strait-laced, upper-class woman Michelle – sitting there now with her designer clothes, her little suede boots, polished nails and strings of pearls, talking so intellectually and correctly about transactions in the City – and that beast within, wanting to devour and destroy the best that lay in sight. The contrast never ceased to astound him. She was so astute, saw through the psyches of merchant bankers and brokers in an instant, but her remarkable insight failed to reach her own unnameable edge, as if it alone were beyond the possibility of intelligent scrutiny.

She was getting in touch now with how she reached towards good things, but then immediately withdrew from them, as if she really had no right to them, or they would pollute her, just like Nina, feeling disgusted at having things inside. They brought to Bruce's mind the image of King Midas, these women, Midas in reverse, fearing that all they touched would turn to death, transform gold into excrement. Whatever was inside them felt bad: their core was noxious and must be emptied out, evacuated. And the more he understood this about Michelle, the more she understood it about herself. Their two understandings grew side by side, emerging from the ground they had worked so hard for so long. The more he liked her, and the more she liked herself, the less her luxuries mattered. For what good was gold that couldn't be enjoyed? What pleasure could Midas take without touch or love? Could wealth console for faulty parenting? Michelle was as marooned on her treasure island, for all her flat in Ladbroke Grove, her house in Tuscany, her Sunday supplement success, as acutely as any prisoner on the rocks of Alcatraz.

Inevitably, Michelle had been alert to the slightest trace of ambivalence in his attitude towards her and it was not until her suffering broke through financial shares and percentages that he had been able to overcome his wariness about her class privilege. He'd been expecting her to leave as she'd left her previous therapists, just like she abandoned food, but two years on and they were still here, battling it out: her unconscious trying to collude with his struggle to unseat her resistances and to face the pain which had precipitated this costly drama, but her natural fear of that hurt flinching away and continuing the cycle of filling and emptying, spending and throwing away, which had become such an all-consuming activity.

Listening to her narrative now, her slowed-down process

of buying and gorging, Bruce sat stunned once more at the
brilliance, the sheer brilliance of the unconscious. It was just
as Freud said: 'The unconscious – that is to say, the
"repressed" – offers no resistance whatever to the efforts of
the treatment.' It is trying desperately, but desperately, to be
heard. Ever since he had become involved with analytic
work, as opposed to the pragmatic version of psychiatry he'd
been programmed into from his medical training, he'd never
ceased to be amazed at the tenacity with which the unconscious struggles to tell its tale. See how dramatically it was
trying to force its way into public with Michelle, driving her
from one delicatessen to another, from one dustbin to
another, in its attempt to be heard, to be free of its pain.
And when things had been so impossibly stuck with Michelle
in the early days, deadlocked in an apparently unbreakable
pattern of compulsion and repetition, her refusal to go deeper
manifesting as very successful attempts to bore and stall him
with talk of bonds and stocks and shareholdings, he'd taken
heart from the one central fact that she kept coming. The
thing that had been driving her to those Jewish delicatessens,
to Harrods, to the best restaurants in Soho, was now driving
her to him, admitting a readiness to stop; it wanted to stop,
but only if he was there, imaging possibility.

It was as if the unconscious was an unruly child, he
thought. It slipped out of the window in the night to join
the grown-ups in the drawing-room, refusing to be
excluded. But the conscious mind, those vigilant adults sip-
ping their coffee, anxious not to draw attention to the cracks
in the ceiling, shunt the child back to bed, 'It's long past
your bedtime', and call in a figure of reprisal most suited to
the times: nanny, sandman, God, father, ghost, wicked fairy,
the horror apparatus of video nasties. 'Children should be
seen but not heard.' Still the adults cannot entirely rid themselves of an imprint on the retina: the image of that barefoot
child in its nightgown seeing right through their social
charms and politenesses, reminding them of what is not said
– a rawness in the expression of a need for love which

adults have left behind. This is what he, Bruce, was to her, Michelle, this is what therapist was to patient: an image of possibility, holding, a chance of someone receiving that rawness, that need, that anger at an eternity of neglect. That was all, when it came down to it, behind all the specific variants, that was all therapy was: that everything. With each hour, the child moved closer and the group of adults, arms opening, became a little less forbidding.

Between Michelle and Sally he had his ritual cup of coffee and cigarette, the weather surprisingly fine enough to take it into the courtyard and sit on the bench sheltered by the walnut tree. Despite several years of therapy work, he still found it a novelty to be able to have these pockets of solitude, so different from those decades in hospitals and institutions with such little opportunity for reflection or peace. Most working activity, he thought, is merely *reactive*, hand to mouth, doing something because someone else expects it to be done, without questioning whether the activity has any meaning or value in itself. It's all functioning, sheer *functionality*, keeping the machine going. Terror that the machine might stop. We haven't paused to consider if life attached to that machine is really worth living or not.

Adi, one of his colleagues at Charing Cross, had longed to return to his native India for precisely that reason.

'Do you ever stop to wonder, Bruce, what all this activity is *for*? You see, to me, and I know I say this because I come from a rural part of India which is so very different, so much of this western society seems to be mere *preparation*. It is preparing to live, but never actually lives, my friend. Like always living in the prelude to a play and never proceeding to the main act. All these functions and machines to function: houses, cars, dishwashers, going to hairdressers, beauticians, dentists, and even, Bruce, to doctors and hospitals, what is it for? In India, you see, they are functions which have to be done so that the main priority can then happen: living, creating, loving, praising God, thinking of God. But here, it is a short circuit and has gone back on itself, a snake eating its tail. The means have become the thing to live for; the means have become the end. The prelude is the drama. So you see, my friend, I cannot live here. I think I even prefer illness to this, my friend, this is too, how do you say, *smooth*. It is too smooth for me.'

Too smooth. That was why he liked working with Sally, he realised, stretching before he closed the French windows, leaving the cup in the kitchen. There was nothing smooth about Sally, she refused smoothness. Should he look at his notes? She would be arriving any moment. What session was it? The last one was 99, Good Lord, had she been coming so long? Session 100, he wrote neatly: Sally, we arrive at a century.

As usual, she was out of breath, having cycled from her exercise class and across London in the early lunch-hour chaos, her spiky hair dramatic against the pastel wall behind the couch.

'Hi, Bruce,' she panted, throwing down her bulging cycle bag near the door and claiming a large cushion leaning against a leg of the Victorian couch which she always refused. He'd questioned her once about whether she felt she couldn't occupy the couch because she paid less, that it was reserved for richer patients, 'real' patients, who, because they could afford more bought the right to lie on the couch, but she'd dismissed that as 'typical analytic jargon'. No, she just preferred sitting on the floor, she always had. Her bed was on the floor, her cushions at home were on the floor, she felt comfortable there: the couch looked like a delivery table and she wasn't going to go through that agony, thanks very much.

Now he waited, blanking his mind into the receptive yet unexpectant screen he knew was necessary. It was like a game of chess: the moves were limited, but the opening gambit unpredictable.

'OK, Bruce, let's not beat about the bush,' she began.

'Oh?'

'I've found out something about you and it's important that you know I know.'

'You've found something out about me?'

'God, I do wish you wouldn't repeat things back at me like that as if you were a bloody parrot. Yes. Two things really, and I know you won't ask me what they are, you'll say do you want to tell me what they are, so I will. The first is that you're married, which I didn't know, but it doesn't really matter one way or the other I suppose. The second is that your wife is a real cow, and I don't know if I can go on seeing someone who's stupid enough to be married to such a mean bitch.'

There was a pregnant pause.

'Would you like me to say it for you, Bruce, or are you too scared about hearing things? – "I wonder if you'd like to tell me more." '

'Would you?'

'Well, I have to, for my sake. You know I've been going to this exercise class each week?'

'Yes, in Shepherds Bush?'

'Well, that's part of it. I lied to you when I said it was in Shepherds Bush. It wasn't. There's no such place as the Tarzan Fitness Studio; I'm surprised you didn't check it out. "The law of the jungle is the survival of the fittest!" Don't you ever wonder if your clients tell lies?'

Not knowing what to say, he paused. *The wise therapist says nothing: if in doubt, do nowt.* 'Hm.'

'Anyway, it was in Knightsbridge'.

'Oh.'

'You know, don't you?'

'The Hollywood Health Club?'

'Yes.'

'You've been going to Marilya's classes?'

'Yes, every week, aerobic work-outs every Friday for the last year.'

'Ah.'

'How was I to know she was your wife, for Christ's

sake? You don't even use the same surname – Dr Stevenson, Marilya Katz – they hardly sound compatible, do they?'

'Marilya still uses her maiden name.'

'Well, anyway, there we've been, working out and bopping away for twelve months, and then today, during the break, Marilya suggests to the class we might like to try a diet she's promoting.'

'A diet?'

'Yes, one of these packet things, don't tell me you don't know she's doing that.'

'No, I didn't know.'

'Wow, what brilliant communication between husband and wife. The left hand doesn't know what the right one is up to, sabotage and hijack in the selfsame unit, wow!'

'You say she's offering a diet in packets?'

'Packets and bars. It's been in the press recently. "Scientifically researched, guaranteed to lose weight, up to four stones in two weeks, without any loss of essential minerals and vitamins." You take one bar or packet of powder with water three times a day and you're supposed to never get hungry and it keeps you fit and healthy and vital, *I don't think.* I've tried things like that in the past, before I came to see you, it's just like eating sweet cardboard, edible polystyrene, and you get really hungry, especially if you have the chocolate or peanut flavoured ones, 'cos they stimulate your desire for sweet things. You end up craving Mars bars and Boosts and Snickers and eating more sugar in between your packet meals than you ever would eating real things. The manufacturers are probably the sweet companies anyway, they're all in league with the slimming production firms. I read about it in *Socialist Weekly*. They're just crap. And very expensive. Works out at about five pounds a day, now who can afford that for a bloody diet?'

'Mm.'

'Aren't you going to ask me what happened?'

'What did happen?'

'Well. Most of the women in the class are members of the

fitness and health club. Actually, I had to cheat to get in. One of my mates does the cleaning there and she managed to steal a couple of the forms and borrow the Polaroid they do the identity cards with, so I've got a pass for classes, but we only did the cheaper membership, which means we can't use their other facilities, the luxury circuit weight gyms, Finnish rock sauna, Jacuzzi baths, solariums, cocktail bars. But then, who'd want to mix with that bloody Knightsbridge and Kensington crowd more than once a week? I didn't tell you about it 'cos the membership's so expensive, you might have thought I could afford to pay you more and then you'd have put my fee up and I'd have had to stop coming.'

'And you didn't want me to know you'd cheated?'

'Yes, that's right. You might have thought I was cheating you about being unemployed, you know, that I'd forged my UB40, that I was here under false pretences. But I'm not.'

In Sally's pause for breath, Bruce's barometer registered the increased pressure of anger, resentment and fear. Ironically, he found himself wondering how Freud would have coped with this one. If his wife, Martha, had been spied upon in glamorous health clubs by working-class patients whose cleaning friends stole their membership? A wife who undermined his very faith?

'I believe you,' he said gently.

Encouraged by his confirmation, she continued. 'In no time, Marilya was surrounded by this group of women all interested in the diet. She's working as a counsellor for it, 'cos they profess to have this personal back-up network of counsellors who talk to you about how you're progressing and keep an eye on your weight and all that, which is apparently what you're paying for. I suppose there were nine or ten women, all rich and glam, none of them really overweight, not anywhere near as fat as I was when I first came here. And I just got really angry. "Don't you see you're being taken for a ride?" I said, "*all* of you, including Marilya? Don't you see it's a con trick, part of the capitalist enterprise?

Who do you think funds these slimming researches? Mars! Rowntrees! They're just gimmicks, pretending to work miracles. You can't lose weight permanently like that, it's bullshit. And anyway who says there's anything wrong with being big? What's so sinful about being the size we are? None of you's overweight anyway. Why don't you spend your money on something more useful? It'll cost as much in a week as a whole week's benefit. It's *sick*!'' And they all looked terribly embarrassed and Marilya smiled patronisingly then carried on blithely, talking as if I wasn't there. I just became invisible to them. Me! Invisible!

'God, I could have killed the lot of them, I was so angry. Especially Marilya, with that jazzy leotard, a new one every week, how many has she got? And that streaked blonde hair, just the right amount of make-up and rings, and all these women fawning on her trying to look like her, Ms size eight or ten Jane Fonda. I was so pissed off, there wasn't any point trying to *say* anything, no one was listening, so I ran out to the bakery on the corner and spent all the cash I'd got out to pay you on cakes, the biggest they'd got. Great squidgy cream buns and chocolate eclairs, jam doughnuts, custard tarts, raspberry cheesecake, Black Forest gâteaux. I had that feeling I've told you about before, that mixture of rage and hunger, I didn't know if I wanted to eat or not, I didn't know what I was going to do with them, I was so mad. But I went back to Hollywood – what a name! – and climbed up on to the roof overhanging the entrance of the building, where they all had to pass out to get to their cars.

'I had to wait ages – they take forever, you know, preening themselves and showering, as if they've got all day to waste – and then they came out, one by one, and when they looked up to see who was calling them, I pelted them with the cream cakes, slap in the face. It was great! Some of them are quite young, yuppie types, and it was wonderful to see them, all this synthetic cream stuck to their well-cut hair, and custard dripping down their necks. It was brilliant! You should have heard their language! All these upwardly mobile middle-class women reduced to crude monosyllables! Unfortunately, I didn't quite get Marilya, 'cos a couple shouted to her just as she was coming out and she dashed back inside, probably to get some official help, so I thought it was time to take to my bike. But I did manage to shove two doughnuts in the exhaust of her Capri and smear thick cream all over the windscreen. Stupid cow. I wrote "Katz is for Cats" on the boot in strawberry jam. It was great. Anyhow, that's why I was late. And why I shan't be able to pay you for today.'

'Mm. Quite a story. I wonder how it came about from all this that she's my wife?'

'Oh yes. She gave us these pamphlets, you see, about the diet, they're in my bike bag, here: "Your personalised weight loss programme" and it tells you all about her counselling role. I'll read it to you – "Marilya Katz is trained in dietary counselling with Bodylines" – that's the firm that's doing the promotion – "and alongside her husband, a private psychotherapist and former psychiatric consultant in the NHS, offers experienced counselling for those with compulsive or overeating difficulties and food addictions." It's very close to the blurb on your handout, and then I noticed the phone number, the same as yours, and put two and two together. I couldn't believe it. Have I really been seeing a con-man all this time? Is she crazy, or are you schizophrenic, or what?'

It was a good question. He wanted to hesitate, to create some time to think, but his instinct to clear himself with her triumphed over theoretical caution.

'Perhaps you have put two and two together and made five.'

'What do you mean?'

'You are worried at the possibility of having been betrayed by me.'

'Possibility! You mean reality, don't you?'

'It is hard for you to let in that betrayals frequently do happen, and need not be utterly destructive. They are not always what they seem.'

'What do you mean?'

'What if I said that I really had no idea this was happening?'

'No idea?'

'None at all.'

'You mean, your wife put out that blurb without your permission?'

'Yes, I mean that.'

'You mean you didn't have any idea that she was doing this dietary counselling?'

'None at all.'

'But you knew she worked at Hollywood, surely?'

'She teaches aerobics in a number of venues. I didn't know much about this specific one, and I certainly didn't know about – what was the name? – Bodylines.'

'Oh.'

'It's hard for you to hear all this. It suggests to you that I am vulnerable too, not omnipotent. And if I can't protect myself from damage, how can I protect you?'

'I'm not particularly bothered about your marriage, to tell you the truth. I expect you can take care of yourself. I'm more concerned about whether you were lying to me or not. But then, if you *weren't* lying, how can I go along with the rest of what you've been telling me? It makes it all a farce. And it's a bit unlikely, isn't it? A therapist not knowing what his wife's up to, *and* them having such opposite values: him telling you not to diet but to get to the root of the hunger, the emptiness, the *feelings*, and her selling dietary products, completely denying what's inside. It's a bit far-fetched, Bruce, like asking me to believe Ghandi was married to one of the Gettys.'

'The whole thing is far-fetched, Sally.'

He could see Marilya trapeze-leaping between them in their mirroring, amazement flooding him at the power of the unconscious to make up such a suitable scenario.

'Are you asking me to believe that the man I've been paying to see for two years because I thought he wasn't deceived by surface crap, hasn't even seen through the woman he's living with? Assuming, that is, that you share a bedroom as well as a phone. Though maybe that's assuming too much, and the number's all you have in common!'

'I have to ask you to believe that, because it's true.'

There was a long pause whilst trust hung in the balance, betrayal waiting in the wings to see which it would claim. His credibility was on the line, whether as husband or therapist, and even if the second could be salvaged from Sally's paranoia, the unsettling of the first would have its inevitable repercussions here anyway. Catch 22.

'I can't afford not to go on trusting you.'

'Yes, I realise that.'

'But that's quite a leap in the dark.'

'Yes. You feel you need some evidence.'

'But I do. To really believe you, I'd have to see you taking some positive action.'

'What kind of action?'

'Leaving her.'

'Leaving Marilya?'

'Yes.'

'Because she's betrayed you?'

'Because she's betrayed *you*.'

'I need to think about things, Sally. All that, with Marilya, that's my issue, outside the bounds of your therapy.'

'But it isn't, Bruce, don't you see? You can't cut off therapy and life like that, for Christ's sake. How could you follow a priest who stole things? How could you be taught art by a man who can't hold a bleeding brush, or learn literature from someone who can't write? You can't be in therapy with someone who's married to a woman like that, who hasn't even got the same values about food or fat or life or *anything*. You're the one who said that the person you're married to, or having a close relationship with, is a reflection of part of *you*, your – what did you call them? Primary something?'

'Primary processes.'

'Yes, that you marry the primary processes, what you've concealed from yourself but keeps trying to resurface. You marry your own contradictions. But this is a bit much. I mean, how far can you go in making excuses for paradox?'

He was silent.

'I mean, here am I, trying to understand myself, not to cram my mouth with substitutes, and how am I meant to do that if the analyst I'm working with is married to a cheat, his primary process is one big deception, and he's not even able to confront it? Where does that leave me when I'm stuck with my self in the middle of the night, trying to resist a jar of peanut butter? I mean, if he's an even bigger failure than I am when it comes to authenticity, if *he* can't cope with compulsions, then what is the point? What is the bloody point?'

She was right, undoubtedly she was right. Was he really willing to put his money where his ideas were, and to let this exposure tear open his comfort and security? Was he ready to lose so much, his slim wife, his sumptuous home? All for this violent woman, with her punkish subculture, her subversive ideas? Was he truly prepared to let his marriage disintegrate for one irate patient, for the sake of her growth and trust? For that's what it would mean for her truth to prevail.

On one level, he could see through it, through all the transference, the countertransference, for he was well versed in the wily plots of the unconscious, anxious to reproduce. He could envisage his supervision group, spectacles poised to spell beware, alerting him to the parallels as history repeated itself. They would force him to recall Sally's childhood trauma, coming home unexpectedly from nursery school, discovering mother having an affair, and mother driving her out to buy some sweets – hence the addiction to sugar – whilst she sorted out this business that Sally was forbidden to reveal to father. And Daddy not believing her when she did tell, and her trust in him and in his faith in her betrayed. Because father didn't want to believe the slander, or to face its implications, there had been no action, no righteous reproach to mother for being unfaithful, and Sally had been stuck hopelessly in the middle, unloved and disbelieved. But even if she *had* concocted this current episode, even if it *had* been engineered by her lost infancy, what mattered then and now was the desperation it trailed: what other recourse did a child have with the whole universe at stake, but phantasy?

But the knots between them were strangling his insight; he was getting confused. Who was baiting whom now? Who was the catalyst around here? He had been hooked into assuming the role of the usurped father, the dead spouse betrayed by a fickle Gertrude, and it was vital he should stand his ground. Yet it was no play: *reality* had caught the conscience of the king, and only habit enabled him to struggle through to the end of the session.

'It seems that you don't know if you can trust me any more.'

'Right on. I don't.'

'As if what you see as my being betrayed by Marilya means that I can be duped and am therefore no longer as omniscient or omnipotent as you would wish. It feels as if I am betraying you.'

'Well, I don't know if it's as complicated as that sounds. It's black and white to me, Bruce. As far as I'm concerned, either you leave your wife, or you betray me and that's the end of our relationship.'

'You mean you expect me to leave my wife as a result of this discovery?'

'I do, yes.'

'This seems to be very close to what happened for you with your parents.'

'You think I've *invented* all this, to repeat what happened when I was *three*?'

'In some ways, yes.'

'Now who's playing into my phantasies of omnipotence?'

What could he say? Touché. Thank goodness her time was

up, saving him from more obscure stumbling in the dark. Either her unconscious *had* invented it all, conjured out of the blue this Oedipal melodrama, or some obscure destiny was indeed pulling the strings of their lives to its Freudian plot. And his tidy analysis brought to its heels.

When Sally had left, Bruce found himself unable to make notes, no appetite for lunch, and he telephoned Dick to cancel their Swiss Cottage swim. It was a cold December afternoon, sharp but dry, and he sauntered through the heart of London, wandering down Marylebone High Street with a vague registering of delicatessens, health food stores, sandwich bars and men eating pies, women watching – one of the few occasions, he thought, when *women* do the looking – food. Then he circled through the squares, past redundant churches with their apologies for faith and grass, till he found a bench in a little triangular patch of park just by Jacob's Well Mews. He was sitting between two carrier-bag pensioners, a man with white straggling hair and string tied round the middle of his stained mac, the kind of man who dialogued with his hat, and a woman, feeding the pigeons strutting over the soiled pavement, the birds' purple chests mirroring her cyclamen-coloured skin. How rarely he sat in places like this, he thought: how confident of rooms he had become.

He knew Sally would disturb things, he'd known it ever since she first arrived at his practice and he'd agreed to the lowest fee compatible with some pretence of charging. He'd known it when one morning she'd said she was bored sitting in the relative shade of the consulting room with spring outside and he'd found himself walking with her, past the Planetarium to Baker Street and Regent's Park, not talking much, just being aware of breathing, blossom, ducks, prams, the light, the texture of the day. He knew it when she'd shed the initial two stones of weight and she'd come bounding in, telling him how now she understood what he'd been trying to tell her, or to get her to see by not telling her: that the fat was not about food at all, but about rage and sadness, about envy of those who *lived*, and she'd searched in her pannier bags for those lines she'd written the previous night. Prowling about in the kitchen as usual, but refusing to stuff her mouth with food to fill the emptiness, she'd created instead her first ever poem: 'In the night we creep to cupboards/Looking for relief./We do not feed our hunger,/But our anger and our grief.' And she had wept and brought tears to his face at the realisation of the extent of her loss and pain, mourning accompanying the gradual shedding of flesh, the two of them *encountering* that emptiness against which the body's weight was such a miserable defence.

Sally had made it impossible for him to derive pleasure from detachment, from simply knowing. She, and Michelle and Nina in their different ways, had made him see that what mattered to them was not a categorisation of eating disorders, but a willingness to *relinquish* theory and to share their particular histories. To know it, to know it as *experience*, in all its primitive state, its rawness, its cost. Against the vomiting at night, the stolen bread and cakes, the mounds of snow, how could he posit theory, supremacy?

Food, he thought, food; had he ever really stopped to consider it before? It was like so much in his life, so much he had taken for granted and assumed he understood. He had written up his theories, in an abstract way, about the relation of food politics to class struggle, formulating a hypothesis that whereas bulimia and anorexia tended to be confined to upper- and middle-class patients, overeating was more of a working-class phenomenon. One stratum felt over-full and needed to shed its excess of solid flesh, whilst the other wrapped itself in a cocoon of chocolate and fat, like eastern women displayed for their size, as if this shared the luxury of wealth. But now he could take nothing for granted – not a bite, not a word, not a heartbeat.

When had he really *tasted* anything? Really bitten or swallowed life? It had all been consumed so mindlessly, so hastily. Adi was right. 'The trouble with your culture, Bruce, is that it is too speedy, always trying to get somewhere, never standing still. And so it misses the point, the still point.' At any second it could disappear or be spoilt. Eternity between each pulse. It was too precious, mysterious, for all this blinkering analysis.

And of course he had been locked in marriage, for he and Marilya were two sides of the same coin, fearing the cutting edge. They had 'lived' together so well by hardly living at all. She with her dieting and bodily image, keeping up physical appearances, he with his paring to the psychic bone. Marilya was on the side that made the rules because they would prove she had won, this latest dieting campaign confirmed it. She would make money by persuading other people they had to look like her. Bodylined, slim and trim, with none of the ambivalence towards life that was evident in Nina, Michelle, Sally. Her relation to food, and to all that food symbolised – mother, love, experience itself – was not a matter of life and death as it was for Nina or Sally. It was about cultivating the right image, being fashionable. Marilya was not only one of the *products* of this age of narcissism, this culture which fostered women as to-be-looked-at-objects and caused all the self-hatred and self-mutilation in Nina and Michelle and the like, but also, by being that, she was one of its salesmen. Sally was right. There was no innocence. Whoever is not for me is against me.

He too. How pleased he had been with his mask, revelling in the peculiar snobbery of having renounced his professional status, celebrating his subversiveness as the Ronnie Laing of the 80s, an *enfant terrible* trampling on dominant psychiatry. Was he really so ill-matched with Marilya? Did he really have the right to criticise her, when their versions of truth had been so double, dulled? They had been stitched into one another's history with selfsame skeins, maturing side by side towards their false maturity. But what had he risked? What had he ever relinquished or *known*? He had kept his house, his mortgage, his marriage, his friends, his cigarettes, his daily habits and addictions, like Freud had his. What did he actually know of the madness, the desperation, that he took women through? Could you lead someone somewhere you hadn't been? He knew nothing, not even nothing, less than nothing. What could they buy with this compromise of a song?

Half-consciously, he found himself lighting a cigarette, noticed the mauve woman's sidelong envy and gave her one, then the man, his fingerless gloves offering cheap whisky in exchange. They sat there silently, an unholy trio in the midst of London's bustle, sending their smoke to even greyer skies. There was nowhere to get to, after all, those crowds were held still here.

In the end all of them, all his women patients, had taught him the same thing: awe. A kind of humility, witnessing such a process of uncovering, discovering: that archaeology of pain and vacancy, anger and lack. And alongside the awe was incredulity, amazement at their ability to face it, to dare to weep and rage, to come right through. For they *were* all women, the ones who saw it out; it was women who were daring to know themselves, and what did he *really* know of their agony, their starvation and bulimia, their bingeing and stealing, their trusting, birthing, longing, dying? Their mothering and unmothering, their nightmares of food, dreams of hunger, these mothers with no mothers, these babies who had sucked breasts which had no life for them, only resentment, anger, guilt, and then been bid to grow and smile and thrive: what did he know of them? These post-war women, mothered by other hollow women without resources, without work, without *joy*. It was a whole generation he was hearing: the other children of Auschwitz.

As he sat there, mouth dry from the tobacco, pigeons scattering from the mongrel which was sniffing round an overflowing waste bin, some words drifted back into his memory. A song, the pricing of experience, a song . . . Yes, he remembered now, how could he have forgotten? It was Shelley, that was who Sally reminded him of, Shelley. That scene with Shelley, years ago and long-erased, a brief affair that had been precluded by Marilya declaring she was pregnant, and leaving him with no option but to stay with her. Shelley, lying, standing, walking, laughing, eating. Shelley, vivacious, alive, yes, so *alive*, her voice like Sally's, he could see and hear her now. What *were* those words she was reciting? Something about experience, yes, *experience*, that was it. Some poet she liked, it must be Blake, how did it go? Experience. *What is the price of experience? Do men buy it for a song? Or wisdom for a dance in the street? No, it is bought with all that a man hath, his wife, his house* . . . His wife, his house . . . his house, his wife . . .

He saw Marilya peeling shrimps, marinading steak, uncorking wine for that evening's supper party. Nina, up and down between kitchen and lounge, craving a taste of the food she was forbidden, fearing her 'blackness'. Michelle, delicatessen queueing for the most succulent smoked salmon, depositing it an hour later, still wrapped in Harrods paper, on an underground station seat for the first keen-eyed traveller. Sally, lobbing doughnut grenades and shooting peanuts at passing drivers as she cycled along Kilburn High Road. This nameless woman next to him, with her broken nail stubs, ferreting amongst rubbish for cigarette butts and half-eaten sandwiches. Deprivation and greed, over-fullness and emptiness, parading the streets. The city was worthy of Marat-Sade, Bethlem turned inside out, its inmates making up the world. Now he saw why bulimia was so apt a response to the times, for this world was indeed sick, nauseating. Too much, just much too much. It made you want to throw up and say no, no, stop, please stop, that isn't what I wanted to take in at all.

One thing was clear: there was no quarantine, thank Freud for that, no one immune. Only some shades of difference. It could be no source of pride to be tentatively blessed with 'in' instead of 'out', mind, wealth, or sanity, no pride at all. It was some inscrutable fate, some other hand that wrote the script for all this interlocking destiny. There was too much 'coincidence'. This last episode, for example, whose unravelling was it? Could it be that it was not Sally who had engineered the dream at all, but he himself, summoning from the outer world just the right players for his own psychic play to be acted out as it was meant to be? Perhaps it was *he* who had hallucinated *her*, so that her words and actions could light the fuse that had lain dormant for so long inside him.

But did that mean that there was, after all, no such thing as an entirely *personal* unconscious? That inner and outer were edging into and out of each other, always, in everyone, everywhere? Then it all became so much bigger, somehow, than Freud had envisaged: it was no longer just a matter of individual neurosis working through, but a *collective* destiny, a merging of fates, that illegible system of concealed connections and paths to which Adi used to give the name 'karma', but which here, unblessed with the recognition of words, remained all the more confusing.

His analytic mind was still churning away automatically, reminding him of transference and countertransference – 'You've been infected by Sally's anger and rage, Bruce my boy. You're feeling guilty at having so much, and at being a man. Don't fall into the trap of acting out: just be aware. This patient is attempting a kind of blackmail, twisting your arm into hers as she enters into a sexual competition with Marilya, her mother, for you, her father. You think you have to make up for the betrayal of the past, and leave your wife, but this isn't psychodrama, Bruce, there's no need to play out Sally's family story. In fact there is no need to give up anything, no need to lose at all.' – but its restraining voice had already lost. He could not be more weary of armchair Marxists who lined their pockets and bought second homes with the profit derived from theoretical discourse about surplus value, than he was of these analysts who spoke on loss and deprivation from their luxurious consulting rooms. For all her melodramatic devices, Sally had made him realise just how weary he was of all the lies. So tired of smoothness, things being smoothed over.

It was too cold to sit there much longer, collar upturned.

He rose to the late afternoon chill, leaving for the more weathered couple on the bench his packet of cigarettes. Hands in his pockets, he paced through the streets again, restless, hungry, recognising that nothingness Sally spoke about. This was what Shelley had touched in him too, this yearning, this unspeakable craving, all else was surface, a peering through delicate lace at death. Yes, he thought, reaching the Outer Circle of the park, crossing the dark canal, yes, this was the real repression. Not orgasms, not sexuality, but *this*, desire beyond desire, unnameable. At last Shelley's departing words were clear, Shelley, in California now, living her dream. The meaning of that other line she'd sent was now transposed into simplicity.

'How can I leave Marilya?' he'd asked rhetorically, when Shelley had tried to persuade him to follow his heart and her to Berkeley. 'She needs security.' And Shelley's look had recognised *his* fear, and her next letter, from the States, with no accompanying address, had been a well-worn page torn from some Jacobean drama, Webster perhaps, some play about a woman, with one speech roughly underlined. Finally he understood it, that line scored so heavily in red ink. Why had it taken him so long, some fifteen years, before experience could throw away the fetters of mere words? *Security some men call the suburbs of hell.* Yes, that was where he had been dwelling: *hell*. The smooth suburbs of hell.

And what he needed now was a telephone, this vandalised half-standing booth in Camden Town, its handset scarred, the stench of pee and fag ends on the floor. It would do, anywhere would do to make a move, so long as it was rough and didn't lie, so long as it was hard and out of hell. For now he needed this: he knew how desperate the need, the need for some rough edges to scrape life against, sharpen his soul.

Future Perfect

Spectrum Three. A huge Victorian warehouse squatting by the docks, recently saved and converted into a centre for alternatives: art, drama, therapy. Bright painted pipes protruding from the walls, scarlet door-handles dis-inviting touch. It was a Saturday, his first free one for months, and Thomas wondered again what he was doing there, surrendering precious spare time to an unknown he feared would be predictable: a drama therapy workshop, a twelve-hour bout of psychodrama. What on earth could have induced him to come? As if he didn't do enough archaeology the rest of the time, let alone digging amongst the skeletons of other psychic wrecks. He must be mad!

From a turning on the second floor he stood and viewed the docks, where other buildings similarly survived through face lifts into shops and galleries, the dirt of history along the quay. A top-heavy set of triangles, fluorescent tubes, flashed garish colours against grey pedestrians, an unconvinced attempt at moving art. It was Tessa who had got him here, forced him to come. 'Oh, Thomas, take a risk for once,' she'd said, 'if you never try, you'll never know.' And so he'd signed his name for this event, unthinkingly, and once he'd paid the exorbitant fee, there was no withdrawing. Reluctantly, tired from broken sleep, he climbed the stairs.

Scanning the list of participants the previous evening, ten plus two leaders, he'd been relieved to learn there was no one he knew. So much easier acting intimacy with people you had never met. Perhaps that was why this existed at all, this therapy business: because *actual* intimacy, ordinary intercourse, had become so damn difficult. It was part of the age, talking to strangers, and he stood near the doorway for a last cigarette, watching these intimates arrive.

A large untidy girl who'd struggled up the stairs, embarrassed at her breathlessness, a crimson motif blazoned on her chest. Its letters, *Colorado*, were completed by the sloping text across her back, *is for hikers*, linking the shoulder blades; either some souvenir from a Grand Canyon trip, or local bargain-basement sale. A punkish blonde, pixie-like, dressed in mourning, skin-hugging black tights tapering to pointed shoes, her metal eyelids radiating scorn. A thin girl who avoided looking at him, tastefully if somewhat soberly dressed. And then some energy, a bubbly redhead racing up the flights, reproaching her companion with a sting more light-hearted than sharp: 'O well, Barry Price, we all know what a chauvinist *you* are', as if acknowledging his sexist sins somehow condoned them.

Behind them, bedraggled and tired, a middle-aged man, bearded, who seemed relieved to register the smoke, and paused beside the window to light his pipe. Thomas realised he loathed the way he was observing people, judging them by appearance and size, as if looks were all. Why *should* size and shape carry so much *meaning*, for Christ's sake? But he was consoled, his sense of the *maleness* of these judgments relieved, when he turned around to find a woman appraising him with just as much interest, the tables turned.

All he could see against the window was this great mass of hair, gleaming in parts with silver streaks, and a loose-cut vest. He followed her up the last flight of stairs, noting heavy antique earrings, tight-fitting black leggings over bare calves, a loose silk jacket draped over tanned shoulders. For a few seconds, he wondered if this was the group's facilitator, but as soon as they'd entered the main room, he could see from the geography of bodies – keeping a respectful distance from the two striking women by the fireplace – that she was just another participant. Those two women were the only ones who remained standing, the younger one, Afro-Caribbean by the look of her, sorting cushions into a large circle and placing boxes of tissues at strategic points whilst the other, tall and even more imposing, was unwrapping a large piece of clear crystal, which she arranged reverently on the mantel-shelf next to some burning incense. The lump of quartz was a protective talisman, the restored fireplace an altarpiece to some forgotten deity.

It was a large room, pleasantly proportioned, with pale lemon walls, arched cathedral windows. Over the renovated chimney breast hung a wall-sized gilt-framed mirror, with baby gold Cupids perched in each top corner, and from certain angles in the room, all the interior was doubled through the looking glass. The floor was stripped pine, var-nished and dotted with dozens of cushions, large and small, of every texture, colour and variety. There was a curtain which could be drawn around one section of the room to create the illusion of a proscenium arch, transforming it into a miniature theatre, and Thomas, who hadn't been there before, had to admit himself impressed by the spaciousness and taste of the setting. Contrasting it with the dark enclosed room where he'd been in analysis for so long, he found himself relishing the light and space, its openness and col-ours. Quite some place, he thought, this stage set, perfect for acting and reflecting, opening up and 'putting it all out there'. Whatever *out there* meant.

It was almost time to begin, and by now there were a dozen people in the room. Sitting cross-legged on a dark cushion next to the girl with the Indian silk jacket – Ger-maine, as she quickly introduced herself – Thomas felt as if he were lowering himself into the stalls of a theatre or the pews of a church. He wondered once again if he had done the right thing to come, or whether the day would be merely another painstaking exercise in coming to terms with the consequences of choices, often mistaken choices, which he made.

The woman leading the group, Miriam Steiner, was easily recognisable from the stunning photograph on her advance publicity. Striking looking – there you go again, Thomas, he reprimanded himself, you really must *do* something about this ineradicable narcissism – American, Jewish, alternating her time between New York and London, she had established a reputation for therapy work over the last two decades, following a career in theatre and dance. Now, somewhere in her fifties, she was an archetype. A tall lean body crowned with a mane of long white hair streaming out like an avalanche of strength around her face. All in black and white, her fine-grained linen trousers, off-white, loosely tucked into very soft, white leather ankle boots, white silk shirt tailored to her lithe body, black embroidered waistcoat, masses of jewellery. A gold watch chain led to the pocket on her waistcoat, a gold bangle on one wrist, various silver and inlaid bracelets on the other, whilst a massive white opal on the middle finger of her left hand, and three gold wedding rings on different fingers, echoed the pearls studding her ears. But even without all the accoutrements, she was stunningly beautiful: that dark Jewish profile, handsome features, mesmerising, charismatic, and his eyes, like everyone else's, were drawn to her. Yes, I will accede to that, he went on, she *is* beautiful, rightly a legend in her time.

With her suave introduction, the group's 'process' began.

'Good morning, everyone. I'd like to give you a warm welcome to today's workshop. I have worked with a couple of you before, and it's good to see you again, but most of your faces are new to me, so I'd like to say hello and welcome to those of you unfamiliar with this form of therapy or with my methods and practice. I'm delighted to be visiting this part of the country again and I hope sincerely that the time we spend together will be mutually rewarding. Let me get a few of the administrative details out of the way first. The workshop runs for twelve hours – a long time, I know, till nine this evening – and although it may be quite intense, we are all committed to staying till the end. That, being as true as we can to one another and ourselves, and keeping confidential anything that happens here, is our only contract.'

Nods intimated signature.

'Any breaks for tea and coffee will be relatively short – ten to fifteen minutes at most – so that we don't lose the momentum of what's happening, and we'll time them and a short lunch period to happen at suitable natural breaks between people's work. I am sure that everyone who wants to will have an opportunity to do some personal work, though I know some of you are here primarily for training purposes. There's no pressure whatsoever to do anything that doesn't feel right for you . . . ' And so on, in the same vein, reassuring, soothing. It was predictable enough, thought Thomas, unoriginal enough, but still needing to be said, safe boundaries made.

He'd done a couple of therapy workshops once before, 'psychic work-outs' he'd jokingly called them, but since he'd been in analysis himself, the ambivalence and resistance to them which he could feel surfacing now had increased. He recognised again that stunned sense of incredulity at the reality of it, or rather its *un*reality: strangers voluntarily meeting to share secrets and intimacies that other cultures and ages would have preserved for the most hallowed places. Mysteries that formerly belonged to the closest lovers' bed, the strictest confession, would be brought forth with as little impunity as Soho nudity: nothing withheld, but 'up front', 'shown'. He could never fully fathom all the reasons that had led to it, this phenomenon of 'soul sharing', a sensational page three of the psyche; as if only this distanced familiarity, this ritualised turning of oneself inside out were safe or meaningful. It was quite peculiar, a public ritual of intimacy which had turned into a secular ceremony, a new confessional beyond the laws of family or church, and equally bizarre.

People now prepared to put into suspense their 'normal'

selves, those masks and personae that customarily covered or negotiated ways of coping with their inner worlds, and prepared to reveal some of the chaos. As Miriam's voice wove in and out of the group, he could see bodies relaxing, thawing, dissolving, sensing permission to let loose their toads and snakes into the room. It was like Coleridge's ghastly wedding feast, all these guests waiting to tell, to unburden their tales; terrible stories of traumatic memories, waiting for disclosure, *dis-closure*, siphoning off the hurt.

As introduction moved clockwise around the circle, people revealing as much or as little as they wished in this initial rite, their life stories emerged in miniature, like some intriguing palimpsest. Through the brief words and more telling silences or body contortions, glimpses of what was unsaid began to come into being. Thomas imagined their self-presentations as a focal point of light, projected backwards to a wider screen, as in a *camera obscura*, where dwelt the travelling side-show of their multiple, and unpresented, selves: dwarves, cripples, madmen, thieves.

Next to Miriam, 'Steve Small', in early twenties, a light mousy beard, glasses, red wool sweater, loose blue jeans. Timidly and hurriedly, looking at the floor in front of him, 'I'm a volunteer worker in a home for the mentally disabled. I've come to learn more about this kind of therapy for using at work.'

Another man on his right, rather older, lined but innocent, his face reminding Thomas of John Berger, and of his Berlin friend, Horst. 'Hello, I'm Colin. Colin Simmonds,' confident, directly addressing the rest of the group. 'I've worked with Miriam before in London and really enjoyed it,' smiling across at her, yet not ingratiating, 'and I've been able to use some of the techniques in my work as an art therapist. I teach art at the college of education. But really I'm here just as much for me. I'm 43, married, two kids, happily married, which is quite a rarity these days' – some laughter – 'I want to learn how to enjoy myself.'

They moved on. Natalie Williams, thin, anorexic, said

barely anything, other than that she was a postgraduate reading history: Thomas had to force his eyes to focus on her barley-sugar bones. Then large 'Colorado' Sheila, as awkward in her words as in her appearance, not knowing whether to talk too much or too little. She spoke in exhaust bursts about her work in a rehabilitation centre for ex-addicts – my God, were they *all* wounded healers here? – and her own nervousness, fear, difficulties with food and alcohol. Thomas wished again that people who were shy wouldn't always insist on embarrassing themselves by exposing so much *more* than less vulnerable people did. It was one of those painful paradoxes, compulsive knifing of one's sores, whatever they were.

Then the bubbly woman who'd berated her friend Barry as they'd arrived, Lee, an aspiring playwright, twenty-six, working with drama in education, keen on improvisations and role play, enthusiastic, energetic – even manic – her gestures always moving, constantly on a responsive alert. Her hair was hennaed vibrant red, her lips a zany pink.

Next to Lee lounged Donna, the angry blonde, whose spiky punkish hair reinforced her message of attack and whose each word launched darts into male flesh.

'The first thing to know about me is that I'm a lesbian. That's who I *am* – a radical separatist – and I have to say that straight away because otherwise groups like this ignore it and make lesbianism an invisible issue.' She wanted to have a baby, but without sex. 'You just get a suitable male to put sperm into a cup: I mean *penetration*'s so ideologically unsound,' and she had given up university and social work to write for a revolutionary newspaper. 'And I have to tell you from the start that I don't like the politics of therapy and analysis. They stink. They're too privileged, too expensive for ordinary people. I've come on this weekend 'cos I want some evidence that psychotherapy can be *political*, can be of some use in the class struggle. I read the interview with Miriam in *Radical Therapy* last month and I want to see if her work's as extreme and far-reaching as she claims it is.'

The conclusion was a petulant so *there*, and Thomas realised he was relieved that Tessa, one of his best women friends who was gay, was not consumed with this innate, irate aggression, otherwise he'd have suspected prejudice in his own reading of Donna's lesbianism as angry and one-dimensional. They left no room for subtlety, he thought, politics that were so confounded with unresolved subjective stuff. And which weren't? Black and white, or red and blue, so crass, insensitive.

Barry, Lee's chauvinist friend, declared himself in sympathy with some of Donna's politics – an administrator in community work, he put himself forward as very involved with radical ways of living, alternative lifestyles – but Thomas mistrusted his manner. Was it just male arrogance, or was there really an aura of something self-congratulatory about Barry that made him quite repulsive? He was a strange mixture of arrogance, anger and uncertainty, pat phrases about left-wing ideology sliding off his tongue, but Thomas knew intuitively that he wasn't there to unearth things in any profound way. The more Barry spoke, the more he incriminated himself, and Thomas suspected that for Barry freedom was neatly synonymous with, and an excuse for, his promiscuity. Behind his lip-service radicalism there were naked bums in the bedroom, South African cans in the larder.

Sitting broadly in the circle, Barry's vast shoulders eclipsed the woman behind him, but when she spoke, her voice came through loud and bitter nonetheless.

'I'm a housewife. I'm only here 'cos the women and mental health group sent me. They've paid for me. There's no way I could have come otherwise.'

'And your name?' prompted Miriam.

'Mrs Biggs. Joyce Biggs.'

She was self-deprecating in a defiant, resentful way, stretched beyond her means both emotionally and economically, one more stress threatening to destroy her with bitterness. Divorced, working class, she had two adult sons still living at home, 'sponging' off her, two ex-husbands who were violent, a history of tranquillizers and alcohol addiction. She looked about fifty-five, but later turned out to be around forty, her eyes casting angry and envious looks around her. Miriam dealt with her cleverly, seeming to take full account of her sense of inadequacy, understanding her class position, but also making it clear through her manner that she wouldn't tolerate any condescension towards Joyce, either in herself or in the rest of the group. There could be no double standards.

Thomas' own turn came next. He wondered what they found as they watched him, with his short dark hair and gold-rimmed glasses, what they made of his studious clean-shaven face and slight Germanic accent. Were they interested at all, or too much preoccupied with their own torn hearts and images to be properly attending to him, or anyone? He'd made a conscious decision to reveal very little today – just the bare facts of his having done a PhD researching into analysis and therapy, theory and practice, of spending some of his time in England, some in Switzerland and Germany – so why was he also telling them he was Jewish? What caused that phantasy that Miriam listened more keenly now? What made him refer to his art, the fact that he spent every spare moment painting large canvases?

Those paintings, stacked against walls and hanging in one-man shows with their reconstructed versions of Madonna and child, icons transmuted and laid over by the horrors of the age. Large canvases of Raphael, Giorgione, Titian, reproduced and redeployed so that the mother-child bond was interrupted by a disgusting modernity: images from twentieth-century history – World War Two atrocities, famine victims, Northern Ireland, urban poverty – and images from advertising – glossy men and women, people reified, synthetic lives – beautifully collaged and painted into fragmented portraits of motherhood. Babies falling from those ample breasts and rose-filled laps; bishops, saints and shepherds from classical foregrounds changed into industrialists or Nazis; the grotesque caricatures of George Grosz and glossy advertising prints of Andy Warhol having invaded Renaissance and pre-Renaissance purity.

What was striking about his work was its tension, how it managed to sustain both that original image of mother and child, in all its confidence and certainty, and to intimate collapse, disintegration. Suddenly the spectator was taken aback, registering that what they were seeing was not, as they had at first supposed, a contemporary version of, say, Fra Lippo Lippi's *Virgin and Child with Scenes from the Life of St Anne*, but a dense and more sinister narrative. That innocent-looking seedy pomegranate in the infant's fingers was a lethal hand grenade, and lying in the canopied bed no haloed female saint, but a harrowed political prisoner, Dolours Price, on hunger strike in Armagh, 1974.

He didn't spell out details here. He'd done enough analysis to know how acutely it related to his history: adopted parents, their involvement with the opulent society of art collectors and critics in London and Europe, many of them Jewish and, like Felix and Selma, in self-imposed exile from South Africa. Most of what he was contending with here was a proud reluctance to let this group know anything about him. For he knew how tempted they would be to reduce it all to some simplistic notion of the *merely* personal, as if all his paintings' pain were nothing but the content of his inner world, and nothing to do with external reality. He didn't want it taken away, this perception he had, which overlaid personal with political and social meanings, apprehending the world in multi-layered complexities. His paintings were not just about mothering in a personal sense, but about a whole lost universe: the loss of the sacred, the loss of a unified vision, the loss of that harmony of self and world, which the Renaissance dyad of mother and baby, Madonna and child, so beautifully epitomised and seemed to be able to take so much for granted.

He doubted there'd be ears to hear, so remained mute, revealing little of himself, despite Miriam's apparent warmth and Germaine's evident interest. He knew the temptation of trying to turn a group into a long-lost family, and spurned the bait. Germaine, too, gave away very little of her personal history. A gestalt therapist, she also worked with astrology, was engaging, warm, her humour deep. Thomas wondered for a moment whether she too might be gay, for she seemed so without unconscious manipulations or projections with men, so – what was the phrase? – 'devoid of guile', but he decided this was his desire expecting the worst. So many lovely women, *especially* therapists, these days *were* gay, he mused, smiling at his self-indulgent and ideologically unsound lament, and he held in abeyance any verdict on her sexuality until he knew more.

That must be everyone, he thought, but Miriam had noticed another silent member on the edge of the circle, half-hidden in the shade of the room.

'You haven't introduced yourself yet. Would you like to?'

This was Bill Davies, the pipe-smoker from the stairs, a shabby figure with creased jacket, in his late fifties. He looked weary, as if life were too much for him. Bill worked in the National Health Service, but felt paralysed there because of his opposition to orthodox psychiatry, a stance which had guaranteed his scapegoating and had for years prohibited promotion. Unhappy with conventional medicine, Bill had tried to use radical forms of therapy in a context which maligned them. He had needed alternative, anti-drug therapies, but as these had become more accessible and popularised, increasingly associated with California, the 'me' decade of hedonism and middle-class luxury, the prejudice of the establishment had hardened from suspicion into condemnation, leaving Bill ostracised on a branch that would eventually wither from their contemptuous neglect. One of Bill's hands, Thomas noticed, was slightly misshapen, twisted, and his identity seemed concentrated there, in that withered left hand, defeated from within.

Bill's feelings about being on the workshop were mixed. His thankfulness that radical therapy, psychodrama, was happening, was surrounded by resentment that it was happening here, 'cloud–cuckoo land', rather than in mainstream medicine. It had become a privileged, expensive activity, almost a hobby – 'though no offence to anyone here', he hastened to add – for people who were relatively OK. A therapy for kicks, 'an *in* thing to do', a glamorised colour supplement attention to oneself, the logical outcome of the eighties.

Part of Bill wanted to reject this whole enterprise, to retain the purity of his lonely struggle inside repressive institutions, but his colleagues' hostile voices, insisting that this stuff was gimmicky, unscientific, inauthentic, inaccessible, also squashed something in his soul, something that knew there *were* other possibilities. Bill's was the kind of mixed response Thomas had seen in people struggling with faith: a longing to be able to surrender to something intangible yet *known*, but this very longing weighed down by a scepticism and bitterness that the doubts could not be countered by anything more substantial than their own hope, their own resilience through the dark night of the soul. As Bill talked of the myopia of some of his peers, vacuum-sucked into the system, still addicted to medication as the anodyne for all ills, 'to them, drugs are straightforward, honest-to-God solutions', his isolation became apparent. Bill was unable to share their lack of uncertainty about themselves: that almost wilful ability to ignore unease when X is sectioned or Y's ECT goes drastically wrong and kills his memory, and Thomas' heart went out to him. There was something of Bill in himself, he knew. Not the same as martyrdom, though very close to it, it was an apprehension of defeat co-existent with an adamant refusal to surrender. Staying with the struggle, because the stakes were high: were everything.

Cynically, whilst Miriam responded, Thomas measured the contrast between them. About the same age, yet whereas Bill was wiped out, Miriam was thriving, the queen bee of individual enterprise. Bill Davies was exhausted by a system which Miriam, by remaining outside, had managed to evade. She had demonstrated that *selling* the soul – the healthy soul – worked, made money, whilst adhering to principles and moral standards inside a social or state-run institution didn't. He didn't know which was better, either morally or personally, Miriam's independent survival of the fittest, or Bill's die-hard refusal to sacrifice nostalgic ideals, but he began to wonder whether both weren't, in their own ways, huge ego investments. Miriam's therapy and philosophy was in the service of the 'positive ego', attached to getting rich and celebrated through her dramatisation of psychic life, really a rising up at the cost of others' inner pain, whilst Bill's was a kind of 'negative ego' involvement, his reluctance to bale out of the dying vessel of the Health Service really a mechanism to strengthen his sense of a moral martyrdom. Was it possible, for all their differences, that they were living in the same place, only in worldly terms her cup was full?

He became conscious through his musing that Simone, Miriam's co-ordinator, a dramatic presence, swirling with colours, black and purple and orange, was saying how aware she was of being 'the only black person present'.

'This often happens in groups of this kind,' she continued, 'though the thirteenth member of the group who had applied to come, Charlie, is also black. Maybe he was frightened of being a token coloured: I think we should register his absence and all that it means.'

There was silence. The stage was set; the group raring to go.

They began with games, silly games to break the ice and ensure they remembered names. Throwing huge cushions, confessing secrets. 'I eat chocolate at night.' 'I wear black underwear.' 'I smashed my husband's car.' And then a more lengthy exercise to loosen up character fixities. It was a simple enough idea, a trading game, a psychic shopkeeping. Simone held a pawn shop, which Miriam owned and could control, where you exchanged some quality about yourself you didn't like for something that you lacked. Two fistfuls of self-denial would buy a jar of self-indulgence. A sack of fear would be replaced by a thick coat of self-assertion. A bucketful of grief purchased a book of tickets for nights on the town, a year of fun.

Most of the bartering was fairly timid. Colin exchanged overwork for more relaxing; Lee wanted some intelligence for laziness; Sheila offered envy of her mother for infinite compassion. But Thomas was not convinced. Bill's attempt to ditch three tons of tiredness for some spirited energy left him wearier than before. Steve's surrender of timidity for irresistible sexual prowess left him terrified; whilst Joyce, attempting to swap worry about money in exchange for a big premium bond win, was told this was against the rules.

'The change has to come from inside: you have to give up something for it,' she was chastened, at which she looked cheated, walking away from the pawnbroker's clutching a shoulder bag of 'certainty the universe will meet my needs' with considerable bad grace.

Then play began in earnest. Miriam invited anyone who wanted to work to stand up and be counted. Donna staked the first claim: she wanted to work on her father, disclosing that he was a Tory MP, and declaring that she 'loathed' his politics, in and out of the house.

'He's a real *pig*.' Miriam walked round and round the room with her, undoing Donna's rage, 'discharging' furiously. Her envy of elder brother who'd gone to a better school, her exclusion from father's world, her anger leading to her own radical politics of revenge seeking to exterminate the male race. Classical Oedipal rivalry, thought Thomas, a latter-day Electra.

But Miriam was turning the room into a world of misrule, a splendid form of carnivalesque: 'Freud says say it: we say play it.' Here was Donna's father, Colin, the right honourable Ronald Eagleton, playing hide and seek under the cushions, giving her a wheelbarrow around the group, Dombey with all pomposity and pride erased. He was the good father, the godfather, nurturing, Donna's face was softer, less belligerent, less taut, Colin was stroking that dishevelled hair, rolling in laughter on the stripped and soft-ened floor.

Lee was similarly satisfied as she took her turn in repairing history. Talking whilst walking around the room on Miri-am's arm of the 'unfinished business' that she had around her brother's death, the group was sucked one by one into her inner world. Joyce played her mother, harried, martyred, self-denying, unfulfilled, pushing her children into jobs, relations, situations she'd wanted for herself but had never dared achieve; her substitute satisfaction at their success never managing to eclipse a deeper resentment and envy at their greater fortune, an envy which manifested in underhand and covertly sadistic attacks upon them. Bill sat in as father, ineffectual, increasingly alcoholic in his own pipedream world, a limp and ageing lounger before fire and TV, deliver-ing platitudes. Thomas was invited to be Lee's dead brother, Simon, victim of suicide ten years before, the living dead, he thought ironically. Germaine stood in for Lee herself, Lee's projection of herself as she would like to be.

The group had become an audience in semi-circle, an amphitheatre at one end of the room, Greek crowd and chorus. They replayed the scenario, the news of Simon's suicide, the resultant confusion, grief, loss, panic, blank iner-tia, Lee's assumption of responsibility.

'I had to try to keep it all together somehow, to stay sane. I had to ignore the whole event in a way, to try to go on believing that things were worth living for, that he'd made a mistake, it was an accident with the drugs, he didn't mean it, there wasn't a family curse, it was all a big mistake. After that, I got into drama more and more. I learnt long parts, I mean really long parts so there were always words, things to say. Beckett's *Not-I*, monologues that went on for hours, anything so as not to have to speak myself.'

Simone passes the tissues, Miriam lets tears emerge, they carry on walking.

Miriam travels back in time, transporting Lee on the magic carpet into childhood. Lee cries in front of her parents: they respond now as they couldn't then, attentive, comforting. Joyce leaves unwashed dishes, holds her, soothes. Bill turns off the TV, repairs her bike. Miriam is a magician, waving away the last scene of death, filling the house with friends, meals, music, talk. She reconstructs a happy childhood scene, where Simon and Lee play together. Thomas lies on the floor, feet stuck in the air, an upside down worm. He can hear giggles – what *is* he doing here? – and Lee buzzes around him, a giant bee. They giggle too. They are four and seven. They get rowdy, roll on the floor, giggle helplessly. There is no one else in the world.

Miriam steps back from the fun.

'What would you want to say to Simon now, Lee, if he were here?'

'I'd want to say . . . '

'Don't just imagine it, do it, Freud says know it, we say show it, show him, show him, tell him now as if he's here. That is Simon. He is here.'

She tells him she loves him. She is proud of him. She wants him to be there always, not to grow up, not to die. 'Please be there always, Simon, please don't go away, don't let them kill you at the hospital.'

'Tell her you are here, Simon.'

Thomas finds it hard to collude. But I'm *dead*, I'm *dead*, can't you see, one of the living *dead*?

'Tell her, show her you love her. Was it an accident, Simon?'

He feels he's supposed to pretend, that the overdose wasn't real, it was just some headache relief he was seeking, all a big mistake, he had so much to live for, and this wonderful kid sister . . .

'I know you're still here, Simon, I know you still love me.'

'Sure, course I do.'

She lets the grieving flow, she becomes guiltless, free.

The waters of her heart stream out, the chorus keens as well. There is a feather touch of death, letting death pass, within the room. But Thomas, Simon/Thomas, feels no part in it. The process is irrelevant to him: he is merely part of their phantasy of restoration, their denial. Now the parents are good parents, and the family is a happy family. He sees the deck of cards on the blood coloured cloth, his childhood in Johannesburg, Mr and Mrs Smiler and their children, Master Smiler and Miss Smiler, Selma encouraging with saccharine.

'Can you give us Master Smiler, Thomas dear?' Her expectation of a pleasing grin – deny catastrophe. And here too the playing of the pack, repairing sighs. The family's restored, the world is free.

'You can go back to your places now.'

Forget Simon. Smile all you Sowetans, the world is free.

And so it goes on, scene after lovely scene, a restoration, making good. Sheila becomes slim and confident, Steve dares to confront father who had undermined his confidence, Barry challenges his ex-partner on maintenance. Miriam makes good, re-writes their history. It's magic, collective megalomania, proof of the power of wishes and unconscious drives.

The new age, thought Thomas, this age in its infancy, was like the new-born child, unable to give up belief in its omnipotence. It needed to believe in its ability to transform everything, and in this sense was no more advanced than the most primitive of tribes. Sitting there, behind his gold-rimmed spectacles, watching the psychic launderette in gear, Thomas couldn't help thinking of Freud, still a hero for all his egotism. Slowly, laboriously, Freud had conducted and collated his research into the buried iceberg, nay, the hidden ice *and* fire of the psyche, subject to none of the impatience that beleaguered this contemporary work. How different it was, Freud sitting quietly in his urbane room at Berggasse 19, Vienna 9, listening intently to the unspoken and unspeakable, to what cannot always be said or shown, the thing that has no words, no shape, compared with this huge playhouse in Birmingham Dockland, *Spectrum Three*.

The practitioners of this magic claimed to do in a week or

a day what Freud had spent a lifetime exploring, beginning to explore, discovering the possibility, and impossibility, of doing. He knew the enemy, the complex intermesh of body, mind, heart, in and out and up and down, the dark vicissitudes of 'psyche', soul. Was it man's impatience that spawned these quick alternatives? The typical intolerance there was with struggle, conflict, ongoing unravelling? This was the get-well-quick syndrome, remaking life according to desire, an infantile phantasy. 'What was it you wanted that you were never able to have? Go for *your* needs *now*.' It was a pressure to go for you-ness, me-ness, more meanness, more being ME, and yet what *was* this *me* that they were trying to achieve?

Here, that burrowing of Freud, awed at the unknown, simply disappeared. Here, the assumption was that everything *could* be said, shown, dramatised, externalised. Here, there were no secrets, no hiding places. Things were 'cleaned up', 'discharged', 'evacuated', 'come to terms with'. Feelings must be extrovert, cats swung against tyrants, cowards killed. A eugenics of the psyche, it was intolerant of darkness, struggle, fear, uncertainty. The aim was to be WHOLE, strong, confident, replete with ZEST, a kind of fascism, determined to exterminate imperfection. He found it hard to determine if the dominant imagery – *dealing with it, getting it out, discharging, coming to terms with, stuff coming up, unfinished business* – was oral, anal, phallic, or simply reflecting capitalist consumption, but it left him uneasy, cringing at the words. Words which were all the more difficult to discard because the things they referred to – death, suicide, mourning, fear, loss – were, despite the ostentation, *real*.

It was a discourse of the sanatorium and stock exchange: hygienic – and costly. Making you feel OK, target success. But what did it have to do with being more *human*, this therapy? He thought of Freud approaching New York harbour in the twenties on his first trip to the States, remarking laconically to his colleague, 'Ah, my dear friend, they think we are bringing them such treasures. What they do not realise is that we are bringing them the plague.' **Where** 'pure' psychoanalysis looked at this plague, staring **it long and** hard in the face, with all its horrors and deathliness, **this mo**dern therapy did a vast cosmetic job. It didn't **want that lo**nely encounter. Miriam and her brightly dressed **cohorts** were latter-day Pied Pipers, paid large amounts **of money to** carry away the dreaded vermin and dump them **in the** Grand Union Canal, the nearest waters of oblivion.

During the brief picnic lunch, which they **all shared ex**cept for Natalie, artlessly professing a lack of **hunger, he** noticed Miriam's ability to create invisible boundaries, **as if her** skill in facilitating psychic exposure in others **relied on revea**ling nothing of herself at all. She was gliding, **walking on** water over the depths of their pain, their mess, **their murky** pasts and presents, upheld by the very undergrowth **that bound** them to their darker selves.

Work recommenced precipitately after **half an hour,** as if they sensed this opportunity to heal themselves **must not** be missed. Bill stepped into the mesmeric circle, **and now** they were walking round and round the room, **Bill and Mir**iam, he slumped slightly forwards, she upright **like the new** Prometheus, rewriting destiny. There was **something poign**ant about the contrast between Bill's scruffy **suede shoes** and Miriam's shining white boots as they **marched side by** side around the polished floor. Bill was waving **his free right** arm, his left held supportively in Miriam's, **as if she knew** that withered part of him needed protection **and caressing.**

'The problem is,' began Bill, 'I feel I might **be on the** verge of a breakdown. I feel like that character **in Chekhov** who's always doing things for other people and it **drives him** mad. He starts hearing things, bees and insects **in his head.** I feel like that. Crowded out.'

He told of his marriages, first to Marjorie, **now Heath**er, the demands of wife, step-daughters – one **a glue-sniffer** – mother-in-law with Alzheimer's disease, **the hospital,** the lack of time. Strange, Thomas thought, **how other** people's suffering, *in extremis*, always tends towards the farcical. It's only inside you know how much it hurts. Was that why Miriam turned it to play? To change the tragic into comedy? It was like Lear, lay on awfulness too thick and it becomes absurd, flakes off into the risible.

Bill talked of his drinking, his despair, his loneliness amidst the demanding activity. They walked, they walked and walked. Now she was exploring Bill's lost anger.

'I'm wondering what's happened to your resentment and anger about all this Bill . . . '

My God, didn't she see? The poor chap had no energy for ire.

'I don't feel angry. Just helpless. The question is, should I leave Heather or admit defeat?' Thomas was watching the event as a TV show, *Double Your Money*, where the audience shouts out advice. 'Open the box!' 'Take the money!' 'Leave her!' 'Let the dead bury the dead!' But Bill was impervious to the chorus, his head in his left hand, wretched.

'I just feel so helpless, dizzy, kind of wanting to stop the world and get off, it's spinning the wrong way, making me sick.'

Miriam nodded, kept them walking silently, trying to undo the terrible sickness in Bill's head.

The audience attention was total, even Barry's nonchalance suspended. Germaine was leaning forwards with her chin cupped in her palm, the silver earrings catching her forearms, utterly engrossed. Only Natalie was removed, unable to participate.

'Do you have any children of your own, Bill?' Miriam's voice was rich and probing.

'No, no, that's the thing. I wish I did. Marjorie wasn't into sex and babies, too frightened, and Heather didn't want any more.'

Thomas saw Bill again as the branch of a tree, pecked and eaten from within, about to fall. He wondered if Miriam too were stumped by it all. What magic wand could transform this? But nothing daunted her; she continued, serene. He wondered if *she* ever woke to nightmares, panicking in sweat, trying to help the night struggle to dawn.

'The pain's greater than the anger, mm, Bill?' He nods sadly. He kneels on the floor and starts to sob. Behind the call to anger lies a sense of impotence, despair.

'I don't think anyone can help me. I don't know what I came here for. Maybe my colleagues are right after all and all this playing around is just a waste of time. Nothing changes.'

'Would it be better to talk to Marjorie, Bill?' A beckoning to Germaine, someone Miriam thinks is strong enough for the projection, to play first wife Marjorie. 'Show Marjorie what you never showed her about your sexual relation with her, the fact you didn't have a baby with her, Bill.'

He sobs more. His tongue is loosened. Sorrow and regret pour out of him. If only, what if . . . I so wanted . . . needed . . . The pain of her coldness, her turning away in the night, her fear of pregnancy. Sobs lurch out of him like an old engine, unaccustomed to this cranking of the heart.

'I wanted a baby with you, Marjorie, I wanted a baby . . . ' How he would have loved it, held it, tenderly, a nurturing father, how he wanted that . . .

'It would be a male child, wouldn't it, Bill?'

He nods. 'Yes, yes, it's a boy.'

'Yes.' She finds a small pink cushion and puts it into his arms where he is kneeling, kneeling in grief and loss. 'Here, Bill, here's the baby you never had and wanted so badly. Hold him, love him, talk to him.'

Bill holds him, the baby, himself, close, tenderly. Thomas can hear Joyce sobbing and Sheila has tears streaming. He can feel some of his own pain rising, his own desire to father, to mother, to be fathered, to be mothered, his own unborn and unheld child like a great ache within him, rising.

Bill is rocking from side to side. 'I want to take care of you. I want to be a loving father to you. Not to all those bloody others out there. To you. To you.'

'Yes,' says Miriam. 'Yes, it is a time for making reparation.'

He promises to make time for this child. Time to play,
make aeroplanes, ride bikes, be silly, time to love and laugh,
time to make proper decisions.

'And time to cry?' prompts Miriam.

'Yes, and time to cry. And let go.' Now he is able to be
angry, to defend his child.

'Show them, Bill,' she urges, 'show what you want,' her
New York voice resounding with the battle cry for freedom.

He shows the chorus, the world, they understand, they
promise to look after him, the child, they see his needs.

'OK. Thank you everyone.'

People were moved by Bill's work. Not many had kept
dry eyes. Miriam made a joke about the number of Kleenex
they'd used, and released the tension, made things 'normal'
again. Time to assimilate, time to digest and distance through
the alkali of theory. Thomas was amazed at her facility in
moving in and out of pain, like a swallow or kingfisher,
dipping and gliding through crises unruffled. He wondered
if she was *involved* at all. He wanted to believe, yet somehow
could not, that Bill's work was real, that it would make
some difference out there in his day-to-day life in the NHS
and harpy-filled Wolverhampton semi, but it seemed
implausible. Was deep transformation *really* possible in this
way, or was it as transitory as the play-acting itself?

He thought sceptically of all the parallel workshops proli-
ferating from west to east, from California to New York,
and rising in Britain from the opulent south west like sap.
These offerings of metamorphosis. *Fulfil your potential. I can
help you discover your REAL self. Train now for the ultimate
mind–body synthesis. Neurosis is caused by traumatic childhood
experience: with our help you can free yourself forever from its
damaging effect. Breathe the breath of life. Rejuvenate your body,
mind and spirit in just three hours with our transformative medita-
tion-breathing-therapeutic-psychic-practice.* Lucrative dreams.

Despite initial declarations, few had really come here for

the theory. They were not in search of *meaning*, but were characters in search of an author to rewrite their lives into OK-ness, refashioning a whole, not damaged, thing. They were not after understanding their neurosis, but seeking freedom from the 'neurosis' of character altogether, and they were happy to sink into their exhaustion after witnessing these catharses. Only Miriam, regal and powerful as ever, was alert, her articulate theories drifting around their shoulders like stale smoke.

His unease and anger increased even more during the weary 'sharing' that followed. Colin was talking about a 'feeling that his life was just a bit *too* OK – if that makes any sense –' and there followed a series of nauseous banterings.

Joyce muttered, 'You should be so lucky!', Simone looked suspicious, but Miriam said knowingly, 'Well, there's always *something* to work on! It sounds as if most of us are here to work on our feeling of something being wrong, whereas Colin's here to find out what's wrong for him in there being nothing wrong.'

And Simone latched on: 'That's right – for us it's what's OK about our not OK-ness and for Colin, what's not OK about his OK-ness!'

The semantics became more complicated as everyone joined in the joke.

'Well, I guess we're trying to rewrite Eric Berne's script about the kinds of transactions and games people play. Instead of his "I'm OK, you're OK", it's more like "I'm not OK, you're not OK and that's OK! It's even OK to feel not OK about feeling OK!" '

Thomas joined the laughter. He was remembering Horst, the friend who had such an uncanny resemblance to Colin, his similar sense of discomfort with too much ease. He could still hear Horst's voice on his last phone call to him that summer of 1983, 'Thomas, how can you be this happy without *dying*?'

Horst had been a scriptwriter for TV doing plays and documentaries. He'd been married very early but it hadn't worked out, he'd not explained to Thomas why. And then, in his early thirties, he'd married Brigitte, a striking looking blonde woman who was an independent film maker. They had three children, a vast house on the outskirts of Berlin, in the Wandersee, all dreams come true. Then one July afternoon, when Brigitte had returned home, she'd found Horst slumped over his desk, three bullets in his head. He'd planned it all, not wanted to leave a mess, neat bandages soaking the blood spilt from his brain, and a long, articulate suicide note, prefaced by a quote from Othello. '*If it were now to die,/'Twere now to be most happy, for I fear/My soul hath her content so absolute,/That not another comfort, like to this/Succeeds in unknown fate.*' Thomas could feel the wrenching inside that he had felt then when Brigitte had phoned to tell him, and it left him with anger at the light-heartedness here.

They were joking about not OK-ness, able to make fun of an inability to let in joy, laughing about that being 'the least of their problems', and all he had was Horst to blacken their complacency. One of Miriam's sentences did reach him somewhere. 'Well,' she was saying wisely, 'happiness *is* one of the hardest things to experience. We all resist it, even though we say it's what we're seeking,' but he was more preoccupied with that gold cherub on the mirror, wanting to smash it through the glass.

They quickly exhausted theory, were having a brief break for cups of tea, and he was watching Barry chatting to Simone, half-listening to them, half-seeing a former lover in the room, the light catching her back. Barry was telling of how he'd been given enlightenment by the Maharaji, enlightenment gained as smoothly as a hi-fi set, but in him it seemed to have blown a fuse. He hadn't been ready for it, any more than he was ready for a sexual relationship that was reciprocal. Barry had a lazy look around his jowls, a man who has something for nowt, before the time is ripe, and observing the lines of dissatisfaction around that otherwise self-satisfied mouth, Thomas saw his suffering, a soul that tried to cheat. And what Barry had done spiritually they were all doing here. They wanted an alchemist to turn their dross to gold, none of the tedium of slow analysis, but big drama, roller-coaster agonies and ecstasies, opera. How hard to take responsibility for oneself. They sought immediate deliverance. Take us from this place of ignorance, sweet therapist, director, please deliver us, for here we can't abide. And helpers rushed along with stretchers, morphine, anodynes, let's lift you from this trench of pain, trying to calm their own despair, or fear.

Sharing cigarettes with Germaine, looking down from the roof area of *Spectrum Three* towards the embarrassed derelict buildings opposite, Thomas asked her what she thought motivated Miriam. It couldn't be altruism, there was too much money-spinning. What unconscious compulsion had driven her to this? A dead sibling, lost parent, premature birth?

'What do you think it *is*, Germaine, that really makes Miriam tick?'

'Well, don't forget she's Jewish.'

'What do you mean?'

'Think of all the Jewish therapists and analysts around. Freud and Klein . . . you should know.'

He laughed. 'Yes, I should know.'

Was that what drove Miriam to this rescue work? Drawing out people's burdening traumas, siphoning boils, stitching up old sutures, despite having no *relation* to these people at all. Was that it? A phantasy of reparation? Her own dream of omnipotence, the Jewish mama righting wrongs? *Don't forget she's Jewish.* She would make time run backwards, pull out the bullets where they lodged in European walls, push back the gas into those leaking German taps. She had been powerless to stop it then, so she would stop it now, malignant destiny; the mother unable to save her unborn children from slaughter would save these vicarious children, rewriting history, making romance. Redeem the times.

'Can it be *just* the Jewish experience, though, Germaine,

can it? Is that *really* enough explanation? I can't help thinking there must be something else, something subjective too, something in her own life. Do you have any idea what it could be?'

Germaine was looking down through the black bars of the iron fire escape, careful, cagey. 'Well, I need you to be discreet about what I tell you . . . not to disclose it to the wrong ears.'

'Of course, that goes without saying.'

'I hope so.'

Sheila was beckoning, they indicated to her they were on their way, walking slowly by the railings as they spoke.

'Funny, isn't it, Thomas, how a good mother comes from a bad one, as if you can't have one without the other: maybe the best surrogate mothers come from the worst real ones, like Melanie Klein.'

'I don't understand.'

'Well, the rumour is – and it might be mere rumour, you know how these things spread – that she had a child when she was sixteen or seventeen. She couldn't possibly keep it, all set for a career in dance, well-to-do right-wing Jewish family, father's political reputation at stake, mother into social functions, charities, protection of unborn children and all that, hardly the most conducive circumstances for single parenting. So apparently she went to London, had the baby, and it was adopted by a rich Jewish couple who were living half the year in South Africa, so they could pretend the child was theirs. All very hush hush, no further contact, that was one of the conditions of the adoption. Some brainless notion of child-rearing then, that the child should get attached to adopted parents as if they are the natural ones, and not allow for any splitting of affection.'

They were in the doorway of the theatre room as Germaine ended her disclosure, and the group looked post-operative, post-cathartic, sprawled lazily over scattered cushions. Yes, he knew that brainless theory. Selma had always said, 'Don't ask', when he'd discovered his adoption during adolescence.

'Thomas, we love you just as much as if you were our own, and you are our own.' That cursed phrase, *as* if . . .

'I wonder if it was a boy or a girl?' he said, casually, as they resumed cushions near the window.

'A boy I think, but don't take this as gospel, Thomas, it might be someone's drunken phantasy or imagination making up a reason for Miriam being as she is. You know how people . . . ' but she was interrupted by Miriam herself taking over the ceremonies for the final acts of disclosure.

The last one to work was Joyce, walking around and around under Miriam's arm, their dervish circle of the room. The Jewish mama undoing the years as she drew back the closed curtain of history. Thomas was only partly attending, partly conscious, caught up in another movement and regression as if that one out there was but a shadowing of his; it was he whom Miriam was holding, he who had fallen through the years, his emptiness lurching towards release.

In his fatigue, hardly having slept after a nightmare in the early hours, he felt that there was nothing now but the walking and the pain, round and round, hers and his, half-real, half-phantasy, till he didn't know if this too was dreaming or waking. He was in Cambridge, cycling by the Cam, a quiet sunny Sunday, on his way to see his professor in Trinity. Soft lilac wisteria was out on some of the old colleges, a sense of spring in the air. He was aware he was having difficulty balancing, for on top of his head was a stack of heavy library books, all thick hardbacks, Freud in the original, and Lacan, weighty analytic tomes. He had to keep upright on his bike, with all these volumes pressing on his skull, as he steered around corners and over uneven cobbles leading down to the river.

In one hand he had a string-bag of groceries for his professor – delicious things from the delicatessen – thick peppered salami, blue cheese, olives, taramasalata, crusty bread, crisp matzos, Gentleman's relish, red wine, for the professor was Austrian and liked his oral delights – whilst with the other he was turning the handlebars right and left, around this incline and that disturbing curve. Near the moored punts he glimpsed a dwarf who muttered 'Can't wait, don't be late,' but he couldn't look away from the path directly in front or he would lose his balance. By the river, though, he knew he had to stop, he knew that there was something in the water demanding his attention.

It was Natalie who had been in the dream, Natalie, whom he'd never met, a brittle figure in a summer frock and straw hat, daisies strewn in her hair, treading in slow motion through long, red-poppied grass towards the riverbank, inexorably closer. But what was it, that drowning shape under the surface, what was it? Natalie, who had walked into the river, lain down in the weeds? No, no, it was a baby, he knew it was a baby, abandoned to the water like Moses, just this baby, he couldn't tell if it was male or female, but very young, its long white christening gown and small embroidered skull cap on its head, about to drown. There was no one else around, only he, Thomas, to stop the baby from drowning, but he couldn't move for all these weighty tomes upon his head, he couldn't dismount, for his father, his professor, was waiting, he mustn't stop or he would lose his doctorate, and he could feel again the familiar panic, sickness, the baby drowning, his mouth crammed full of death, each second nearer hell, screaming, clutching for breath, his lungs blocked up with weeds and tar-black water . . .

'Come, come,' Miriam coaxed, midwife to agony, her woman's voice, her mother's voice, a voice to sleep by, moving to the past. Was it he or Joyce now, curled on the floor, a few months old, a few weeks old, days, hours, alone, hearing father thrashing mother, unable to stop the pain to her or to herself, mother leaving, helpless, helpless? There was crying, her crying, mother's crying, his crying, anguished sobs, time having stopped, held in suspense at that moment that swung like gallows from eternity. He saw someone stopping father, saving mother, reversing time, and he could feel Miriam bending over Joyce, Germaine leaning over him, concerned.

'What is it Thomas, what is it? Who's left you? What's happening to you?' And she taking him up in her arms and rocking him as Miriam was rocking Joyce, soothing, being the mother she needed, he needed, the mother . . .

He was in a place where language couldn't reach, a place of pain and longing and desire, before consciousness began. Mind and body were not, had not learnt division; time and space were not, had not begun, not known. Somewhere before mirrors, before screams brought recognition. There was only this nucleus, this cell of him, unformed, alive, waiting, at one. He was with the rest now, being rocked, lifting Joyce slowly from side to side, a vast cradle of the world, of all of them, rocking her body, rocking his body, holding her from the ground, back and forth, crooning, caressing this fifty-year-old, day-old baby, and she lost to it all, he lost to it all, lifted and rocked before a life of violence and isolation, before deprivation.

And in this new beginning was the world. And the world was love. And hurt was not, hardness was not, council estates were not, orphans were not, nor poverty nor pain. Just softness, light, warmth, peace, caressing, flesh, these soft sounds as the women moved, their breath mingling, their voices humming, soft sea-shell of the seven worlds, holding and holding, on and on. Slowly, after an eternity, they lowered her, lying beneath a blanket on the ground, quiet, peaceful after lifetime's storm. Some were sobbing at the healing, some were awed at the witnessing. The room felt lighter, cleansed of Joyce's resentment and hatred, a catharsis had occurred.

'Good,' says Miriam, 'good.' It is finished. *Consummatum est*.

Noticing with surprise that hours had passed during that birth, Thomas slipped into the hall for a cigarette to steady his hand, and sat with his feet on the scarlet handrail, inhaling the tobacco deeply, trying to catch air his dream had denied. What had happened to him? Where had he been? He felt shaky, no longer in control. Germaine was approaching, smiling, asking him if he was all right, he must deal with this trembling in his body, his limbs trying to spasm, there was nothing to hold him, he must distance, let himself distract, freeze.

'Are you OK, Thomas?' Germaine was there, Simone was there, they could see something was collapsing.

'Yes, I'm OK. I mean, I'm not OK, and that's OK!' The half-joke sounded feeble, unconvincing.

'Is there anything we can do, anything you need?'

Only some holding I never had. Only the impossible. Only everything.

'No, it's OK, thanks, I'll just have a couple of cigarettes, then I'll be fine. I'm just tired, I didn't sleep too well last night.'

'Maybe you need company,' Germaine suggested.

He smiled, 'I can't think of anything nicer,' but still the pain and panic raged inside. Nothing was enough; nothing could repair. The rent had gone too deep.

'What's your family situation, Thomas, do you have parents? Brothers? Sisters? Are they still alive? Or wives?'

'I'll tell you later. At the moment, it's too painful.'

She understood, said nothing, stroked his arm. Her hand was caressing the plastic poles which stood before a drop of several hundred feet, her Indian snake rings sinuous.

'What's happening in there now?'

'Oh, it'll be mostly theory now, winding up.'

'Mutual congratulations and things.'

'Don't be so bloody cynical, Thomas.'

'Sorry.'

'But yes, it'll be something like that.'

Thomas hated his resistance. He loathed the contempt he had for the surrender he so longed to make. He too wanted to make a mess in public, but with Selma and Felix for parents, he'd never messed, he'd kept his sounds, shapes,

contents, to himself, had learnt to be contained. He wanted
to put his chaos in the room too, but his was unacceptable,
he was the one that Miriam would not sustain. And he was
envious of the others rocking Joyce like that without self-
consciousness, envious of them held by Miriam. He would
have liked to have been able to suspend his disbelief too, to
let go in what an inner voice insisted was a puerile, an
infantile, way. He wanted to share their discovery of a
mother figure, larger than life, to counterbalance all the badd-
ies of the inner world. But his scepticism was too strong.
His mentor was Freud, always fully human: *they* show, I
know. Freud never leapt into the woods, did not succumb to
deities or gnomes; Thomas could not betray him for this
new divinity. His resistance stood as solid as a prison wall,
concrete, invincible.

Hanging on to his arguments, he determined to take a
strong grip on himself for the last hour, desperately holding
together his sense of disintegrating, falling. But Miriam's
words of theorisation intervened, drifting through his
unsettled mind like sounds of a foreign language when
dozing on a train, unsure what country you are in. Thoughts
were spinning, not even thoughts, connections, memories,
realisations which were impossible to contain. *Don't forget
she's Jewish.* Miriam was fifty. *She had a baby when she was
seventeen.* He was thirty-three. *A boy.* She was seventeen
years his senior. *It went to a good Jewish family in London for
adoption.* In 1956, when he was born, she was seventeen.
They were from South Africa. It was the year she'd gone to
Britain to produce her unwanted foundling, the year Selma
and Felix had returned from Johannesburg and taken him
into their childless family. So what if, what if . . . no, that
was beyond the wildest dreams and dramas of *Spectrum
Three*, what if . . . No, no, no, it couldn't possibly be true.
It was more far-fetched than a Shakespearian romance, all
ends well-tied. But what and if it *were*? *Don't forget she's
Jewish.* Their blood was what they shared. They were the
same race, the same family.

Her words floated in and out, counterpointing his dreamy associations.

'. . . Much more than verbal . . . traumatic experiences get lodged in the body and psyche . . . deep . . . visceral . . . somatic . . . pain . . . Freud . . . psychosomatic . . . neglected . . . mothering . . . healing . . . restoring the good enough mother . . . finding the lost mother . . . sharing . . . lost mother . . . mother . . . mother . . . mother . . . '

The phrases seared him, re-opened the tear even wider. *Mother . . . mother . . . mother . . . mother . . .* He too wanted the wound taken away, this bloody scream of history stopped. He too wanted a righting of wrongs, an eternal reparation, life lived *as it might have been.* Those leaking taps. *Don't forget she's Jewish.* So am I. *So am I. And what about the bullets in my wounds?*

What if the child she abandoned in infancy *was* him, and fact were stranger and stronger than fiction? Could he reclaim this woman, Miriam, *as* his long-lost mother? *Was* she the mother, he the son? What if the future *were* perfect, in reality, not phantasy, and the embryo present all the time? But how could it be true? Mind split with madness at the thought. Head pulsed impossibility, desire. Was he going to risk making an idiot of himself and say to this stranger, yes, you are right, and more than right, for this theory is founded upon solid rock, you are indeed the long-lost mother? Part of him yearned for it to be true, this phantasy, this Mills and Boon. He hungered for permission to hold out his heart.

But another part yearned equally for it to be false. He imagined Freud on his death-bed, refusing to soften, unable to drink tenderness, adamantly denying God till the end and beyond. Anything except his pained version of the truth was too facile, too infantile, the stuff of dreams, offending hard-won knowledge for which he had sold all. But what if it was Freud, after all, who *was* wrong, Freud the sceptic? What if God really *did* exist and fairy-tales were true, and the magic of primitive tribes dancing every dawn and dusk *was* the reason for the sun rising each day? What if behind the sleep of reason lay not only monsters and vampires, but angels, benevolence, goodness, light, light. What if . . . ? Not only plagues but healing, light, light . . . *light* . . .

They were completing business, congratulating one another, noting ambitions left undone, remembering their bargains in the pawn shop and singing promises to unseen selves. Germaine had them in stitches, telling about an 'encounter-type weekend' she'd been on, where everyone had to be naked, yes, physically naked for two days, 'to get used to being together as we really are, trying to like the bits we hate', those sagging breasts, bellies and bums, and how they'd sat in a circle, a dozen of them, passing around a massive chunk of raw pig's liver, some pagan ritual to get them closer to the elements, their 'primal' selves. Though only half-listening, Thomas too smiled at the vision: twelve middle-class therapy addicts, social workers and teachers and mental health volunteers, sitting around with blood trickling down their thighs and arms, pig's blood spilling in their laps. He laughed at the absurdity of it. But it was a laughter which hurt.

Wasn't this too a public disembowelling, getting their innards out, passing their hearts, spleens, livers around the room? He imagined other parts of animals being handed between them too, goat-tails and ears and testicles, ridiculous, ugly, and his face grimaced bitterly at the absurdity, tragic absurdity, that they should be so *out of touch* they needed these raw rituals to feel blood to know what lay inside themselves. It was a civilised version of bloodbaths, bullfights, or brawling in the streets. It was what the goddam century, for all its barbarism, had lost: to *know* we feel; to *witness* one another bleed.

The others were full of positive resolutions, the kind you make on return from a vacation, only this time it was as if they were all about to start a lifelong reprieve from work. They promised they'd 'have much more fun', 'spend money on themselves', 'give more priority to silly things, to going out, and seeing friends, and feeling good'. Sheila was going to 'stop worrying about what she weighed'; Lee would 'stop visiting her parents out of guilt'; Donna would 'confront her father in real life and get what she needed to do her writing and a degree'; Steve would ask out the girl at the mental health bureau; Barry would pay less maintenance and 'sort things out', but his eye was still roving, his body lounged against Simone's cushion. And Natalie remained silent. Nothing had changed for her. She'd occupied the royal box, but still the drama, life, was external to her, too lethal to be risked.

Thomas found himself getting impatient and weary as he listened to the thanks and effusive acknowledgments. Couldn't they see that their real dramas were off stage? What had the day achieved? Miriam had made a good few bucks and some of her charisma might have rubbed off on them. But would their lives *really* change? The pain they all lived with, the pain of this godless culture, *that* stayed, that couldn't be reversed. You came into the world, a script clutched in your hand. Could one day change the writing on that foetal wall?

It was 8.30 p.m., the workshop drawing to a close, farewells being said. Miriam noted his silence, inviting him to share.

'You seem to have withdrawn from us Thomas, is there anything you'd like to say before we end? I wonder if you're still holding on to some of that scepticism? What's happening with you? Is there anything you're not saying, any unfinished business with any of us here?'

The stock market wasn't closing without a chance to cash in all his bonds. And what a chance of the spotlight: Hamlet, Oedipus and Perdita rolled into one. The stage would ignite, the warehouse go up in flames of recognition, anagnorisis such as this chorus had never seen. Again, the TV audience yelled and cheered, 'Go on, Thomas, open the box, open the box,' but he stayed silent. What could he say? 'You're my mother'? He wasn't an idiot, he couldn't say that, and anyway, was it true? What was truth? *Everything possible to*

be believed is an image of truth. But where did the possibility
of belief come from?

You had to think about things, weigh them up, decide,
discriminate. I am like Natalie, he thought, frightened of
becoming Sheila, the fat one, starving myself because I don't
want to be deceived, because I don't want to choke on this
rich sugary philosophy, *as if.* It keeps me cold, empty, but
true. True to the century, a kind of loyalty. What was it
Felix had said, when he'd revealed he wanted to begin analysis? '*Hang on to your neuroses, they're all you've got.*' Are we
meant to deny damage? Meant to pretend there was no
bloody cross? No Buchenwald? Give him neurosis, *let him
be mad, sweet heav'n, let him be mad,* but let the substance that
was *him* remain.

It was hot, he was weary, crazy, there had been too much
drama. Things like this didn't happen, he was tired, it had
made him dream up the whole thing, it was all regret at not
having 'worked' himself, that had made him concoct this
final drama. It was wish-fulfilment, projection, megalomania, a gratifying phantasy of omnipotence to remedy neurosis of abandonment. He knew the theory, he knew the
words. O thank you father, thank you Freud, he knew the
bloody words.

The arguments in his head went round and round in a
dance of death, hostile figures in his skull scything down the
horsemen of reparation. Another few moments and it would
be too late to turn back the clock. Miriam was flying back
to New York tomorrow; they would be entered as case
histories in her file, part of her impressive train of achievements, her surrogate children, held and repaired. Maybe she
was their mother more than his, for he couldn't share her:
he refused to have her as a mother substitute, yet another
one. He needed to hang on to possibility, Miriam's *real*
mothering, to an eternal universal yes, but to do so, she
must stay a myth: the possible *reality* of her must be denied
to keep her endlessly affirmed.

Once again, he must lose her, this time knowingly, consciously embracing loss, for he was tired unto death of the whole damned philosophy of make-believe, that bloody Vaihinger's *as if*. He was the one she'd left behind, thirty-three years ago, the one rent she could not repair. He wouldn't be seduced.

'Anything to share, Thomas?'

Nothing, mother. 'Nothing, Miriam.' Except I wish that I believed. *Oh, how I wish that I believed. That the future was perfect. That my redeemer liveth.*

Good, she says, good. It is finished. The others are embracing, exchanging addresses and numbers, appreciating. He watches Miriam pick up her pure white jacket – serene, smiling, letting Simone tidy the room – his mind hallucinates her body swollen with *his* form, hears *her* screams as he forces through her to the world. She is leaving the room now, he wants to call her back, but can he stab her in her brightest hour? He holds his cigarette, inhales impossibility; oh let it go, surrenders, let it go. Someone must lose. As Brecht once said, *Who built the pyramids?*

They gather lighters, papers, bags. Germaine is waiting for him now, suggesting they join Colin, Barry, Lee in the bar. He wonders if they'll spend the night together, is lying in bed with her, telling her the drama he hasn't acted, his masochism turns into nobility. Germaine touches his cheek, strokes thighs and belly, curls into his arms. She points to a new series of paintings, filled with mothers and infants, Christ protecting the Madonna from invading death.

'Are you coming, then, Thomas? Don't you feel like a bit of normality after all that heaviness?' passing him his jacket and nodding to Colin that they'd meet them in the bar, noticing his hesitation. 'You know your trouble, Thomas Winkler, don't you?' mocking, 'your trouble is, you don't like happy endings.'

He smiles ironically, sadly, that barbed wire stretched from east to west, piercing the flesh of refugees. Horst's body sprawled across the desk. Draping his coat over his shoulder, he walks towards the stairs.

'I can see I'm not going to get away with anything with you, Germaine, am I? You can read me like a book. Don't be so damn astute. Don't you understand? I'm a child of the times: I'm Jewish. Of course I don't trust happy endings.'

'Just because you don't believe in them, Thomas, doesn't mean that they don't exist!'

'But don't you see, Germaine, it's just like this version of therapy. It's too seductive. The politics are so dubious.'

'But Thomas,' she says, laughing, adjusting her silk jacket on the naked brown flesh, shutting the door with certainty against unsettled ghosts, and hooking her arm into his as they descend the half-lit stairs, 'Thomas, the politics of seduction always are!'

The New Jerusalem

It all started with that phone call Stephanie made just before she left London. I think it was sometime in mid-July, yes, the date must be here on my moon chart, because I was keeping a religious record of every bloody hormonal event. Late Sunday evening, July 10th.

'Emma?'

'Speaking.'

'Thank God for that, I've been trying for ages. It's Stephanie. What a relief, to actually get you and not the answerphone! I can't tell you how I *hate* speaking to those machines: my whole life these days seems to be spent trying to get past impersonal bits of metal or decoding silicone chips. I could swear my mother's got a very authentic-sounding answer machine that she programmes to talk to me, whole blinking dialogues! Come to think of it, Emma, how do I know it is really flesh and blood your end, and not some sophisticated computer?'

'Well, I promise you I'm more than just a voice. In fact, I'm bleeding profusely at the moment, so . . . '

'I know. "Only women bleed." *Raving Beauties*, right?'

'Right – so I think I'm the real thing!'

'You've still not managed to get pregnant, then, Emily?'

'No, I was a couple of days late this month, but it was a false alarm.'

'I'm sorry. You'll have to tell Paul he's not trying hard enough!'

'My God, if he tried any harder, I think it would drop off!'

'That's better, it's nice to hear your dirty laugh again. Anyway, what about the rest of life? It's really nice to talk to you, by the way, I don't half miss you.'

'I do you too. The trouble is, this baby thing affects everything else, it's making me feel I'm no good at anything.'

'But that's crazy, and you know it. Remember what Kate Chopin said anyway.'

'What was that?'

'*Anybody* can have babies: an *oyster* can have babies. The important thing is to be a person.'

'I know, I just really want a baby. It would be kind of giving birth to myself, if that makes sense.'

'Only too much. It's probably why most women have kids. New lives, phantasies of new lives. Still, it will happen eventually Em, it's bound to. There must be a soul up there *somewhere* that could use a good mother.'

'I know, that's what I keep telling myself, it's just a matter of time.'

'You're probably having to wait till the right person's ready to reincarnate. Maybe they're even still alive!'

'Well, so long as it's not Maggie Thatcher or Dennis, I don't mind. I don't want blood poisoning.'

'Quite!'

'Steph, I'm sorry I haven't written all this time. I've been meaning to, but . . . '

' . . . "but I'm a lousy correspondent" . . . '

'Exactly, so it's good you've phoned, you can let me have your new address and everything. How does it feel to be leaving the flat?'

'Weird, it's really weird, a bit traumatic. Do you know, this is the only place I've ever had that's been all mine, that Yvette didn't find or choose or pay for. In fact, I was trying to work out the dates just now, Em. When was it we first moved in here?'

'It was at the end of our first term, wasn't it? You got the flat in December and we moved in at New Year, just before your nineteenth birthday. I was there three years, and you've been there another four. So you've had it for seven years.'

'Good Lord! As long as that? Quite a symbolic number then, seven . . . it doesn't feel that long, four years on my own here . . . '

'Hardly on your own, Steph, come on, I'd hardly call your past few years on your own!'

'No, that's true, it's not exactly been a den of chastity. But *underneath* I've been on my own. I mean, I've paid all the bills, and there haven't really been any permanent fixtures, not worth speaking of . . . !'

'But what about this new guy you hinted at in your card?'

'Soll, you mean, beautiful Soll?'

'Yes, is he likely to stick around?'

'God, Em, I hope so. I can't stand one more crash landing. Well, that's why I'm phoning really, to tell you about it all. He's the main reason I'm leaving London. We're not only going to live together, but we've found a place to stay in Glastonbury, a kind of communal house where various dancers and alternative types live, and we're going to try basing ourselves there for a few months at least.'

'Glastonbury! But what about work?'

'Well, Soll will travel as usual, he does gigs all over the place, and there's quite a demand for African dance around Somerset, especially the Bristol–Bath area, so he should be able to pick up some regular classes there. He's wonderful, Emily, and a superb dancer, mm. I'll carry on with my dance and maybe learn some astrology or something too, there's plenty of scope for that. I mean, it's King Arthur's country, the astral centre of England, the very heart chakra of the nation! Beautiful landscape too. Mind you, almost anywhere would be after Stoke Newington, wouldn't it? The Seven Sisters don't exactly take much beating!'

'You'll love being in the country, Steph, I couldn't live anywhere else now.'

'I know. And it'll be so good to walk down the street without worrying about getting mugged – Alice got attacked again last week, did I tell you? She lost sixty quid. And to get away from all the noise and pollution. I had the radio on just now whilst I was packing and they've discovered yet more nitrates in London water. You may as well try mouth-washing with sulphuric acid as get any safe liquid out of the tap within fifty miles of Westminster, it's disgusting.'

'So when are you moving?'

'Sorry, I was getting carried away. We're going next Satur-day. Soll gets back from an Amsterdam show on Friday, and we've got a couple of friends to help us move some stuff in a transit van, so it shouldn't be too bad.'

'Quite a drive, though, isn't it?'

'It's about three hours on the A303, and we'll leave early before the traffic builds up, well at least that's the plan. It'll be OK. Peter's quite heartbroken I'm leaving the flat.'

'The landlord? Is he still downstairs?'

'Yes, as jovial as ever. He said I could sub-let if I wanted, but I told him I need a new start. I've got to get away from London. After all, Yvette's still here, and you've got to cut the apron strings sometime, even if they are elastic enough to stretch from Richmond to Cockfosters.'

'What does she think about it all?'

'Oh, I shan't tell *her* till it's a *fait accompli*. Then she'll probably find five minutes in between patients to leave me a message on the answerphone wishing me a wonderful *vita nuova*.'

'Well, I hope the move goes well. You will send letters and things won't you?'

'I will, even though you hardly ever reply!'

'I know, but I'm not as verbal as you. I reply in kind, I send protective vibes and things through the ether.'

'Well, I shouldn't be needing it so much there, the holy

pastures of Glastonbury, England's green and pleasant land . . . '

'It'll be different energy, that's for sure.'

'Actually the house isn't in Glastonbury itself, it's a few miles away, shall I give you the address?'

'Aha – I've got a pen ready . . . '

'It's Sage Farm, Pilton.'

'Is that all, no road? No code?'

'Oh damn the code, I'm not putting post-office workers a step closer to redundancy by using the code; no it's quite small, it'll find us like that.'

'Isn't Pilton where they have the pop festival?'

'Yes, we'll have our fingers on the pulses of the nation's anarchic youth and latter-day hippies every summer.'

'And deafened eardrums!'

'Oh, I'm used to that with Soll's music. Fantastic drumming.'

'What's the phone number?'

'No, no phone – we're going to be living very simply, no telephone, no television, no microwave, no dishwasher. Getting away from all the indispensable mod-cons for a while.'

'You'll probably die of culture shock.'

'Yes, we'll have such severe withdrawal symptoms, deprived of London stimuli and carbon monoxide, we'll be on a life-support system of Radio One, no even worse, Radio Two, within a week.'

'Radio Four, actually. That's what they all listen to up here.'

'Really? Yes, I suppose it is. What's the news your end, anyway? How's the café? What's the latest in the onslaught against roast beef and Yorkshire pud?'

'It's catching on. There's enough students and health freaks around to keep us sprouting beans, anyway. Funny though, I keep looking at all these students and wondering what they'll end up doing with *their* degrees. I mean, did I *really* need to know about the demography or politics of South East Asia to bake spinach quiche in a Yorkshire backwater?'

'Don't see it like that, Em, where's your militancy gone? Do some affirmations. *All my knowledge is useful, it has made me the person I am.* Don't be demoralised. You might have a daughter who really wants to know about the Third World!'

'That would be nice.'

'Anyway, keep trying, keep it up as the actress said to the bishop. Maybe playing mother earth is just a temporary role. Listen, I must go now.'

'I *do* hope everything goes well on Saturday. You will write, won't you?'

'Of course, I promise. I'm saying a ritual goodbye to this place for both of us, don't forget. God, is that really the time? I must go. Talk to you soon Emily, bye. Take care. Lots of love.'

'Bye, Stephanie. Bye.'

I always kept Stephanie's letters. It was something about female contact, but also more than that, something about *her*, her inner world, our friendship, that I was starved for. They would keep me going from one week to the next whilst I counted the menstrual days and tried to convince myself that Paul's version of closeness was enough.

August 4th

Dearest Emily. How's about *this* for the new Jerusalem? Picture is of Glastonbury Tor, primeval energy of the mound just out of frame! Doing lots of dancing, walking, loving and more! This beats the City any day, or night. Practising some ancient fertility rituals I can do here for you! Love Steph. xxx

August 31st

Thanks for your letter, Em, you see you *can* write when you let yourself get your hands out of that sticky fermenting dough for just five minutes! Pleased to hear Paul's livening up: maybe he just needs educating, like the rest of them. Stick at it, kid!

You asked me to describe life here, you don't know what you're letting yourself in for. But as I've got a bit of time on my hands – Soll's up in Birmingham for a few days – I'll have a go. Next time I'm travelling with him – in the next few weeks his company's got workshops coming up in Exeter, Reading, Nottingham, Leicester – ridiculous really, when we moved to get some peace and quiet, but I'm getting pissed off being left behind like some patient Griselda. He's so sexual, I can't bear it when he goes off, feels like the worst possible abandonment. He's *such* a dancer: it just makes you want to *move* all day! *All ways moving*, our new motto.

Being here is quite an experience. The house is a cross between an old farmhouse and semi-Georgian mansion, sitting on the edge of a hill which was an ancient settlement, probably an Iron Age fort. Soll and I are sharing a large room in the front of the house with a splendid view across green hills and valleys to Glastonbury – vivid *emerald* green with blue tinges at dusk – with the sea floating on the far horizon. At sunset, the tor gets haloed in a glow of orange sun, terribly beautiful, the world at its most intense and poignant as it disappears. It feels quite magical.

That's the operative word: *magic*. Glastonbury thrives on it, survives by selling it. *Hundreds* of 'healers', astrologers, psychics, mediums, I never knew half of them existed, so many therapeutic possibilities even the most divided psychopath would have to admit surrender. I mean just listen to the A to Z of therapy round here! Acupuncture, acupressure, Alexander technique, alignment therapy, American Indian medicine wheels, aromatherapy, astrology, Buddhist movement, colour and chakras, connective tissue work, crystal therapy, dance therapy, dietary therapy, drama therapy, dream therapy, energy balancing, flower remedies, gestalt therapy, hair analysis, handwriting therapy, herbal medicine, homeopathy, humanistic therapy, hypnotherapy, iridology, Jungian-Senoi dream work, kinesiology, massage, meditation, metamorphic technique, mind clearing, NLP (neuro-linguistic programming), osteopathy, palm reading, polarity balancing, postural integration, psychosynthesis, rebirthing, reflexology – believe it or not, they can tell everything about you now, you know, just from the pupil of your eye, the ball of your foot, or a strand of your hair (mine's getting very grey beneath the highlights!) and maybe there's one I haven't found yet that works from the bum! – regression, Reichian therapy, reiki, sand-play therapy, shiatsu, smile therapy, Taoist therapy, TA (transactional analysis), vibrational healing, visualisations, white magic, yoga, Zen, Zoroastrianism, and all.

Amazing mantra-sounding phrases everywhere. *If you can walk you can dance. If you can talk you can sing. You Are Beautiful, You Are Free, You Are True: You Were Born That Way.* What more could one ask for? God? Ah, but he or she is here too, inside you, you're not allowed to forget it. *You are total love manifest in perfect physical form.* It's all here, the dawn of a new age, a new humanity!

I expect Ma would see it as one huge *placebo*, all very colourful and seductive, trying to tell a broken society it feels good, and I must admit there's precious little scientific explanation for anything. Most of it seems to work very *mysteriously*, magically. But then, magic has its charms. Everything's about light and liberation: *Rainbow End* Café, the Glastonbury *experience, vibrating with colour – awakening our rainbow bodies* and *Arthur*'s sacred this that or the other. What Haworth is for the Brontës, Glastonbury is for Arthur Rex. Though, as yet, there's no King Arthur toffee or parkin (more's the pity – miss your ginger parkin, the very gooey kind!)

The strange thing is that, despite all the commercial crap, some of it *is* real. The chalice well, for example, is very special, it feels quite holy to be in there for a few hours and see people sitting quietly meditating or praying or being still amongst the flowers, a sacred (I had to correct that from scared – I wonder why they slip so easily into one another?) spot. But for the rest, it's more jumbled up, and I'm totally confused as to what's sacred and what's secular, Glastonbury seems to have got them utterly blurred: half myth and half plain banality. Shops, for example, crammed with esoteric knick-knacks, rainbow skirts and candles, Indian shirts with little bells and dangling mirrors, crystal balls, Tarot cards, stone eggs, amethyst and quartz pendants, fountains of holy-well water trickling over the carefully arranged polished crystals, tapes of New Age music playing, soothing pipes and harps mesmerising you so you're floating away and only too happy to spend anything from £5 to £50 on a huge slab of quartz, or crucial guide books on loving relationships, how to let go of fear, contact your aura of liberated energy, be *free*.

Weird, you just start getting carried away, drifting into the Book of Revelation, a new heaven and a new earth, all death and sorrow and crying and pain passed away and tears from eyes wiped clean, when you're suddenly outside on the pavement again, and it's a dull Tuesday afternoon, bedraggled locals looking grey and haggard, a couple of pregnant women wearily pushing heavily laden prams up the street to the local mouldy Gateway, and a rake-like pensioner getting incensed at some long-haired, leather-jacketed youth who's just ridden his Yamaha within two centimetres of his front toes. And the music that was in your head somewhere and those rainbow promises of the free bounty of the fountain of life feel like mockeries, grating against this reality, Thatcher's seedy Britain. It's quite peculiar, makes me wonder if I've left Stamford Hill and Stratford East behind after all.

Anyway, I'm currently knee deep in most suitable reading whilst Soll's away, soaking up Arthurian epic and romance like one of your delicious herbal baths. Almost half-way through Marion Bradley's long novel, *The Mists of Avalon*, escaping into every mood-drenched page. Have you read it, Em? It's the Arthurian saga told from a female point of view, wise prophetic women and sybils like Morgan le Fay: brilliant account of how their spirituality and sexuality was repressed by the spread of a male-dominated Christian religion and its oppressive letter-of-the-law-logic and rationality. What else *can* you fight against that with, but magic? At least, what's come to be called 'magic', but our use of the word's rather debased, like the practice. It's very powerful, I think you'd enjoy it. Too heavy to send you in the post – it's a kind of cross between *Lord of the Rings* and a medieval *Gone with the Wind* – but do try it, if you can find time in between your tassajara cookbook and ovulation calculations!

I wonder sometimes how the bookshops and small presses make any profit at all from such specialised publications, though. After all, the market for esoteric lore is hardly able to compete with Mills and Boon, is it? Soll says they're probably all in league with one another, that the marketing and production of all these spiritual gimmicks is carefully managed. He suspects that the whole apparatus of the 'alternative' therapy and healing world feeds into and subsidises these presses, and if we looked into it, we'd probably find it's all an outpost of Robert Maxwell or Rupert Murdoch's empires anyway – or Proctor and Gamble, cleaning things up! But Soll's such a cynic because of his experience in Africa, I think he could sniff conspiracy in the nursery. Still, I do know what he means: that other book I mentioned to you ages ago, *The Aquarian Conspiracy*, might have a more sinister meaning in its title than we imagine!

Fortunately, the biggest plot of all isn't visible down here – I'm happy to say I haven't detected the *slightest* trace of psychoanalysis – and you know how keen my senses are when that Big Brother, I mean Mother, lurks around! Must go now, that's enough depletion of the rain forests with all my writing for one day. Good luck with the new opening hours and the conception! Lots of love, Steph.

The news of my positive pregnancy test came through in late September, my diary's marked in jubilant red ink, YES, so it must have been that month she phoned me from a local village. Ditch something, I wrote the number down on the inside cover to call her back. Ditcheat, September 21st.

'Hey, Emma, that's fantastic news, I'm so pleased for you! A summer baby! Now you'll have to believe that the witchcraft of Avalon is all it's cracked up to be: I put some seeds on the Tor and did the ritual dance and fertility chant in the full moon, when the planets were at their most auspicious, so there you are! Ancient technology: works wonders! It's so exciting. Can I be godmother, or whatever the secular equivalent is if you're not having a Christening?'

'Of course you can Stephanie, but don't you remember that time in the flat once, when we talked about babies, and we agreed we'd like to be at the birth, if either of us had kids?'

'Hey, you're right, I'd forgotten that. You mean you're inviting me to the birth?'

'If you'd like to come.'

'I'd love to, wow, that's one date I won't miss. I'll be there, Emily, come hell or high water. Thank you. I bet Paul's pleased.'

'Over the moon. It seems to have inspired him, he's been doing all kinds of creative things, like knocking out the alcove in the spare room, building a false floor, loads of odd jobs.'

'Excellent. Mind you, he's probably only too relieved to have a bit of a break from all the enforced sex!'

'Probably!'

'How's your health?'

'It's all right, except I've been having really weird dreams ever since I got pregnant. Makes me frightened to go to sleep. A sense of being haunted. Do you think that's normal?'

'Don't ask me, I get that without being pregnant! It's probably your hormone level adjusting to the invasion.'

'Yes, I suppose so. Anyway, what about you Stephanie, how's things with you?'

'A bit frustrating, really. Soll's away again for the week, and I'm rapidly discovering this crowd in the house are not exactly my scene. Staying up all night on the Tor waiting for a cold sunrise, or meditating around candles and incense all evening without any talk, is not really my idea of bliss. I'm even missing London streets and the telly, let alone Screen on the Green! But I've got to stick it out for at least a year, or I'll have Yvette down my throat with an all-knowing "I told you so." She doesn't know the half of it: the goddess worship at dawn would absolutely freak her out, and as for the coven of witches here – *real* witches, can you believe it? – she'd probably have them, or me, or all of us, *committed*!'

'Has she met Soll yet?'

'God, no, I haven't even told her about him. After those scenes with Bob last year, do you remember, when Yvette got so earnest at three in the morning about his "reluctance to engage with reality", as if the poor guy was out of work through some indigenous indolence and not because of the high unemployment rate in North Wales, never again. I wouldn't let her near any more of my men with a Freudian umbrella! When we split up, Bob said, "Steph, I still love you, so let me give you a bit of advice. Don't take your next lover home to mother for approval. She's too conservative. These political radicals always are." How right he was. No, Yvette can keep her head shrinking for her paying clients. I don't want Soll any smaller than he is – neither in his mind nor any other part of his anatomy!'

'Do you think she'd mind him being African?'

'Oh, she wouldn't refer to it explicitly, but she'd note it in the recording machine she dictates to her brain before sleep every night like some goddam *robot* – "Note this recurrent peculiarity in Stephanie: feels compelled to react against dominant social and sexual mores" – or words to that effect. You don't know how fortunate you are, Em. Better no mother than a bad one, I reckon. But how on earth did we slip into my least favourite topic of conversation? Let's get back to the good news. You're going to carry on working?'

'That sounds like an order.'

'It is.'

'Yes: anyway, I can't afford not to. I'll work as long as I can. It's due in the middle of May, but the first one's often late.'

'*First* one? You said that as if it was a prelude to other things. How many are you thinking of having, then?'

'As many as possible.'

'Good job you're not in China.'

'Why?'

'You're only allowed one. Penalised after that: reduced benefits.'

'Well, the same thing happens here in other ways.'

'That's true. Your politics are returning at last. Never mind, you can have my quota – I'm only too happy to have all my kids vicariously.'

'*Stephanie*, give us a chance, I haven't even had this one yet.'

'Sorry. Don't let my cynicism about mothering rub off on you. Hey, talking about money, Em, this call's threatening to run up your phone bill to astronomic proportions, we'd better stop. I'm so thrilled about the baby, it's wonderful; Soll and I will invent a new dance for it and I *swear* I'll be there at the birth, the fairy godmother, OK? So, is it my turn to write next, or yours?'

'Mine.'

'Good. Take care then, Em. Bye for now, lots of love.'

'Bye, Steph.'

November 8th

    Emma – Sorry not to have replied before now, phantasies of having infinite free time when I moved were naïve optimism. Been travelling around a lot the last few weeks. But Soll's away now and a marijuana crowd have finally made their noisy exodus, thank Krishna, so I'm revelling in unaccustomed solitude and can sit down with my feet on the cat and write to you.

Had mother to stay for the weekend and bonfire night – like childhood again, nostalgic but quite a strain. Surprisingly, she took Glastonbury seriously at first – well, seriously enough to bother to notice what was happening here – said I was wrong to think she only 'approved' of London analysis. 'The world's large enough for all of us,' she said, and when she actually *bought* a large amethyst crystal amidst the running water of *Shambhala*, I thought the world was turning on its axis and the New Age finally spinning in. But, predictably enough, it went rather awry. The amethyst turned out to be for a friend and the circle dance I took her to in the late afternoon on Saturday was an unmitigated disaster. It was so embarrassing. There was me hoping she'd get in touch with some mystical earth energies, sway that psychoanalytic poise a bit, become the rich soft mother whose arms I could fall into without ambivalence, but the inmates of the *Glastonbury Experience* were determined to do everything to put a spanner in the works of my phantasy life – Stephanie's desires wrecked on the wheel of the mundane world once again – so what's new?!

First of all this woman leading the group, Nanette, who really fancies herself, is floating around like some preening magpie in her mirrored skirt and jangly jewellery, hardly noticing what anyone else in the group is up to. The fact that most of them had never been to a circle dance before and were about as agile as Les Dawson on *petits points* totally escaped her. Instead of running the group so that it feels relaxed, Nanette gives off the air of sly superiority, raising the competitiveness at least fifty degrees and getting everyone galloping much faster and nimbler than they know how. The smoothness of something as easy as *misir lou* and *nebesko kolo* became utter fiascos, collisions of bodies and bellies going opposite ways, returning to meet themselves, as if the M5 had suddenly opened traffic lanes in every direction and there's a complete log-jam. I could hear Yvette's mind doing overtime, ticking over like an unstoppable machine, looking at Nanette, thinking 'Mm, some unresolved narcissism here,' and at the circle, 'Oh dear, difficulties in group management here, too much ambiguity, the misleading parent.'

But to cap it all, the woman next to my darling mother in the circle – why did it have to be *that* woman, right next to her? – having immense struggles dancing in her tight skirt and stockings, proceeds to a dramatic strip-tease down to bra and knickers. The woman is neither slim, nor elegant, nor young, and despite me feeling sympathetic to her wanting to be able to move properly and all the thoughts running around my head warning against dominant ideology about age and size, it's utterly humiliating. She's middle-aged, flabby, making clumsy gestures trying in vain to imitate Nanette – who is meanwhile continuing her ethereal wavings of arms and hands above her head and quick twistings of hips and feet – but every attempt this near-nude woman makes at a Swan Lake performance only draws more attention to the ineptness of ageing grey flesh. Honestly, Emma, it made me wince, it was so sad. And the whole group was like that woman, slightly seedy, trying too hard, with none of the lightness and grace I'd wanted to impress Yvette: the charm of the Aquarian age.

Yvette didn't say anything, but then again, she didn't need to. Her face spoke volumes, I could see words like 'exhibitionism', 'Oedipal competition', in every silent look. (The live music was being played by an all-male band, *watching* us, so of course we were all in competition for the father's love, what else?) Such a contrast with the Richmond propriety she's used to: after all, her patients only *talk* about their desires to flaunt and display – they don't actually act it out in public. All the time we were in Glastonbury, these crude dramas were being pushed in front of her eyes. It happened again in the house, a crowd of weirdos just 'happened' to drop in at tea-time, some traveller friends of Joey who lives in the basement – patchouli oil barely disguising bodily stench – as if there was a plot in the town to vindicate her and condemn me, to prove just how crazy people *are* without analysis. Everybody associated with me, and me too, were all on show with our defects, our autism, just for her benefit, to demonstrate how clumsy and useless we are without her. I became that child on the bridge in Munch's *Scream* – all mouth and agony and the world encroaching – what a weekend! I was praying for the tor to release some of its devas and swallow me up in its magical darkness.

And of course, she ended up with one of her famous theories about the place; she has an answer for everything. We were merrily tramping through a mulch of orange leaves, autumn soaked in the lanes beneath the mound of the tor – the tor, by the way, is a giant breast and the Tower of St Michael on top of it an erect phallus, so there you are, mother and father in one, both sexes nicely united, which is why all these delinquents are so keen to go there, reconciled with their persecutory parents at last! 'You see, Stephanie,' she said, 'Glastonbury is a place which is attracting people who can't accept *reality*, who can't face *ordinary* complexities and difficulties. All this frantic striving after white light, this longing for the dawn of a new era which is all sweetness and peace, is trying to get away from ordinary struggles with hatred and anger and pain, *inner* persecution. Hence what you refer to as the "weird" energy. There's nothing supernatural about it, there never was: that weirdness, that sense of the uncanny is simply people's own buried awfulness. It's because they're not taking responsibility for their darker sides, for the full range of their emotional natures. And so the things they don't want to look at are lurking around streets and buildings, which is why you keep feeling you're walking into pockets of darkness. So there *is* a weird energy around, but it's nothing to do with demonism, just the weirdness of human nature: it's what people are trying to leave behind. But it's not about good or evil spirits: there's no such thing.'

She's always told me that, ever since I can remember. No ghosts, no angels, no devils, no fairies, no Father Christmas, only mothers and fathers and animals and yourself. I realise now that must be why she left my father, though she's never said so. I don't think atheists and believers make very good bedfellows, do you? His faith must have incensed her: maybe she was jealous of it, as if he'd got another lover. Anyway, she went on as we trudged along the Somerset levels, reminding me of the vampire myth – Dracula – how vampires can't see themselves in the mirror, for they have no reflection, they are already shadows, and how they are created by precisely this kind of splitting. Bad parts of the psyche disowned and put out there, beyond the body. 'All the darkness they can't accept in themselves is getting projected out and deposited here, in the town and on these ancient mounds,' she said.

It was dark by the time we got back to Pilton, and I felt hollow inside, as if the whole experience of Glastonbury had changed: Yvette had irrevocably altered it for me. I've been feeling hollow ever since, horribly empty. Glastonbury couldn't be an opening into Eden any more, it was just a refuse site, a dumping ground for unconscious rubbish, damn her. Can she leave nothing unspoilt? What really made me mad, though, was the *coldness* of her analysis, dissecting human nature as if she didn't have a heart. Maybe it's she who is the vampire. But I *shall* make it work here *in spite of her.* If only I could find some other dimension, somewhere between the dry land of analysis and the red sea of Glastonbury, wouldn't it be wonderful. If those dissolving mists of Avalon were real!

Sorry, Em, I've been drinking whilst writing this and I forgot it was a letter to you and not my journal, so please forgive the lengthy invective. You're lucky, even if it has felt like a big gap to you – at least you feel free enough to be someone else's mother! Maybe it *is* a way of giving birth to yourself. I hope the morning sickness soon abates, it sounds grim. I reckon this letter's long enough to last you another couple of months! Take care. Write soon. Much love, Steph.

November 30th

In front of one old log fire. Dearest Em, Your letter helped clarify a lot of things about Glastonbury. Yes, there must be *some* genuine mysticism, maybe that's why I'm here. Nice to think of Joseph of Arimathea sticking his staff into the ground and it blossoming into a hawthorn tree. The disciples certainly travelled around more than they're given credit for. But I've not heard that idea before, of Christ going to India and being buried there: makes sense, though, doesn't it, India, the navel of the world. That would account for all the pilgrimages there now, but what a cheat for all those devout Christians labouring under the delusion that Christ's body is gracing the Holy Land, and saving all their Green Shield stamps for guided bus tours round the Dead Sea. My father must be turning in his grave at the very thought: heresy! By all accounts, he was pretty unyielding when it came to the gospels, interpreted them rather literally. Mind you, if it is true, it would explain some of the mess in the Middle East, wouldn't it? It's much less protected than we thought. God playing hide-and-seek with his own body – what a joker!

I should stay for Christmas, shouldn't I, and see if the thorn bush by the Abbey really does flower every December 25, but I've promised Yvette I'll go to her for the yule-tide farce. Soll will be in Africa – he promises this will be our last Christmas apart – and his prophecies are usually quite accurate (he predicts a son for you, by the way, no wonder you feel invaded!).

I'm wondering more and more how much of this place *is* authentic and how much it's all just illusion. What *is* the relation between pagan spirituality, Christian mysticism, and the Arthurian legend? Is there any? I can't accept Yvette's theory that it's *all* different levels of illusion, like the spoon-bending business. It feels to me like there's some kind of spiritual core here that's got overlaid, a strong primal energy that can't be disguised despite all the junk on top. I've met a woman here who's into astrology, Anna, terribly transcendental, waist-length black hair, who's hooked on to the idea of this being the lost Atlantis, and that spiritual essences are trying to communicate here, to reach through into the human realm, to teach us things. She's into channelling messages from them, can you believe it? But she's dead normal apart from that – she's even got a PhD in anthropology, so she can't be a complete nutter (or maybe she can, knowing academics!).

There has to be *something* in it. Why else the incredible convergence of people and energies here? Maybe there was some ancient druidic or Celtic essence, a deep knowing spirituality, possibly associated with women, that was focused here, then this Arthurian stuff, male heroism and power displacing it, getting merged with the masculine rule of the Church, and now, with our generation's rejection of that, there's openings for spiritual forces to come in again, and so all this New Age paraphernalia has got imposed on top, some of it superficial, some of it trying to reach down. It's made more confusing because the top layer is simultaneously dredging up the layers underneath and reclaiming them, like those shots of houses after bomb blasts, with the front wall missing and all the floors and stairs visible simultaneously. But that's the kind of archaeological image Ma uses, heaven forbid!

December 10th

Sorry, delay in posting this, will just add a word. Soll's already left for Africa, and I miss him dreadfully. I think I need to do something about this – we've had too much time apart, and I cannot cope with any more separation. I might try one of the quacks in town in the New Year. Sue – that brilliant dancer I worked with in Camden Arts Centre – she did a show at the Roundhouse that weekend you came down, satirising marriage and motherhood, brilliant, do you remember? – Whoops, I've probably said the wrong thing again, no offence to you, Em, you're obviously loving being pregnant – long sentence, but anyway, Sue's living in Glastonbury now too, and she's seeing this therapist who she reckons is brilliant. Sue's certainly changed, no longer gets week-long depressions, is much straighter with her anger, and earning money for the first time in a decade. I might give it a whirl in January, despite all past reservations about the couch. Will write again before Christmas. S.

December 20th

Where on earth did you find that book on Atlantis in the wilds of Yorkshire? Just what I needed to read on the train and counterbalance the library at home. All these analytic Horatios. There are more things in heaven and earth, Herr Freud, than were dreamt of in Vienna. Here's a small present for you. Enjoy your last baby/child/adolescent/offspring-free Christmas for fifty years, and make the most of the erotic possibilities! Love to Paul: impending fatherhood obviously suits him. Maybe having kids gives people a *purpose*? If I survive the yule-tide unpoisoned and uncommitted, I'll write you in the New Year. Have a great one and Xmas. Best love, Steph xxx

Jan 10th

Back at Pilton, thank God, just about alive. Who on earth invented it? Two weeks of stuffing bellies, starving hearts and minds, smiling and feeling villainous: horrific! They certainly fiddled the calendar craftily to make mid-winter darkness coincide with God's incarnation – maybe Soll's right and He too has shares in Fisher-Price, Cadbury's, Bernard Matthews' turkey farms and Marks and Sparks, but I can't believe His taste would sink so low as to relish the junk we got served up on TV: I'd forgotten the obscene crassness of it, those lobotomised chat shows. Yvette videoed the films she wanted, but that liberated time for us to talk, heaven forbid, *being* together!!!

She restrained herself from doing too much interpreting, except when she had some other analysts to dinner – and then, when they asked me where I was living, she had to point out that the other name for Glastonbury was *Avalon* – and of course what's her Richmond address but *Avalon* Terrace? Implying I'd not got away from her at all. Have you ever thought of the word *smothering*? Notice how it contains *mothering*? Different origin – it's Scandinavian – but still, the verbal similarity is striking. There's no such thing as 'coincidence', I learn that more and more.

And then they started laying into unqualified therapists. Yvette said she'd had to bail two people out recently – one man and one woman who'd done intensive bioenergetic work or TA groups or something and they'd gone round the twist – so that prompted the lot of them to start telling their horror stories about wrecks from alternative therapy who'd ended up being committed. Honestly, talk about prejudice: you mean *they're* not concealing any suicides or failures?

My New Year resolution, despite all this and previous vows, is to see this therapist/astrologer in Glastonbury who Sue swears by. I've got to find some way of really *living*, so I'm booking an appointment for next week. Send some protection! Happy New Year again. Love S. xxx

Thanks to a badly sprained wrist, I'd been unable to write since Christmas, so Paul dropped her a line for me asking her to phone and reverse the charge. It was early February when she called, freezing snow: I remember worrying about how bleak it must be for her having conversations in cold telephone booths at the side of empty roads.

'Emily? Hi, it's Steph here.'

'Hello, shall I call you back? Give me the number, the usual one, Ditcheat? . . . Good, now we can talk as long as we like without those dreadful bleeps.'

'How's your hand?'

'Oh, it's improving. Hard to cook with no right arm, though. We've had to get a student in to help in the café. Did you start your therapy?'

'I did, that's why I haven't been in touch, I'm sorry, I've been a bit preoccupied with it.'

'Tell me.'

'This woman, my therapist, she's terrific, Emily, not at all what I'd expected. Stunningly beautiful physically, thick auburn hair, grey eyes, superb face, a bit like Jacqueline Bisset, sort of dreamy looking but very intelligent. Not the usual mother figure at all. And very perceptive, she understood exactly why I was reluctant to go: so astute about my childhood. It's exactly what I need. She does astrology too, but only if you ask for it.'

'What's her qualifications?'

'Do you know, I didn't ask, but there's framed certificates on the wall. I think she did some training in London and in Eastern Europe somewhere. She has a foreign surname I can't pronounce, but her first name's Eva, and she's a Doctor, so I guess her credentials are good. She's got masses of clients here already, almost everybody I know has started seeing her and that's the best recommendation. You could have all the qualifications in the world and still be a lousy therapist.'

'Isn't it expensive?'

'It is rather, it's as much as analysis, though not so often, but I discussed that with her and she has this long-term credit system I've signed into. I needed to prove I could make a commitment, she said.'

'Wow. Well, I hope it helps you sort things out, Steph.'

'I'm sure it will, I feel better already, she's brilliant. And such an exquisite room. Thick white carpet, white cushions, a green bronze statue of an Egyptian cat, massive ivory goddess, incense, candles, utter luxury and peace, dreamy. You even have to take your shoes off. But anyway, Emmy, it sounds like you've been in the wars, what's happening?'

'Well, I had that accident when I sprained my wrist, bent back the hand, quite painful, but it happened because I'm so bloody tired all the time. I just daren't sleep, you see, those nightmares haven't stopped, every time I lose consciousness I can feel things possessing me.'

'Really?'

'Yes, it's as if I don't know who I am, and some force is trying to take me over.'

'That's not like you, Emma, I thought I was the paranoid one around here. Do you think you should see someone?'

'I just keep thinking of awful horror movies, you know, *Rosemary's Baby* and *The Exorcist*, *The Omen*, really scary.'

'What's Paul up to in all this?'

'He's getting a bit impatient, thinks I'm being irrational, so he can't help being patronising: "Oh, it's because you're pregnant, stop worrying, nothing's going to happen. There's nothing to be frightened about."'

'People are always condescending about fear and paranoia till they feel it themselves. I hate it when men get like that, "Stop being so het up about things, you're getting *hysterical*." Yuk.'

'I know. It's hard for me at the moment though, Steph, to know what I'm actually experiencing, you know, as *reality*, and what I'm imagining. I don't know if I'm asleep or awake. Reality feels very unreal right now.'

'Look, if I find someone for you to see, will you go?'

'You mean a therapist?'

'Yes. I'm sure Eva will be on some kind of network through the country. I can ask her, anyway.'

'All right, I'm so desperate with this insomnia, I've got to do something, or I'll go mad.'

'Good. I'll drop you a line after my next session, OK?'

'Fine. Thanks.'

Feb 17th

Dear Em, Eva recommended someone in Whitby for you, a woman who did the same training as her and she says she rates her work very highly. Dr Avril Wolpe, on 382798. Do at least have an initial talk with her: that's free! Don't be defeated by the nightmares. Love Steph.

March 3rd

Just a quick note to say that's great – I had a feeling you'd go and it would work. Told Eva, she's pleased she could help. Strange, having your first session on Leap Year day, but maybe it's a bonus rather than part of the general unreality. Maybe it's going to be something special, extraordinary. Try and let yourself see it that way. Meantime, here's a card of my favourite spot: the chalice well garden. Best love, S.

March 30th

No, this therapy business isn't at all what I'd imagined either. Fascinating, though. I'm really pleased we're doing it at the same time, especially with therapists who have similar backgrounds, it makes me feel closer to you than ever. I sometimes wonder how weird it must be for them, if they know each other and realise their clients know each other – a right complex network!

Make a good play, wouldn't it, a husband and wife who are therapists, seeing clients who are also married, but not knowing their partner sees the partner, and them inadvertently becoming rivals, urging the clients to go for different things! Damning the other therapist without knowing who it was – it could cause both marriages to break up! Or two therapists who hate each other, separately seeing patients who are partners or friends, and encouraging hostility, at first unconsciously, then perhaps consciously, in order to attack the detested colleague! Trying to get the rival's client to crack up to prove the therapist was no good! Maybe all clients are just pawns in some gigantic game played by analysts! On the other hand, though, you could have clients who take revenge, bringing completely false stories, inventing all their dreams, telling only lies – after all, what *is* history? Or a trainee therapist who's really a novelist in disguise, and he invents a whole case-load to take along to his supervisor, a very experienced old analyst, who delves into all these characters, and gives him all the rich material for his next novel. Fantastic! It hardly bears thinking about, does it? The permutations are infinite!

What amazes me is how on earth they fit it all in. Eva never seems to get tired or look at all under par, yet she must see at least forty people a week, her timetable's overflowing, and then she works weekends too, residentials: whenever does she manage to eat or sleep or look after the boring necessities, let alone have *relationships*? It sounds like Avril's made of the same stuff: do you think they live on royal jelly? Bloody superwomen. Maybe they just don't have close relationships, maybe they just live through their clients. But how can people be so perfect? Eva's never missed anyone's session, she's never late or ill, she never fails to say the right thing: there's something about it that's too good to be true. Even Mother had the occasional flu or mistook the odd half-hour! Strange, isn't it? Especially that neither of them is taking any break for Easter or summer. Why don't they need one? I shall have to find out what their secret is, some elixir of eternal life. Maybe she sleeps on a very powerful ley line!

April 1st
I must have been prophetic when I said that, Em – today I discovered where she lives: Avebury, in Wiltshire. There's old stone circles there and a white horse nearby on the hillside, doubtless that's what takes her travelling into the ether each night for recharging! Eva says there's various places of particular spiritual power in Britain – Yorkshire, of course, and Cornwall, Devon, Glastonbury, the Malverns, even London – apparently Kew Gardens are used by very advanced spirits to determine the destiny of Europe. (Bet Ma doesn't know that – invisible powers on her doorstep, across the very road – and she thought she'd gone there for the tropical plants!!) Eva's philosophy, the polar opposite of Yvette's, is that you have to contact and surrender to these higher powers, cosmic forces that rule your karmic life. You see, Mother always used to say, "At some point, Stephanie, you have to make a *conscious* decision about your life," but now I realise Eva's right, and it's the opposite that's true: letting the *unconscious* make decisions for you. Going along with dreams.

Anyway, if tapping into the deepest energy levels makes us as healthy, wealthy and wise as Eva and Avril, we'll not be doing too badly. I expect with all that universal vitality pumping into you, your wrist's improving, but if not, don't worry about replying, I'll be in touch again soon. Love Steph.

April 14th
I'm writing back straight away, Em, 'cos you sounded in such a state in your letter. Your nightmares are really horrific. I don't want to side with Paul, but maybe you *are* worn out with the pregnancy? Frightened of the birth and aftermath? I know what you mean about having mixed feelings about therapy, but that's all par for the course. Actually, I think it's OK that Avril isn't taking any breaks in the summer, Eva isn't either, they're just really committed. I know it feels a bit much for Avril to expect you to

pay all summer, even over the baby period, but then you might need to see her, and if she keeps a place for you, it is time she's otherwise losing.

I've had a similar dilemma: Soll wanted me to go to Spain with him in May for a month, but I can't afford it whilst I'm doing this therapy. Eva was just unyielding about it – either I commit myself to this, and work things through with her once and for all, or I may as well leave. No room for compromise – she's a hard taskmaster. Soll's disappointed, says it's defeating the object, that therapy was supposed to be bringing us closer. I have to trust him whilst he's away, but I can imagine him going off with someone just out of frustration or anger, and how can I blame him? I've also had to take a part-time teaching job to pay for Eva, the interest on my loan was getting out of hand, so I can identify with your cash flow problems. Hard, isn't it? Love S.

April 23rd

'Stephanie, I was hoping you'd phone today, you must have picked up the telepathic messages I was sending you.'

'Why, what's wrong? Is it something about the baby?'

'No, there's nothing wrong with that. Except it's moving around like a young calf, legs everywhere, and I'm massive, you wouldn't believe it. I wouldn't even be able to walk into that kitchen we had in the London flat. No, I think I'm going crazy, Stephanie, I'm really scared.'

'What's happened?'

'I just can't cope with seeing Avril any more, I got really thrown by her today, I can't cope with it.'

'Go on, tell me.'

'I've been having these nightmares, night after night, but last night it was so vivid, it really was happening, it wasn't unconscious at all, it actually happened.'

'Go on.'

'God, I'm shaking just remembering it. I couldn't sleep,

you see, the baby was thrashing about so much, so I got up
and went for a walk.'

'On your own? In the dark?'

'It wasn't that dark, the moon was out, and I walked along
the street up to the Abbey.'

'To the ruins?'

'Yes. And I was walking around the churchyard, feeling
the wind, smelling the sea, when I realised all the grave-lids
were shifting slightly and figures struggling out of them.
They were all women, Stephanie, all women with long hair,
they all looked like Avril, they *were* Avril, flicking back
their hair as she does, all standing and sauntering around the
churchyard. And it was then that I realised.'

'Realised what?'

'She's a vampire.'

'*Emily*!'

'Don't you remember, Stephanie? The Dracula Story?
Where Dracula came from?'

'Transylvania.'

'Yes, but he came to England via Whitby. They disem-
barked here, by the Abbey.'

'Emily . . . '

'And here they are again. His agents. This sinister presence, Avril, it's one of his evil agents. And she's out to get
my blood. All our blood. They started coming after me,
following me around the tombstones and then down the
main street, everywhere I turned, these identical women,
smiling, knowing they would soon have me. They're out
for us, Steph, I won't be here after the baby's born, I know
that. I can't bear it, I think I'm going mad, I don't know
what to do.'

'But it was a *dream*, Emily, a vivid one, a realistic one, but
only a dream.'

'No, Stephanie, that's the worst thing of all, it isn't a
dream.'

'What makes you think that?'

'Well, I had a session with Avril today, and I told her what had happened in the night, and she just smiled, supercilious, and in her smile I could see the smile of the vampires, exactly the same, half seductive, half malignant, as if confirming I was right. And she said it was a common phantasy, to feel your therapist wants to kill you or is in a plot against you.'

'There you are then, that's the explanation.'

'Ah, but it isn't.'

'Why not?'

'I had to go into the loo, in the middle of the hour, my bladder was bursting, and there was blood on all the towels, fresh blood.'

'No.'

'Yes, there was. So I went back in and said I needed to stop coming, that I knew she wanted to have me totally under her control. She was so cool, like a machine. She said I'd made a commitment, and if I gave in now to the part that was frightened to continue, she couldn't answer for the consequences. I think she's possessed, Steph, mad: *one* of us has to be. I don't think I can bear seeing her any more, I'm scared she'll end up killing me, taking everything from me.'

'Emily, calm down. Just take it easy, calm down. Is Paul with you?'

'No, not at the moment, he's working long hours, we're so short of money.'

'OK. Let me think. I wish I could come up and be with you, but I've got all this teaching. I'm sure this is just a temporary set-back with Avril; I fight Eva all the time. There must be some natural explanation for the blood. I really don't think you should stop going, it's helped you ever so much till now; you've coped really well with the pregnancy. Maybe this is the last stage in working through something important about your inner parents. Don't panic, Emily, just hang on till the birth. I'll be up for that, and I'll send you some healing every night, and phone you again at the weekend, all right?'

'But Steph, what if vampires . . . '

'Emily, it's all the pregnancy. Don't worry.'

'OK Steph, I'll talk to you at the weekend. Bye.'

April 29th
Dearest Emma, Sorry I didn't get through on the phone,
I tried several times, but no lines available – must have
been that storm. Hope your sleep's settled down now, and
Avril's sorted things out. Soll's back briefly and we've had
a bit of a row, so can't write now. Let me know how you
are. Love S.

May 9th
Yes, of course I remember *The Stepford Wives*, it was at
Screen on the Green, wasn't it, we went with Mo and
Sarah, and had an Indian meal afterwards. Such a relief to
know we weren't the only women who felt like that –
that you get cloned into marriage and motherhood. But
I'm still not with you. What exactly do you mean, "That's
the unreality I meant . . . and the names: A*v*alon, E*v*a,
A*v*ril, A*v*ebury . . . my Dracula dream begins to make
sense"? You're not usually as cryptic as that, I don't get
it, am I missing something?

I think it's a bad idea to stop seeing Avril: I don't think
it's so easy doing it on your own. But maybe you'll start
again after the summer. I'm all packed up ready, so don't
forget to ring me the minute you think there's any signs
of the baby, no matter how premature or a false alarm.
Be sure you get hold of me, here's a list of all the phone
numbers of friends and work, you can interrupt whatever
I'm doing – even if it's the middle of a session!

Things with Soll deteriorating: I'm angry with him 'cos
he's away all the time, he's angry with me 'cos I moan
about it, but don't go with him. I suspect he's finding
Glastonbury a bit boring, but now I've started this therapy
I have to be here all the time. What to do? Love Steph.

May 13th
These awful dreams you're still having, things attacking
your eyes, needles puncturing, aeroplanes diving into

them: maybe in a previous life you were killed or blinded through arrows or knives entering your face? And the vampires might be linked up there too. Eva's been explaining to me that it's the stores of impressions from past lives that form the deepest layers of our dreams, and she's trying to put me in touch with some of my past incarnations so I can really understand myself. It's fascinating: maybe you should do the same and get to the root of the nightmares.

I've agreed to go on a special retreat with her next week at Avebury, to explore past lives. I need the distraction. Soll left last week, and I have this irrational feeling he's not coming back. Probably just my own fear, but there's a chance he could be invited to teach on a dance programme in the south of Spain for the summer, and he's not left anything valuable here. The hope is that if I get to grips with past incarnations, I'll know where this disastrous pattern with men comes from, then it might change. I'll try to find out if you and I have known each other before too. I'm sure we must have had a previous connection, I can't imagine feeling closer to another woman than you. I expect Yvette will turn out to have been something peculiar, a downtrodden slave in some Southern plantation, or my step-daughter! I'll let you know anyway, assuming I return from the ether! Love as ever, Stephanie.

That was the last letter. On May 16th and 19th, I received picture postcards, covered with handwriting which was even wilder than usual.

The White Horse, Wiltshire. *And I heard as it were the noise of thunder, one of the four beasts saying, Come and see. And I saw, and behold a white horse: and he that sat on him had a bow; and a crown was given unto him: and he went forth conquering, and to conquer. I am talking about the speechless full moon!*

Stone circle, Avebury. *And there appeared a great wonder in heaven; a woman clothed with the sun, and the moon under her feet, and upon her head a crown of twelve stars: And she being with child cried, travailing in birth, and pained to be delivered . . . And she brought forth a man child, who was to rule all nations with a rod of iron: and her child was caught up unto God, and to his throne.*

And the woman fled into the wilderness . . . Escaping reasonableness.

I left it for a week, trying to deny what I knew, but the baby was about to arrive and I'd promised to try to reach her. It was the day before the birth that I finally telephoned her mother, not caring any more how she classified me. Tired with a body that had never been so full – who had invaded me? How could I keep this sleepless other inside me? – I had given up trying to hold a self together.

'Hello, is that Dr More?'

'It is.'

'This is Emma, Emily Lang. I used to share the flat with Stephanie in Seven Sisters, I don't know if you remember me.'

'Emily, of course I do, hello. How nice. Stephanie told me you're having a baby, has it arrived yet?'

'No, it hasn't, but that's what I'm phoning about. Ever since we knew I was pregnant, we've been planning that Steph would come up for the birth. I really want her to be here, and she really wants to come, but if the baby hasn't arrived naturally by tomorrow, it's going to be induced, so I'm desperate to find her.'

'Well, she doesn't call me very regularly, you know. I've no idea where she is, I assumed she was still in Pilton.'

'No, she's not, she hasn't been there since the weekend before last.'

'Well, perhaps she's visiting friends somewhere.'

'No, I've tried all the numbers she left me. No one's heard anything from her. I'm terribly worried. She normally phones every few days, especially just now. I know something dreadful's happened to her, carried her away.'

'No, I don't think so. What kind of thing do you mean?'

'Oh, you'll think this is ever so stupid, with you being a psychoanalyst and all that, but I have to say it, because it's true. Some conspiracy's got her.'

'Some conspiracy? What on earth do you mean, Emily, some conspiracy?'

'A conspiracy of . . . therapists.'

'A . . . *conspiracy*? Of . . . *therapists*?'

'Yes, it's been going on for some time. You see over the last few years, powerful forces and figures have moved into areas where the ground is best tuned for receptivity – ancient energy fields that were prepared long ago, places like Glastonbury, Avebury, Whitby – it's a New Age take-over.'

'A take-over?'

'Yes, it's very clear, well organised. It works through a network of therapists. First of all they get you hooked into complete dependence on them, you see, then once you're paying all your money into their system, they gradually invade you till you're part of their universe, completely absorbed into their empire of mind and spirit. Can you understand, Yvette? Yv . . . Oh my God, oh my God!'

'What's the matter, Emily? Is it the baby?'

'Christ, I'm so *thick*. I've only just realised.'

'What?'

'You. Your name, your bloody name: Yvette, you're in it too. Eva, Avril, Avebury, Avalon, Ivy, Yvette, you're all linked up, you're in it too, of course you are, right opposite Kew Gardens. It's true. It's everywhere. Oh, God.'

'Emily, what on earth is going on? I think you'd better get the doctor in, dear, perhaps you need some sedatives. Listen, sweetheart, it's all right to be frightened the first time you have a baby. Of course you're scared, you don't know what's going to happen, lots of women become extremely irrational just before or during labour, it's completely natural: your biochemical framework is having to cope with an incredible strain, your hormones can easily become unbalanced. It's inevitable you feel somewhat anxious, even depressed. You feel the whole world is against you right now, don't you? Maybe you're thinking about your mother, is that it, and you don't want to have to go through it all? But Emily, that was nearly thirty years ago, childbirth is much safer now, you'll be all right. Really, everything's OK, sweetie, it's just your anxiety about the birth coming to the surface in this way. Don't worry. Now, is there anybody there to take care of you? I've forgotten your boyfriend's name.'

'I knew you wouldn't understand. Can't you hear what I'm telling you? Stephanie's disappeared. Your daughter, my closest friend. She's gone. She's slipped through the time-space continuum, passed into the mists of Avalon, back into previous incarnations . . . '

'Emily, you're getting hy . . . over-excited. It won't do the baby any good.'

'*Hysterical*, you were going to say, weren't you? You wanted to call me hysterical.'

'Yes, the word was on my tongue, but . . . '

'I knew you'd have some bloody rational explanation. You can't hear anything different, can you? Nothing outside the left half of your bleeding brain! Stephanie was always going on about it. How you call everything hysterical when you don't understand. Men and women. Even her Dad. She told me. Anything too slippy for your couch, just hysterical, barmy, mad. Freud's Dora. *Hysteria*. They denied the world was round you know. They were frightened of falling off then as well.'

'But Emily, whatever gives you the idea I'm frightened? I think you've got rather caught up in Stephanie's phantasies, my dear. I'm used to Stephanie's games, you see, and this is doubtless another big ruse on her part. She's probably gone racing to Tanzania after Soll and is very cleverly covering her traces. She was always on the move, she used to run away all the time. She'd go to any lengths to try to deceive me, to convince herself she's omnipotent. No, whatever mess she's got into this time, it's just part of the same pattern she's always displayed. Drawing attention to herself somehow, wanting to be different. Wanting to be a bird, a fish, to fly. She's always had a penchant for melodrama, been subject to delusions of grandeur. Everything has to be extreme, larger than life. Why else do you think she's living with a black African dancer? Mm? If he exists, that is. She's invented marriages before now.'

'It's always fucking phantasies with you guys, isn't it? Letting you off the hook. Phantasy this and psychotic that, never stuck for an answer.'

'If only you would understand, Emily. Stephanie lives in a world which is most fragile, where the dividing line between phantasy and reality *is* utterly tenuous. Sometimes she'd even fake a suicide to get me to worry.'

'And *you* have the nerve to call *us* paranoid, hysterical. Christ, we've got nothing on you!'

'Stephanie will be back when the phantasy is spent, and the money. She'll turn up again when she needs hard cash.'

'Ah, but that's where you're wrong, Doctor More.'

'What do you mean?'

'She won't be back, I'm certain about that. Wherever she is, in this world or the next, she'll not be back. I've got the proof in front of me, the writing: how Stephanie's gone, been taken up into the new Jerusalem, standing beneath the tree of life, and . . . '

'There you are, you see, thinking she's found God. Just like her father.'

'No, it's not as you imagine. She's gone, gone forever. At least, she won't be back as Stephanie.'

' "She won't be back as Stephanie"?'

'No. I understand it now, it's all falling into place. She had to escape you somehow, of course she did. She's right, you're too tyrannical, you wanted to programme her. So she's left the body she had as Stephanie in order that her soul should re-enter this one, the one inside me. She's going to reincarnate as *my* child, *my* baby, she wants a *real* mother at last.'

'A real mother?'

'Yes, a real mother. Not an analyst: not part of the conspiracy.'

'But my dear child, you're quite insane. You're talking as if you really believe I *am* something inhuman.'

'Of course I am. Stephanie told me about your answer machine – how you can programme it in advance to reply to people, how you're protected from real contact, as if the rest of us are glue and you're scared to get your hands sticky. *You're* the one who can't bear this normality.'

'Oh dear, Emily, you *are* in a bad way with your pregnancy, aren't you? You're being *awfully* fanciful, you know. Isn't anyone there with you? It's terribly sad: you're talking just like Stephanie, as if you don't believe in the possibility of real concern.'

'Of course I am, of course I'm talking like her. I *am* her: she is within me now. She and I are one.'

'I do wish you'd drop this. The way you both carry on, anyone would think you didn't live in the same world as the rest of us. Or that there really *was* a conspiracy somewhere, some kind of superhuman plot . . . '

'Exactly, Doctor More, exactly, *Yvette*. You know the saying, don't you? *Just because you're paranoid doesn't mean they're not out to get you*. I'm not the one that's denying reality round here.'

Torn pages of Stephanie's journal, with neither address nor date, arrived next morning, May 29th, the day of the birth. I put them with a pile of her letters and some personal papers in the spare room, but Paul's mother stayed all that week and the ones following, to 'help', and they managed to get lost in her zealous efficiency. Weeks later, I looked for them everywhere, frantic to find clues to our sanity, that place where laughter slept, but my child's grandmother intercepted me at every turn.

'You've got *real* things to concern yourself with now,' she said. 'I don't want to hear any more of these horror stories, this nonsense about witchcraft, people disappearing without trace. Reincarnation, indeed. You've got to think of your baby, Emily, you don't want him drinking in nightmares with the milk, now, do you?

Motherhood's about surrender, sacrifice, responsibility. It's about being in the *real* world, womanly, dispossessed. You have to give things up, phantasies. And life became implacable from then, pulling against my breasts.

Living too many years upon the threshold of insanity, forcing the lock. And now my body's key. Doors hanging loose.

Reaching for nothing, diving through closed hoops, I have upset the ark. Tasting the best that could happen. This water.

The two of us, I and not-I, stepping upon the net. Nothing ahead. The speechless full moon comes out now.

The Eye of the Buddha

Ilse sat through the third persistent ringing of the phone, unperturbed. It reminded her of the repeatedly practised alarm drills at the school where she used to work, when various anti-fire technologies seemed to have been programmed to interrupt things at just the most crucial moments, when the kids' hands were thickest in red mud and clay. Then, her resistance to the summons to the yard, her impatience at being pulled away from all the rich imaginary forms, had invariably attracted the wrath of the headmaster, but now she could afford to be more indifferent to criticism. Not until she'd reached a stage with the painting where she could suspend it without damage for a while did she wipe her hands on an old scrap of denim and prepare a coffee in readiness for the next inevitable call.

'Ilse, is that you? At last, thank God, where have you been? I've phoned at least half a dozen times this morning.'

'No, Samuel, four exactly.'

'You mean you were in all the time?'

'Yes, I was in.'

'Hell, Ilse, I do wish you'd pick up the phone when you're there, or at least get an answer machine so you can leave a message when to call back. It's ever so inconvenient, you know. What on earth were you doing, *meditating* or something? Well, we won't go into that now. Listen, I haven't got long to speak, there's a supervision seminar I've just nipped out of whilst they're having morning coffee, but we need to talk about this solicitor's letter.'

'You may need to, Samuel, I don't.'

'But you can't do this, Ilse, you can't, it's crazy.'

'It depends what you mean by crazy. Maybe I *am* crazy, but it doesn't worry me.'

'Look, we've both got to be reasonable about this, it's the only way forward.'

'Depends what you mean by reason, Samuel.'

'God, I'll have to go back now, George has just put his head round the door – yes, I'm on my way . . . ' she could see that impatient gesture of his, brushing his hair back off his forehead, he never *walked* anywhere, always on the run, ' . . . look, when can I phone you to talk properly?'

'Whenever you like. I'm not going anywhere.'

'But this isn't talking, Ilse.'

'Depends what you mean by talking, Sam.'

'Oh, damn it, the money's . . . ' The phone was slammed down peremptorily at the other end as he was cut off. She could sense his exasperation, as he made a gesture of frustration, 'Bloody hell, George, women are impossible, especially ex-wives. She's going round the bend,' and his colleague's concurring pat on the shoulder, 'I know, I know.' Sam was anxious to have her behaviour represented as some kind of malicious retaliation, the revenge of the spurned woman, whereas all she was doing was sticking her ground, sitting tight. This time, she wouldn't lose her nose to spite her face, no matter what the accusations.

She didn't mind solitude any more, at least not periodically. It let her digest things. For over two years she had been in shock, she supposed, at the denouement, for the deepest betrayal is like cancer, you never really believe it will happen to you. During that time, she'd still had to function, robot-like, feelings buried and on hold, for how can you collapse when there are lives to sustain around you? It was spring '85 when Sam had moved out, Walter was just doing his A levels prior to pilot training, Jacob would take his the following year, '86, the same time as Minna's O levels: it was no time for disintegration. Only now was there a chance to assimilate and feel, to unfold, roots finally released and allowed to spread and seek whatever it was they needed.

The worst thing was the unexpectedness of events, how foolish it had made her appear, not having known or guessed. She'd been supporting him all the way, had thought she knew who she was dealing with, but suddenly she'd had to recognise a stranger, a psychotic within their midst, a fraud. A Freud. For could it not all be laid at his door, this disaster, was it not a tragedy wrought by that cold man of Vienna with his penis-obsession and his fat cigars? If she hated anyone, it must be him, that urbane diplomat of the unconscious, that strangler of souls. Was it not Freud who had declared death to things of the spirit, he who had defined her light as darkness and her open mind as mad? He it was who wanted to cast her into disrepute, declaring she did not belong.

She could hear Samuel now, being comforted by his peer group, interpreting her stroppiness. 'Give it time, Sam, give it time, she's understandably hurt, give her time. Still no luck trying to get her into therapy, I suppose?'

And his dismissive retort. 'Some fat chance. She hardly moves out of the house, and the nearest analyst – of repute – who doesn't know me is in Cambridge, she'd never go back there. But there must be some *legal* expedient, she can't get away with this, it's outrageous.'

That was him all over: expedience, the politics of a Machiavelli. She had to show him what justice was, what truth.

Fortunately, her solicitor was prepared to fight for her right to everything. She was one of the few friends remaining from their academic years, and as contemptuous of Samuel's second wind as only a woman can be who has also been left in the lurch of imminent middle age for an ebullient girl, still bright-eyed with the surprise of having sprung successfully from an embarrassing adolescence into a triumphant adult sexuality. It had been harder for Carol than for her, though, for Michael had conducted his affair virtually under her office window, with a blonde secretary half Carol's age and a mite of her intelligence: all the effort and wisdom that Carol had given and garnered over the decades rendered futile by this slap in the face, this knife in the vagina.

Thanks to Carol she hadn't lost her home, a beautiful Suffolk long-house, with mullion windows and thatched roof, despite Sam's utmost efforts to persuade the courts that with the three children away at last, it was far beyond her requirements and that he had a right to half. He wanted his share of the money released to buy a Hampstead flat with Lyndall: they'd found one near Belsize Park with a separate entrance which he could use for his practice, hence his urgency in seeking a settlement, but he was still in the process of appealing his case and after nine months of wrangling, the battle still raged.

It was complicated by the tricky issue of the book, the famous book. This was what the fuss was really about. Sam had started telling everyone he'd finished his lengthy study, *Ego Splits in the Narcissistic Personality*, just as he was becoming sadly aware that the rift from his wife was making their legal separation inevitable. It was, he maintained, a huge work that ran into two volumes, part of a series that Cambridge had commissioned. In the last stages of writing and editing, however, it had been transferred on to one master disk which he'd entrusted to Ilse to correct and tidy up on their home word processor, just as his affair, unbeknown to him, was gathering the untimely impudence to go public.

He upheld that Ilse, presumably motivated by jealousy and anger at losing him – an anger, he argued, with typical analytic symmetry, that would be magnified out of all proportion to the actual incident because of the loss of her father in the last year of the war, when she was only two – had then hidden or destroyed the disk, thereby negating several years of important research and thought. This loss threatened to undo his career and reputation, for the disk contained crucial client records that were utterly confidential. He claimed he didn't know if she had completely destroyed it or had merely concealed it somewhere with a view to blackmailing him with the promise of its future release, thereby strengthening her fight for the house and estate, but he had gone to every length to try to track down his lost baby: bribes, threatened search warrants, writs. The only recourse left to him now, it seemed, was some declaration of her mental instability. Sectioning, of course, was too shameful for an analyst, but some kind of 'proof' of a major psychotic disorder would give him the vindication he needed to restore his dented public image, and this was his latest tack.

It was quite a feat, she had to admit it, masterly. He *was* quite knowledgeable in that area, narcissism, he *had* taken a book contract with Cambridge, he *had* talked at length to colleagues about how it was developing and shown them notes and drafts of work in progress. How were they to know it was all a grand phantasy concocted against his fear of failure? How many knew of his mother dying when he'd gone to public school and his haunting sense of responsibility for destroying her, atoning only by writing and succeeding in one institution after another? Who except she could say it was a massive lie? A deception he didn't acknowledge even to himself, so out of touch was he with his own reality.

As she'd explained at length to Carol, it was all fabrication. Why would she have spent months transcribing or editing his manuscript? She wasn't even interested in the ego, never mind its tables of division and multiplication; she wouldn't have got involved with the project in the first place. After she'd been able to relinquish teaching and concentrate on her own work, she'd never have resumed that kind of mindless wifely support and self-annihilation. It was all a myth that Sam had conceived to save his face at not having delivered the goods on time: a device for covering up his own procrastination and laziness, trying to conceal the time he'd wasted screwing around, giving her the blame and responsibility for his non-deliverance of the manuscript.

She and Carol weren't quite intimate enough, she knew, for Carol really to know whether she was telling truth or lies when she said she knew nothing of the whereabouts of the supposed book, and she herself wasn't sure whether or not Carol did believe her. But the important thing was that Carol acted as if she believed: what mattered was that she wanted to believe; or what was even better, was that she seemed to want not to believe but to be able to act as if she did believe, thereby fulfilling her own need for a wily revenge against men. It was a perfect foil. Truth slithered and slipped between their respective solicitors like some jellied eel, head and tail quite indistinguishable.

What surprised her most was Sam's surprise, his indignation at her behaviour. It reinforced all her scepticism about therapy in general and his brand of it in particular if he knew so little about basic human nature. What kind of analyst was he, to be shocked at hardness, to be confounded at retaliation when a life's work had been demolished? When she objected to Lyndall interfering with the kids, he had even tried, with characteristic charm, to sweet talk her into tolerance.

'I don't know why you're being like this, Ilse. We've known each other twenty-five years, a quarter of a century, we've had twenty-three years of married life, how can you let it end acrimoniously? It really amazes me that you can be like this. We always agreed that if the time came when we felt the relationship had outgrown itself, we would say so, that we wouldn't go on just for the sake of the children. We both agreed that, you know. Why can't you accept what is more gracefully?'

He was one to talk, she thought. When had he ever accepted what was? Wasn't he forever trying to chop and change and undermine – the fabric of society, institutions, and now the psyche? Had *he* stayed with the difficulty of what is, the day-to-day ongoingness of life, with old paths overgrown and the way forward unclear? Had he welcomed ageing and changing, admitted the impotence of knowledge to control death, in the end? No, when the mid-life crisis chimed, he had rushed off to the distractions of metropolitan splendour, to the seduction of training and affairs and getting known in another brave new world. He hadn't wanted to hear what the clock was telling him about transience and death, the body wearing out like an old car. He hadn't been prepared to drink life or death gracefully, but only life greedily, as he always had, grabbbing the day.

There was a steady drizzle now, but she needed some air, and walked with Nell, a mongrel despite Sam's preference for pedigree, to the bare flat land and the woods beyond the village. She crossed the bridge, where the River Dove meandered southwards beyond Eye, breathing in the delicious smell of ripe summer. She liked these sinister Suffolk skies, the wet air and nettles, loved the September harvesting of crimson hips and haws, shining blackberries, heavy elderberry trees, weighed down as if in latter days of pregnancy. She drew her hands together as she inhaled, pulled spiritual energies to the top of her head and then down the chakras and the spine. *I am part of the infinite universe. I extend my love to all life, visible and invisible.* How she enjoyed this air, this space. She'd never tired of the country, for all the warnings that she'd miss urban life, her London of the late 40s and 50s, then Cambridge of the 60s. She never missed city life, never. How could anyone crave pollution? It was madness.

But then, madness was popular. Anything that made an excuse for psychotherapy, analysis, was in. It was ordinary life, this banal day-to-dayness that was out. They always had to do things to it to make it tolerable. It had to be interpreted, understood, catalogued, written about, refined, like all the other natural substances – bread, vegetables, air – it had to be improved and spoilt. She brought her arms up sideways for a second time, hands clasped and turned, palms upwards to the cloud-filled sky. *I am at peace. I am. I am.* These bloody analysts, she thought, as she drew the energy down through the base and sacral chakras to the earth. They mutilate the mind: dismembering, dividing, splitting apart. They don't know how to live, to be. They render simple-ness imposs-ible, even though that's what they claim to be straining towards, just like they're surprised when you give them an eye for an eye and a tooth for a tooth. As if the human depths they claim to be plumbing shouldn't really be *that* nasty underneath, not *that* vindictive, not *that* murderous. *I am part of the earth, the fire, the elements, the air.*

She slashed some teazles with her pocket knife to take a tall bunch back for the outside hall, hurled a couple of sticks for Nell, then undid her hair and let the rain soak face and skull. That's good, she thought, that's very good, just feeling again. That's what they're missing, in their counselling chambers, these simple pleasures, wind on skin, rain on tongue, love in the heart. Making time just to experience things. *Root my feet in enduring things.* She remembered how Sam had laughed when Minna had come back from her first alternative therapy weekend: it must have been the summer of '84, just before this giant farce uncurled itself. Minna had been narrating the day's activities and described a slow-motion exercise they'd done.

A group of them had stood in a circle, she reported, hold-ing one another, swaying from side to side, then backwards and forwards, then they had very slowly learnt to walk, putting one foot at a time in front of them, so they really *felt* and experienced every one. Sam said it sounded like kindergarten, it was silly, and Minna nodded, 'Yes, there was a chap there a bit like you, Dad, he got bored with it, it was too slow for him, and he walked out half way through the morning. You'd have hated it, Dad, there was hardly any talking, people didn't really get to know one another at all on a social level. But it was funny, I quite enjoyed it. After lunch, we progressed on to bouncing a ball! One bounce, then two, then sharing it between us, it was really slow, but you actually *felt* it all, noticed what you were doing, you know? Co-ordination's an incredible thing, do you realise that? Then we spent an hour with a partner just getting to know them, without talking, you weren't allowed to say anything, it was brilliant. I was with this really lovely looking guy, called Jonathan, and we spent ages just looking at each other's hands, then arms and necks and faces. God, when you know what a miracle the human body is – it was fantastic! And feet, wow, tendons and the shape of the heel and the instep . . . '

'I hope yours didn't smell as much as they usually do, Minna,' Samuel had said in his clumsy attempt at a joke, and that had successfully thrown cold water on the whole episode.

'Oh piss off, Dad, you always know how to spoil things, don't you? I s'pose you and that lot in London don't have bodily functions, do you? You don't sweat or smell, and you certainly don't *menstruate*, do you?', slamming the door behind her.

And when she, Ilse, had tried to talk to Sam about being more sensitive, he'd guiltily turned on her too, 'Well, honestly, what a crack-brained idea of therapy. Part of the Esalen mob, wasn't it? How much was it? A hundred? That's a week's analysis, for Christ's sake.'

'I don't know why you swear by such an archaic dead god. I thought there was only one Jew deified around here and his was a five letter name beginning with F.'

'Oh, go to hell.'

That was one of the last weekends she could recall him being around Long Cottage. Then the frequent 'conferences' began, and the weekend 'consultation' work at the Tavistock, and like an idiot she'd believed it all, *credulous* heart.

And yet he'd had the effrontery to accuse *her* of a selfish obsessiveness. Simply because she'd gone on strict macrobiotic diets or Buddhist retreats, spent nights without sleep to meditate or remained silent for several days a month, he'd accused her of abdicating responsibility.

'You're becoming positively cranky, Ilse, you know that? Let's hope it's the menopause, at least that would explain it . . . '

But then, he'd always been unable to leave her or anyone to pursue their own path without criticism or contempt, for he couldn't tolerate difference. It wasn't only that his particular preoccupations became so all-consuming for him that there was no other reality: this was on a par with the rest of the family expecting her to go along with every enthusiasm, Walter with his planes, then his pilot training, Jacob with his guitar and sax, Minna with her life drawing classes. No, she could have tolerated Sam's shifting fanaticisms on that level. But the way in which they became ardent faiths that were the *only* way to redeem mankind, that was what she found more difficult. Initially it had been his Marxist sociology, trying to subvert the state by teaching the Frankfurt school in the midst of the flowered quadrangles of Trinity College. But that intellectual firecracker had burnt out and the next explosion had been psychoanalysis, the most enduring – and expensive – craze. He'd bought Freud's *Collected Works*, hardback copies of the twenty-four volumes of the famous Standard Edition, as earnestly as he'd stacked the shelves with Marx and Engels, Althusser and Durkheim, ten years previously, but he refused to admit it was a fashion. This one, finally, was *it*: this was what the others had been trying to find.

'They always say that with new religions, new gurus,' she'd admonished him, careful to put the brakes on, knowing only too well his tendency to steam ahead and crash into disillusionment. But once again, this was the exception that proved the rule. It was, apparently, her 'envy' and 'resistance' speaking. Envy. The angry feeling that someone else has what you want: the desire to take it away from them or to spoil it.

'I think you're jealous, Ilse. First at Cambridge, you were angry with academics there because you didn't have a degree, only a teacher's certificate, and now it's the Tavi, you're angry with the analytical world because you haven't been in therapy yourself, you've only got meditation and your Buddhist teacher and that's not the same kind of privileged relationship. Now why don't you seriously think about going into analysis for yourself?'

Why was it they always called it sour grapes when you didn't aim for what they said you wanted but you couldn't have? Grapes were not what she was looking for.

'I don't need to.'

'Everyone needs to.'

'Why?'

'To make them more aware.'

'My eyes are fully dilated, thanks.' *I am at peace.*

'But psychoanalysis helps you get at the *meaning* of what you're doing. Now why, for example, are you and Minna obsessed with drawing, mm? Why is it that the two women in the house are always painting and drawing? Especially double fruits and vegetables, or the female body. What explanation do you have for that, mm?'

'I don't need one, Sam, I just want to enjoy it, to notice and celebrate what is.'

'You see, it's highly significant that it's the *female* body you both keep re-presenting. You're trying to re-create the lost mother, the body of the mother, to re-find the mother's breast, the good breast.'

'So what?'

'What do you mean, so what? Doesn't that excite you at all, to know that?'

'Quite frankly, Sam, no, it leaves me cold. It seems to me that you're busy trying to understand what we actually *are.* You're doing it at third remove: ideas about ideas about ideas about being or having the mother, when we're it. We *are* what you're missing. We *are* what you lack. You're the one that's split off and divided, not us.'

'Oh, you don't know what you're talking about, you're so naïve sometimes, you should read some Melanie Klein, you really should, it's all in there.'

'What do you want me to do? Start painting naked phalluses to prove I'm normal? You expect me to celebrate heterosexuality with *our* sex as it is?'

But his jacket was half-way down the drive, his anger vented on a therapeutic walk for Nell.

Once or twice when Sam was in London all week and the kids at school, she had tried leafing through some of the books and papers in his study, but she was left feeling like a squirrel hammering for hours at some nut only to find the kernel empty, or a much easier seed close on the ground. The positive statements in Klein seemed so self-evident, such natural truths that her meditation accessed so much more easily, that she couldn't see what all the fuss was about. She read:

> To be genuinely considerate implies that we can put ourselves in the place of other people: we 'identify' ourselves with them. Now this capacity for identification with another person is a most important element in human relationships in general, and is also a condition for real and strong feelings of love. We are only able to disregard or to some extent sacrifice our own feelings and desires, and thus for a time to put the other person's interests and emotions first, if we have the capacity to identify ourselves with the loved person.

What was there to disagree with here? *I desire a oneness with all life which travels beside me.* Of course there was love and hate in each of us, and of course it was a lifelong struggle to balance and battle them out in ourselves and in relation to others, but what was new about this? Did it need all these words? Weren't there easier ways to unblock the ducts of the heart?

But it was the elaboration of theories into quantum mechanics, that perversion of loving from an art to a science that really sealed her rejection. What did these complex graphs and tables have to do with love? She puzzled for one long winter's day over the pristine copies of W. R. Bion, slim volumes placed reverently next to Klein, but found their contents were either dazzlingly unfathomable or, beneath their abstract formulae, remarkably unremarkable. Paging through the smooth paper she found sentences and even paragraphs which she read appreciatively, like poetry, vaguely sensing their meaning, but where they could be unravelled from their Laingian knots into some straight clarity, they too stated the obvious, spelling out to her that analytic thought, like Marxist theory before it, had finally become so complex that it had to overstep itself in sophistication in order to capture the simple.

We may make a distinction between milk and love by appropriate classification . . . we may say that milk is a material substance and is related to alimentation and is presumably dealt with by the digestive tract. Love on the other hand we may regard as immaterial though comparable with milk for the mental welfare of the child. We may place it in one or more of a number of different categories that philosophy, religion and other disciplines place at our disposal . . . The milk, we may assume with a degree of conviction we cannot feel about love, is received and dealt with by the alimentary canal; what receives and deals with the love? The question may be a formulation based on inadequate thinking . . . It may be useful to suppose that there exists in reality a psycho-somatic breast and an infantile psycho-somatic alimentary canal corresponding to the breast.

Concentrating on the ideas made her tired, and she lay on Sam's sheepskin rug in his study, wondering. *Open your hands and feel love energy between your palms.* Maybe *she* had the resistance to thinking that Bion was talking about. *Place hands in an attitude of prayer over the heart.* Maybe she *was* the schizoid character who couldn't act or think but only dream, living her life split into an eternal reverie. Vaguely wondering about the time, wondering if Minna would be returning soon, she flicked back the page. Here, she read that 'The activity we know as "thinking" was in origin a procedure for unburdening the psyche of accretions of stimuli . . . ' and she felt even more confused. What was the aim? To think? Or to get rid of thinking altogether as being merely second best, processing unwanted stuff? Was all this riddle of psychoanalytic thinking a shedding of blocked stimuli? Too much input? What was what? What did they need this science for, why had they invented imaginary organs? After all, that thing they'd called the 'psychosomatic alimentary canal', what was it but the heart, that simple thing that man has always known and feared to face, the good old-fashioned *heart*?

The books made her feel pleased she had chosen less stressful forms of knowledge, more ancient ways of integrating body, mind and soul. It was only Sam who found her choice anathema, denouncing her practices as anachronistic and self-indulgent. He couldn't adjust to a speed slow enough to stand on one foot at a time, let alone to staying still. Carol had told her he'd complained of all this to Michael as far back as their Cambridge days.

'What Ilse needs is something *social*, active, vigorous, like car mechanics or woodwork. If she won't get into politics, I'd much rather she did something useful, instead of all this quietude, alternate nostril breathing, you can't imagine the weird lengths they go to. It's so passive, what earthly use is it? She even thinks he *talks* to her – the Buddha! – can you credit it?'

His impatience had escalated when she started maintaining silence and doing thrice-daily meditations.

'Look, Ilse, all this *I am part of an infinite universe* number is an eastern practice; it was formed for a specific age and civilisation. It's totally at odds with the needs of this culture, don't you see? You can't divorce the physical practice from the social structure like that. Meditating, fasting, then eating seaweed: it's absurd. Before you know where you are, you'll be praying and going to church – some advert for the wife of a Marxist lecturer! *Sound the OM three times in attunement with God and the cosmos.* Try telling that to a working-class housewife in Sunderland! Don't you see, you can't fit a round peg into a square hole. You can't just demolish or side-step western culture like that, it's a whole philosophical tradition and rationalism that has to be taken on, respected, transformed. The best revolutionaries – Marx, Freud – have tried to *change* what is through *understanding*, not through copping out.'

Their progressive estrangement, far from being healed, had been intensified by Sam's increasing involvement with psychotherapy. The polarity between politics and social issues on the one hand, meditation and spiritual activities on the other, grew more acute, and she soon realised it had been naïve to suppose that psychoanalysis was about tolerance. For Sam, the idea of having a soul was even more taboo now that its unconscious origins were known, and he became annoyed at her pictures of mandalas and venerated yogis on the walls. Anything to do with the spirit, the slightest mention of things spiritual, made him angry. It was as if squatters had crept into his mind overnight, she thought: he was terrified they might dismantle the elaborate decorations he'd hung there so carefully over a lifetime. Over many lifetimes, in fact. But the mention of this idea incensed him too. It was the last big row they'd had.

'Ilse, don't mention reincarnation again when we're in the middle of a dinner party, *please*. It was bad enough when we were at Cambridge, you coming along with these crackpot ideas of eastern mysticism, but at least the abstract liberalism prevailing there let you entertain possibilities about anything as theories to be tossed around. . . . '

'Yes, about as nonchalantly as shuttlecocks,' she'd interrupted, relieved she'd had enough wine to make her articulate enough to counter Sam's solid arguments with a bit of eloquence. 'I doubt if their ideas would be very substantial if it came to dying, or indeed really *living*, for them.'

' . . . But when we've got members of the Tavistock panel

here, Ilse, it's a bit embarrassing, to say the least, to have
you coming out with notions of problematic mother–child
relations deriving from bad karmic ties in previous lives and
having to be worked through in this one, and said with such
conviction, as if you really believe it. It's just the same as
that time you told Professor Taylor at Cambridge that maybe
the blacks who were being victimised in the Civil Rights
movement had been repressive white landowners in former
lifetimes and had to put the credit sheet right. I mean, this
was a guy who'd written a study of slavery in the South! It
took me months to put that one right again. Honestly, half
of them thought I'd married an imbecile, you know, or that
my ideas might be only skin deep. And now with the Tavi
crowd! Well, it makes me feel I haven't put my own house
in order. And as for that tasteless joke tonight about the
KGB – that was really infantile!'

'Oh, did you think so? I quite enjoyed that one.' She
laughed again, she had enjoyed it, their discomfiture. It had
been a large buffet supper and as the hostess, she'd been
moving between them with wine, peanuts, olives, catching
fragments of their competitive talk about credentials. One
had come from the BAP, another from the IGA, that balding
overtalker from the WPF, letters shooting around, GAS,
CAC, BAP, CAP, SAPP, YAPP, killing all illegitimates
outside their own orthodoxies. And then Anneliese, a Dutch
friend of Ilse's who was staying with them whilst she did
some work with disturbed adolescents, fell into the trap of
expressing her admiration for Patricks, one of the better-
known and more vocal anti-establishment therapists, with
whom she had done some training. The siblings fell on her
like wolves.

'Oh, Patricks! The trouble with Patricks is that he doesn't
have any one theoretical position to which he particularly
adheres, does he? His theoretical allegiances are all over the
place.'

And Anneliese's face had fallen, puzzled by their intolerance. At this point Ilse, quick to react to predatory behaviour,

poised to leave the room to answer the door-bell, said loudly, 'Actually, Anneliese's position is close to that of A. S. Neil. She believes in working towards a humanity that doesn't *need* analysis. She's like me: we come from the KGB.'

They looked dubious, was this some training institute they didn't know?

'The KGB?'

'The Kleinian Good Breast!'

She could hear from the hall that no one laughed, but Sam had coughed and covered up the pun. 'Oh, that's Ilse all through, irreverent! The KGB. Ha ha! The KGB!'

So she'd smiled again after they'd departed, listening to Sam's familiar invective as she leant lazily against the kitchen work-tops and fiddled with discarded corks. *I am brother and sister to all life. I extend oneness to all.*

'What do you expect me to do, Sam? Keep quiet, and sit there like some dumb animal?'

'You don't mind keeping silent when it suits you.'

'Well, it doesn't suit me when all these privileged Oxbridge and Tavi touts are sitting there spouting fourth about relationships and connections and they haven't got the least idea about karma or the past associations between people that have accrued from endless incarnations, millions upon millions of them. If you ask me, they're damn ignorant. They know as much about the human psyche as a whale knows about the Gobi Desert. Do you really expect me to play deaf and dumb and mindless to boot?'

'Ilse, it's not that, it's just that you're speaking different languages, you're using a discourse they don't understand.'

'Discourse my arse, Sam Todd. What's wrong with speaking plain English? It's still capable, you know, for all your Marxism and psychoanalytic deconstruction, of calling a spade a spade and a spirit a spirit, and as far as I'm concerned, both are equally substantial. Certainly more substantial than some of that esoteric crap you were all bandying around tonight. Instead of the Cambridge days of Althusser and Derrida and Lacan, now it's Meltzer and Bion and Bick.

Honestly, if each name you all dropped had really presented itself as what it was, we'd be knee deep by now in pigeon shit.'

'You're obsessed with it, aren't you?'

'What, shit? Yes, I know the term – *scatology* – you probably use it as a joke in between sessions – "Oh, that one's a bit *scatty*" – or maybe you haven't the wit for that kind of repartee. They're a dour lot, if you ask me, Sam, no sense of humour, pompous, no that's not quite the right word, *sanctimonious*: they've found their holy of holies in the psychoanalytic encounter and anything else is definitely, but most definitely, out. Garbage. And you're rapidly becoming one of their neophytes, and that really depresses me.'

'If only you'd go into analysis, Ilse, you wouldn't feel like this. You're angry because you're feeling excluded, rejected.'

'Well, who wouldn't with so many cold shoulders to rub against? Don't you see, Sam, I DON'T WANT TO HAVE ANALYSIS, I DON'T NEED IT ANY MORE THAN MOST OF THIS GLOBAL VILLAGE NEEDS IT, AND I'M NOT GOING TO HAVE IT. I need other routes to sanity. Other kinds of peace.'

'Oh, I know, Ilse. The mantra meditation exercise. Hands at solar plexus pointing to the earth. *I am. I am at peace. I am a thought form of the universe of light.* That's real sanity.'

'Oh, piss off, Samuel. You're always right, aren't you?'

'It would seem so.'

That was the rub. Behind their increasing sexual and emotional rift, this utter incompatibility of ideas about the path to truth. It was from then onwards, as the obstinacy of her resistance to sharing his path really sank in during his training, that Sam had begun his affair with Lyndall and stayed in London more. But it wasn't Lyndall who had stolen him. It was a tempting set of thoughts. It was an ideology.

Yes, that was when he'd started spreading rumours about his book, building up expectation. At first, she'd been taken aback, but then, thanks to her mantra meditation she had realised what was happening. As he lost her, he'd needed to create an object to replace her, a baby that he then held her responsible for losing. The book was a cover for his guilt, something stolen from him when the actual theft was his. He was destroying his family's life and the terrible burden of blame had to be ditched on to her shoulders.

What staggered her was the tenacity with which he'd clung to the myth, as if her own sense of reality was so tenuous as to be utterly malleable, mere putty which he would imprint and set and which would never falter, for when she'd tried to introduce some of these insights, he'd laughed and ridiculed what he called her laywoman's version of Freud.

'Displaced guilt, ha ha. You've picked up some basic tools, and now you think you can make electricity, but you'd better forget it, Ilse, before you get your fingers burnt. Look what happened to Victor Frankenstein.'

That was the day she knew the tide had turned and he was no longer amenable to reason. She owed him neither body nor soul: she wouldn't climb the pyre. Let him call her a witch to save his sanity. She knew that game.

It was chilly now, the summer was definitely waning fast, and she strode home quickly, hungry for cheese and wine. These long days were so very good, so slow, the novelty of not having to negotiate the needs of three children and one husband was almost worth the cost. *I am at peace.* Time at last to paint and meditate, to think what we were here for on this earth, sounding the OM. Sam maintained that the point was to strengthen the ego, to create a human identity beyond fragmentation and splitting, but that was the pride of the mind speaking. She wanted to see ego and mind dissolve altogether, to get out of the cage of personality. You had to disappear in one great wave of surrender. *I am part of an infinite universe. The light exists through me.*

Several times, before their split was irreversible, she had tried to explain.

'Sam, we needn't be incompatible like this. Can't we have our different means? All paths end in the same place, you know. I just don't rate knowledge like you do, I never have. I don't want to be able to *think* all the time: I don't value Cartesian thought, the left side of the brain like you do. I want to live from the right side of the brain, the side that's in touch with the heart. I want to follow my intuition.' But behind his tolerant veneer, she could see he was bored. The words meant nothing to him. It was already too late, long before his head was in Trinity College, or he fathered her children, or put his foot in the door of the Analytic Institute. The script had been written long before. This merging and this loss had been sketched out before his body had a flesh: it had emerged when his soul chose this particular path. Karma. You could not swim against that tide. Yet there was no point saying any of this. It was 'an alien discourse' to him, a foreign language. *The sun of the father gives forth light, the arms of the mother give forth love.*

Pouring another cup of herb tea after lunch, and sitting watching the light in the window, she leafed through her journal and looked again at the paper she'd found in Sam's study. It was a paragraph he'd copied out from one of Bion's books called *Learning From Experience*, and he'd neatly inscribed in the margin 'This is Ilse – exactly – a mask of arrogant incomprehension as a defence against what she fears and cannot understand, against what takes me (father) away from her.' The passage read:

> Some patients who are concerned to prove their superior-
> ity to the analyst by defeating his attempts at interpretation
> can be shown that they are mis-understanding the
> interpretations to demonstrate that an ability to mis-under-
> stand is superior to an ability to understand.

Yes, she thought, even my resistance to understanding has to be understood. He thinks he knows it all. But what's so special about understanding? What good is it? When it comes to the bottom line, understanding doesn't have any meaning. She reached out her arms in a gesture away from, then returning, to the heart. Only love has meaning. *I extend my love to all life, visible and invisible.* Knowledge vanishes away, but love . . .

The phone interrupted her pot of tea three times. The first was Carol: the hearing had been deferred pending further legal evidence, but Sam's solicitor was behaving as if he knew his ground was becoming increasingly shaky, and she was optimistic he wouldn't pursue things much further. Then Minna, she'd be coming home for a few days with her new man, Martin, a fellow art student at Leeds.

'I know you'll think he's a bit like Dad, he's interested in Marxist approaches to sculpture, and I'm afraid he's not a vegetarian either, but he's a lovely person, Mum, ever so good looking. Will you get some nice food in for us, please? I'll do the cooking.'

Finally David, a writer she'd encountered some weeks previously.

'Could I speak to Ilse Van-Meir?'

'Speaking.'

'Oh, Ilse, hello, you may not remember me, but we were both at the Lama's last visit at the Buddhist Centre. We had a talk about Kundera's novel, *The Unbearable Lightness of Being.*'

'Oh, yes, of course, I remember.'

'Well, they're showing the film of it at the Arts Cinema tomorrow evening in Colchester, and I wondered if you'd like to go?'

'Yes, I'd love to see it, I didn't know it was on. What time does it start, shall we meet there?'

She could feel a new warmth vibrating in her aura. *Light in the pillars of the body, chakras hum.* David tomorrow, Minna and Martin for the weekend. *Oneness with life, my fellow travellers along the path of light.* Austerity had its limits, even solitariness should never be sustained for long. There had to be this movement in and out, a flowing between self and other. Even the body could not remain impermeable: always something or someone was trying to move, to reach back into it. Spirits attempting to get in or through. She raised her palm, the fingers pointing past rain-spattered glass, sounded the OM.

Spurred on by the rise of energy, she could work more quickly now, determined to finish the painting she'd been working on since Samuel left. It was a work which had been commissioned by the Meditation Centre for their main hall, and at the centre of the vast canvas, surrounded by mountains, paths, Sherpas, flowers, and light, with detailed miniature panels in each corner, rested the compassionate figure of the Buddha, the folds of his flame-coloured garment shimmering in the silver afternoon. As she completed the last section of the Buddha's face, Ilse laughed brokenly at the irony of events. There was Samuel, really convinced that she was mad, her spirituality a hysterical defence against loss. And here was she, knowing that Sam was suffering from a great delusion, his analytical world a massive edifice against the fear of his own destructiveness, his death. Both of them were merely living through their predetermined scripts, but the problem was that their authorship had nothing in common. Sam's came from an understanding ego, that must *know*, whilst hers was from a soul trying to unpick the tangled web into which it had chosen to fall, the warp of her ego shuttled by crossing threads of family and history and time. Endless hostility: the mind striking and madness spitting back.

'It's all right for you,' she shouted, berating the radiant Buddha with a handful of brushes as he calmly watched her. 'Go on, adjust the creases in your robe, I expect they're not catching the light properly or something. That's it, have a good laugh. Grin away. No problem. You've already made it, haven't you? You know what it's like to be God. You don't have to put up with this mess any more. You know what it's like being here? In the bloody chaos of the late twentieth century? All these divorces and wars and people cracking up all around you? It's bloody awful. Inside and out. Crazy. Go on, don't let it trouble you, just carry on smiling. You can afford to: you're not in the midst of all this insanity.'

But with the final touch to the painting, a gleam of white in the Buddha's left eye, the phone started ringing for the fourth time that afternoon – it would be Sam once again for a longer talk in which their madness could lock horns – and the canvas chuckled as the words of the Buddha sang out into the mirror of her studio.

'Oh, but I am, I am. I'm in the very midst of it. I *am* the midst of it. I always was. I always am. Everywhere. Father and mother. Visible and invisible. Formless behind the form, one only behind multitudes. I always will be. Silence and speech. I am. I am. Earth, water, fire and air. I am.'

'Ilse are you there? God, I do wish you'd get to the phone quicker.'

'*I am. I am. I am at peace. I am. I am. Infinite universe. Travelling light, I am. I am.*'

Hideous Progeny

   To say I wish she'd never walked across the threshold of the consulting room would be putting it too mildly. I'd damn her from existence if I could. Her and her demons. *Demons!* Can you credit it, me using the word demon as if it signified? Me? I would have kept that plaque outside the door well covered if I'd known. She, introducing such absurdity, such hell. I'd like to think that it was phantasy, never began.

It was a cold spring morning, early, there was frost still on the glass. A Thursday it must have been, for I'd put the bags of rubbish out. I had no idea what to expect; she'd merely telephoned to book the hour.
   'Dr Brown?'
   'Williams-Brown, actually.'
   'Right. I'm Beatrice Morelli. Bea for short.'
   'Would you like to take a seat? I mean, the couch?'
   'Sure.'
But she wouldn't lie down. She kept on turning round, watching my face to guarantee discomfiture. It was too subtle to be called openly provocative, the way she crossed her legs, or shook her hair across her breasts, and yet it was insinuating, pushing her body deep into my mind. Within minutes she told me she had been bereaved: her husband had been drowned whilst on an Adriatic yachting trip, she had

some problems releasing the grief. She'd made some kind of vow she wouldn't sleep with other men, 'But then I feel so sexual all the time, death and sex are so close, somehow, aren't they? Why do you think that is?' And now was feeling stuck within herself, her life, relationships. She had one child, a son, but he no longer lived with her, had moved abroad, and so she was alone, feeling the lack.

The talk was desultory at first, at least in tone, referring casually to death and loss and fears as if they were mundane affairs, a car tyre burst, or some forgotten name, and though I registered the facts, they had little effect. Perhaps my mind was somewhere else, I was preoccupied with my accounts, for Jane and Claire were always buying clothes, getting us into debt, and so the things that come from that first hour are just the skeleton. Skeleton. Ha! Already this damn language slips, insists on introducing death.

Fortunately, despite some people finding the ethics dubious, I often tape-recorded work. It removed ambiguity, and then if I was too tired, I could listen again, in the dark privacy of night, letting the sessions become reveries where truth might shine. I don't doubt there will be hostile critics who might read such practice, and indeed many of my activities, as suspicious, but I cannot withhold what I regard as the truth. I have received the inevitable venomous letters from angry feminists saying that this is proper vengeance for putting my nose into what was 'none of my damned business', that all analysts are merely capitalising on other people's suffering, mostly women's, and that the point is to transform the *world*, not suck its refuse dry. But I have decided to defy gauntlets of feminist hostility. I will raise up the flag of honesty, declare the truth, though their envy would turn half of the species green.

I will be frank. It is true that initially I did gain something from the publicity around this affair: what people term the 'gutter press' gave it some coverage for quite a little time, and *capitalising* could be thought to be an apt reproach, for who goes into this business out of charity? But those funds didn't last long, they could hardly compensate for the inestimable cost of losing my prestigious practice. The fact was, I wanted the truth publicised, for I was always loyal to trying to understand: that was why I went into therapy in the first place, analytic therapy, for what other way is there in a secular age towards an enlightened humanity? That's what I had always assumed, anyway: that darkness would be filled with light. Ever since my student days, I had been following the footsteps of Freud, one of the last in a long procession of humanists, arguably indeed the very greatest of the secular humanists. *In place of id, there shall ego be. Let there be light.* But I digress.

You've possibly heard the outlines of the case and their inevitable embroidery by those sensation mongers in the press, but I hardly need remind you that these are not to be trusted. What can't be transformed into melodrama as it's told? As a therapist, I lived with drama all the time, became aware how even the minutest incident can be altered, be magnified by pain or misery into Gothic proportions. But here, we find undeniable traces of operatic material, as if we were indeed watching a replay of the Shelley life story re-worked and transposed into the late twentieth century. Which, in a way, we are. But whereas with most cases I would say that the *as if* remains as if, phantasy, here the *as if* and *it is* become too close, and inner and outer have become inseparable.

That's what I hate her for, most. That disrespect for knowledge; that desire to cheat me with the rules; trying to bring that craziness into the universe, confound our best attempts to understand, pull down the walls that keep us from the pigs. Have you ever spent hours looking at a boar? Those massive balls, those mad white eyes, pink-rimmed with too much blood? She's happy now, you see. She's got me there. Within the sty. She just wanted to prove that women live outside. Beyond the norm. Hm. Yes, that *was* hm, and not a snort. I can still talk, goddam it, I can still transform offal into words. I haven't yet succumbed to her design. She hasn't killed me off. I still believe in the nobility of *homo sapiens*, in being civil, civic. This present mockery that contrasts so acutely with my past, far from refuting what I believed, merely confirms that I was right, that the primary endeavour is to stay human against the odds. That is what being *human* means: to keep the shit beneath your head. And here we gobble reason with other scraps. Where id is, why there, *there shall* ego be.

But you are getting confused. You want to know. The source of all despair, Beatrice said, wanting to know. All right, I'll tell the tale. Sadly, it is so unlike what I'd planned. It will come out all monstrous, messy, mucous, covered in blood. And I had wanted it so otherwise. Such a neat case history, ordered, significant, explained, put chronologically: she did this, I said that, and then we understood. That's not what I have for you now. Things are too raw, the hate rises again, these women making things unkempt, impossible. I say women, because I cannot separate them any longer into discrete unities. Beatrice, Mary, and that dark other one, unnameable, myself, no not myself, they have become the only thing, scorching my suffering, twisting the blade.

It is so chaotic, such disorder prevails. But it is true. I will tell it as it is, nothing extenuate. My records and her own account, even though she claims I tampered with these, made them more crazy than they were. No, I have not changed her journals – they show her madness much more brilliantly than anything I could invent: illogical scraps, dreams, fragments, rambling philosophy, literary quotes. I merely present them to you, interspersed with our sessions, in whatever order I could make, and the many undated ones I have merely stuck together to give some shadow of coherence. I feel like Frankenstein, poor Victor Frankenstein, handling the broken bodies of the dead, stroking and patching them to life. *Disjecta membra*. Fragments of the dead. *The dead. The living dead*. But let me not anticipate, you think I am rambling again. I struggle like this with sanity: want you to understand. Always I had contempt for disorder, always paid homage not to chaos, but to what it shades. The erect centre from which things collapse: the noble mind o'erthrown. *Look on my works, ye Mighty, and despair!*

Fortunately, I can let you listen without interruption to some of the most important monologues from the first sessions, for I not only taped, but edited and ran them all together, not just to listen to in the darkness, but to have more sense of logic, continuity. Yes, it is true, after a while she did lie on the couch, legs sprawled, long legs. I forced myself to stare the other way. She started off by talking about vacancy, despair.

'The worst thing is the emptiness. A feeling of things being, well, hollowed out, unreal. Yes, it's been like that as long as I can remember. Wandering around the house in search of my father. He sometimes sat at his desk, pretending to write, or put on great shows of entertainment, hoping these *nouveau riche* friends would line his pockets with silver, but he wasn't ever there for me. There was a wide hall, ever so dark, like I imagine the gates of hell, with figures round the door lintels, a grey oval mirror, full of people talking to the shadows in the corridors. He just wasn't there. No, there wasn't anyone there. Except my sister. And she was haunting the stairs too, even more shadowy than me. It was as if I should have been somebody else. I should have lived before. Or after, I don't know, but not then, not to them. To him.

'I knew you'd ask about Mother. Mother wasn't there either. Or perhaps she was, in the passageways, not quite ferried over. She died when I was born, you see. The afterbirth had not come out, some of it stayed inside. As if I'd left part of myself behind. Strange, isn't it? Birth being death. Killing your mother by being inside her or coming out of her. It makes you wonder if you shouldn't move. They're the same thing anyway. Birth and death, life and death, it all merges together in the end. There is no difference. I always wanted to be dead, really. I still do. Then I'd be with her, wouldn't I? I'd get to know her then, I'd have one. All these people who complain about their mothers. They've no idea. Just this hole. Just this space where there should be someone. There's no one there to mediate between you and the world, no one to talk for you, no translator. So you never really learn the language. You're forever in this foreign country.

'He made us learn it though. Language. He'd have pulled our tongues out if we didn't. I always felt I lived inside an adult brain. I had to read before I was four. The crummiest old leather-bound books, the Bible, and Milton and Shakespeare, words and words and words. But they're mixed up with other things: smells, darkness, tastes, pain. My first memory of bodily pain is of a fire. One of the women helping made a huge log fire in the kitchen – maybe there were guests coming for a literary supper – and it was so bright, vivid hot colours, orange and red and yellow. I wanted to touch them and put them inside me. I wanted to eat that heat, it might get rid of all the coldness, make me feel alive. So I put in my hand to get a big mouthful, but then everything was pain, intense pain, searing pain, and a scream and a shock and scorching skin, I watched it shrivel up and show the flesh. And a message came down from father that he was writing an important document, and not to make such noise. And the woman bandaged my arm, and told me to try to read to take the pain away. I can always see fire. Fire and ice. The two hells. Burning cold and freezing heat, those places where the world begins and ends.

'You've no idea how much I hated that house. It was always empty. Why did that building remain alive when Mother's house was a coffin? I had that paralysed arm, oh from early on, no one else knew why, but I knew that it was the fire. It was that burning, burning, I could feel it every time I went for something bright, oranges, sunlight, red camellias, the arm was paralysed with scorching pain and kept me in the dark. There was a doctor Cline who had me sent to Bournemouth for some bracing sea, then Scotland. It was wonderful there. I loved it. I stayed with a family called the Baxters, in Dundee I think, so kind they were.

Mrs Baxter cajoled me to eat, sweet things and soft honeyed desserts. That was the first time – I think I must have been in my early teens, yes it was just before I fell in love – the first time I really knew what food *was*, what a delight it was, how you could enjoy things, sucking, swallowing, tasting such different textures. For me, Paradise is very earthy. It's about the body being happy. About not wanting, not having gaps, getting exactly what it needs, no more, no less. But always I fell from it. Went back to the blackness, hunger, words.

'That's all we ever got. We were fed words: breakfast, dinner and tea, consuming books. Father had remarried by this time, and we got dreadful food, predictable and dull. Guests got a nice claret and cheese, but we got the frugal English fare, without any flair. Grey maggots that sank into your stomach lining, putrid vegetables, nothing red or alive. I never let my stepmother kiss me. I had this horror of her mouth. I always had a fear of embracing her and then opening my arms and feeling death, her body that I'd just caressed turned into a stiff carcass on my lips.

'Funny, I got quite good with words, I don't know why. I didn't particularly like them, to me they always feel like second best to something else, but they went in easily, even long, difficult ones, and I became skilled at re-forming them, reproducing them, as long as I can remember. I didn't even try, it just happened. But with Frances – my sister, well half-sister, really – it was different. She could never get the hang of them. Father got so impatient with her, called her stupid, imbecilic, but I was the apple of his eye. He would call me into his evening gatherings, showing me off to his men friends, talking about my 'precocious intellect'. He said it was 'quite masculine in character'. It was a kind of seduction scene, really, but my tits were Milton and Plutarch my arse.

'You know the myth about Athena, sprung out of the head of Zeus, his favoured brain-child? It was just like that. No real mothering at all. But it was even worse for Fanny – that's what we called Frances. Mary Jane, our stepmother, loathed her, and she didn't get any defences from father for being intellectually brilliant as I did. She wouldn't talk to me much either – maybe she was jealous, I don't know. I didn't have much time, actually, I was in his study all day. Anyway, she was the first family corpse. Yes, I said corpse. From Latin *corpus*, meaning body. She took an overdose. I suppose you imagine it's the least painful way to do it, progressive oblivion, but it can be agony. Think of Madame Bovary. Arsenic.

'Anyway, Fanny did it. Got out of it. Out of herself. Amazing, really, I never thought she'd have the guts. I'd already abandoned things by then, I was in Europe. She was the one left at home, playing dutiful daughters. Why dear Papa chose that auspicious moment to reveal to Fanny her true parenting, I'll never know. Probably a stupid caprice. Just when I'm off gallivanting around France and Italy with the in-crowd, there's Fanny paralysed at home with a step-mother who resents her and a father who despises her, hanging on desperately to a thread of faith that makes life worth living. Then father comes along and cuts that thread at its only firm holding point: her legitimacy. Suddenly she isn't even his: she doesn't belong. She is the bastard daughter of a corpse and rake. Once without a mother and now without a father as well, who is she? She's illegitimate, a non-being, one of the dead.

'I wish I could mourn her. I'd like to talk to her. I miss her. I miss you, Fanny. It wasn't that I didn't want to be with you. Don't you see? I got forced away. They separated us by envy and competition. It's what they do. I wasn't strong enough to stop it, and I didn't understand. But we are the same, don't you see? Behind my mask, just the same vacancy, the same despair. I envy you your refusal to compromise. You took your death to where it belongs, amongst the dead, but I still carry mine around with me. I wasn't powerful enough to stop him throwing you to obscurity, I couldn't get you back home to be buried. But your death is more powerful than words, Fanny, it says how intolerable life can be. You had the honesty to quit, to say *there is no meaning to it all*. I shan't let them forget.'

You will agree that we covered, or should I say un-covered, quite a lot of ground in a short time, and I had to congratulate myself on the dexterity with which I'd intervened. Within a few sessions, I had enabled her to find some early traumas, memories, working on loss of mother, sister, with all those attendant feelings of anger, grief, and deep futility: it was remarkable how logically, how speedily it fitted into place. For some time we continued in this vein, until all the essential details of her early years were known, and it would be as easy to interpret as to summarise the facts, but I will allow you to hear more of her own wandering; it gives a flavour of her bitter mind.

'I've come to hate men, you see. Though hatred is too clear a word, too unequivocal. It's more a sense of inner collapse, a despair they will never understand. Some deep resentment that they will not try. And I don't just mean men. I mean the *masculinity* in people. I don't think *you* can hear me really. I need a female audience. I mean, what did they ever really *know*? You, I'm talking to you. Do you think you know something? Theories, language, thoughts? Did you ever know a knowledge which hasn't engendered death? Genesis is the greatest myth. The fruit of the tree of knowledge is sorrow, and guilt, and grief that increases a thousandfold and cannot be erased. Knowledge clings to the mind like lichen to a rock. This is why women go mad much more easily. They're trying to shake off that lichen, but it can't be lost without losing the mind itself. They have to crack open the whole of the rock.

'I can't tell it chronologically any more. I've had enough of time. Chronos, King of the clock. Chronic. I'm feeling choked, strangled. Clock time is masculine, pedestrian, inane, a fear of soaring in eternity. I need to be more free of things that choke my spirit in the dark. I hate the restrictions you put on time. I need to be more free.'

Those were the exciting early weeks of initial disclosures. She talked quite freely about the death of her mother, and Fanny, even Pearce, her husband who had drowned, but then we entered that familiar territory of therapeutic stalemate. The same material, the same infertile ground, ploughing dull furrows of despair, emptiness, defeat. Although the pieces of the jigsaw were numerous, there was a sense of incompleteness. Something was missing, something she was avoiding bringing out, some hideous monstrosity she wouldn't tell. For all these dead bodies and lives, though linked by blood and love, were *outside* hers, and yet she spoke of having some monstrosity *inside*, which didn't quite link up. I knew that there were theories about *the bad object* a person can carry inside, when they feel they're containing something that feels heavy and black, but with Beatrice, I sensed that it was something more. Something else had invaded her, something more sinister, some presence from *out there*. But it was resistant to being moved. Spring moved to summer, then to autumn and then the early morning hours of her sessions were full of the darkness of the previous night.

Maybe this something that was yet unsaid linked up, I thought, with Bea's block about work. I haven't mentioned that yet, have I? I'd forgotten you didn't know. One always thinks one's own dramas, being so big, are broadcast to the world. She was a film producer, you see, freelance, made fictionalised documentaries about revolutionary figures, artists, all women – Wollstonecraft, Woolf, Pankhurst, Kahlo, Kollontai, you know the kind of thing: productions for Channel Four and independent cinemas. She wasn't quite as well known then, though, not as she is now, and she'd come to me because she'd got this block. She couldn't work. It coincided with Pearce dying, but that didn't seem to be the only point. She said she wanted to get on, she had to get this film made, work was the anodyne for grief, but every time she looked at films or cameras, approached the cutting room or desk, she had this kind of black-out. She went dead.

'I can't describe it to you. But it's as if I've just stopped living. There's all this hollowness and I fall into it. A pit. A darkness. It's not disintegrating, for there's nothing, no me, to disintegrate. But every time I think of working, there's this pit opening.'

The balance tipped that morning when I asked her directly what the project was that she was working on currently.

'Mary Shelley. Author of *Frankenstein*. Didn't you realise?'

I must admit I was surprised. Now she reminded me, I'd vaguely heard of her, Mary, as Percy Shelley's wife, the Romantic poet's wife, but I hadn't realised that it was from the pen of such a woman, mixing with the foremost intellects of the day, that such things had come. Monsters. Monstrosities.

'Yes, that's right, the horror story *Frankenstein*. She wrote lots of other things too, but that's the one that's stuck in the popular mind. I made a documentary about her mother, you see, two years ago, Mary Wollstonecraft, but that was easier. Wollstonecraft was a radical feminist, in her way, for her time. She fought with men on their own terms. She was rational, whatever *that* means. But Shelley, she's another thing altogether: irrational, locked in, mad. It feels like facing the world's depression, the abjection of women through the ages rolled into a stone against my heart.'

Bea had this tendency to melodramatic turns of phrase, what one colleague of mine would call women playing 'tragedy queens'. I had become quite used to it by now.

'Is that the problem behind your block? Women's depression? Or your own?'

'Both. How could they be separable? We're carved from the same granite. Look at Fanny, look at my mother, look at me. What killed us all? You think gender's *irrelevant*? Can't you see what's under your very nose? That you're the man whose coffers get filled up and I'm the woman paying to lie down upon your couch? At one time you'd have had to pay for the privilege of staring at a woman's legs for a whole hour. You think sex is coincidence?'

She used to get angry that I didn't take more notice of women's depression, deaths – poor Fanny's suicide, for instance, or Frida Kahlo's pain – but I knew that she was wanting to distract attention from the anger with her own father, that really it was he who had not noticed her enough. This idea, mind you, only enraged her all the more. You can hear from her language – I have this too on tape – that she was holding no stops when it came to expletives or blasphemies. I've edited the very worst to save embarrassment.

'Clever fucking bastard, aren't you, Godfrey? Think we're so bleeding bright, don't we, with our public school background and medical training? Mm? Let me tell you a few things straight. Straight. Without devious strategies, without there being any unconscious motives. First, I am OUT-RAGED. Not for me. Not for me alone. For women. For Frances. And all the rest. Women in mental homes. Women on benefits, pills, meat hooks. Outraged, angry, furious. You comprehend the terms? What a fucking nerve, trying to talk that anger away as *my* stuff, my personal unconscious material! What if it isn't? What if it's more than me, and it's *real*, out there, *fact*! You understand that word, fact?

'Second, you don't know the first bloody thing about it. You've never been there – where you call crazy. I can tell that by just looking at you. By the way your house is. The way your face is, your clothes are. You've never bloody been there. So how can you know? Anything? Anything that matters about women, life?'

I was familiar with such furious moods, of course, and let the anger run its course. It was like a tantrum. When the child has cried enough and hurt its fists against the wall, it stops. It learns to stop. It has to learn: there is no other choice.

Moreover, I wasn't prepared to enter into an abstract debate about sexual politics. I had enough of that on a domestic scale with Claire and Jane. Once or twice, by the way, Beatrice asked for details of my family life, but I was prudent enough to give only sketchy hints. I told her I was married, and that we had a daughter who was just fifteen. But apart from such minimal facts, I was admirably mute. I didn't tell her any names, nor that Jane was my second wife, and Claire the daughter from Jane's first marriage. It's important, you see, to give an impression of stability, of permanence. I didn't want her thinking I was defeated by death, or impotent.

The only trouble was that the consulting room was situated in the basement of our Victorian three-storey house, and on the ground level you could look easily into the living-room and kitchen – one big room which stretched back to French windows and enclosed garden at the back – so she could have witnessed or heard things going on. We tried to keep the blinds partially drawn, but there are always days when you forget, and maybe she perceived more than I knew. Somehow she must have infiltrated into the house, got to know Claire, left doors and windows slightly on the hook for her familiars to call.

But at that time, I knew nothing. I concentrated on the narrative. I wondered where all that darkness had been before; where it had gone to in her infancy. And then she told me about her writing, about death. She said she used to sit upon her mother's grave for hours on end, reading her mother's books, or writing stories, poems, secret letters to her mother, herself. She used writing like therapy, to have a silent listener. She was reluctant to share with me what was inside, but one day, by happy 'accident', I discovered some of the early and late journals and had access to that inner world. She'd sometimes bring them in, you see, to share the details of an old or recent dream, and I would manage, in the hurried confusion of bags and coats and payment, or during her visit to the bathroom, to remove a few pages from her file – loose-leaved, it made it easier – and then contrive to return them at the next session. No, I don't think that's dubious morality, I mean fair's fair and in order to work well, I had to use whatever information I could glean. Of course, I took the opportunity to photocopy them.

I was right: she had confided to those sheets far more than she had ever done to me. Some pages were scored heavily, as if in anger she had pressed the pen through to the back, others had only a couple of words sprawled in thin pencil right across the page, like bodies pulled upon the rack. Of course, they were mere fragments, but they said much. The first extracts I read covered that early period of our inter-action, and provided valuable insight into her transferred feelings to me. As I thought, what she concealed was sexu-ality: she had ideas of seducing me, wanted me laid!

Like most female patients, she needed to believe that I was attracted to her, that she might seduce me as she hadn't been able to her father. For she was rapidly slipping into phantasy, a world marked by an inability to separate inner from outer. She would acknowledge my judicious readings of her dreams with looks that mixed appreciation with flirtation, attempt-ing to show ridicule in order to disclaim her deep sexual attraction and desire for me. So despite that tone of disil-lusionment which you might register in her journal entries, it is important to remember that she was struggling to deny reality: her ineradicable longing to seduce.

10 March 198–. To Islington: first session with Williams-Brown. Pompous old fart, gives nothing of himself away. Looks very solid and immovable. Old man of the unconscious sea. An ageing Byron, thick black hair bit long over the collar and bow tie – daring, daring! – cultivated wildness. Did I imagine smell of cigars or Turkish ciggies, inevitable symptom of analytic background? Feel like shock-ing him into spontaneity. Told him about some basic insecurities. The basement smells slightly of urinated walls. Upstairs looked plusher. Wife? Housewife? The garbage was stacked rather anally.

18 March. Things proceed with God. (Godfrey. He was taken aback that I knew his name. 'I'd prefer it if you referred to me as Dr Williams-Brown,' he said with condescension in his floppy voice. 'But Godfrey,' I replied, 'Godfrey, surely you're flattered when women want to use your Christian name? Godfrey sounds much more intimate, more phallic, don't you think?') I bet he thinks I want to get him into bed. They usually do.

20 March. He has some insights into dreams and things, but rather formulaically. The kind of detective who'd catch the murderer only if he left the clues in the right place. No intuition. He knows the theories, but has he been there? I doubt it.

25 March. God finding me a handful. Can't cope with me talking about the transference, being too explicit on sex. He can't contain the leaking libido: it's wetting his nice couch! I lead him on a bit – naughty, I know, but I've got to have laughs somewhere. Despair still clicking its heels: I pretend not to notice it.

Lunchtime wandering around the Egyptian section of the British Museum. Hieroglyphs, mummies, hybrid man-beast deities. They had a form in which to put the monstrous then, life-death: is it the modern age that's made it so unspeakable?

Besides these dated entries were pages which were less obviously referring to external events: dream-like reflections of her own internal world. And this was when Mary began to come more to the fore, and things began to turn.

Tired, central London and back. Morning in British Museum Library again. BM, the Blessed Martyr. Reading Mary Shelley's letters in a cardboard box. The real thing! Papers she touched and scrawled, held to her mouth. Embarrassed at enjoying touching them – kept looking round in that very proper, polished reading room to see if anyone would catch me – mustn't have such fetishistic pleasure – like masturbating, too obscene. Strange, to be able to stroke the actual objects like this, the letters she produced, papers that real woman once sat down and wrote. Like holy relics, magic objects, linking her with me, making us one, despite the centuries. Two pairs of hands holding her writing, hers on one side the page, and mine the other, like The Two Fridas, joined by an umbilical cord.

(This, I later discovered – by watching Bea's documentary films – referred to the title of a famous painting by the Mexican artist Frida Kahlo, whose work is punctuated with themes and motifs strikingly parallel to Mary Shelley's – at least as Bea interpreted them. Birth, still-birth, death, women's anguish and suffering, the characteristic iconography of female despair. *The Two Fridas*, from 1939, depicts two women – the same woman, herself and her double – side by side on a bench, one hand joined, but their hearts literally exposed and also linked by a large red artery flowing like a placenta between them. A surrealistic image, it suggests that the life of one depends upon the life – and death – of the other, united as they are against the loss of men and an aborted sexuality. I mention this because the painting, and all of Kahlo's work, seems to have had powerful reverberations for Beatrice, and to echo many of the unconscious preoccupations she discovered in her own relation to Mary Shelley/herself.)

Disturbing was her despair – her urgent note to Claire, imperative, COME, COME, who's there for me? I must have you, please come. And then the passing of the panic, urbane sanity remade.

God's losing face. Can't manage my anger. The point he misses is that things have to be lived through, and not just talked about or understood. You can't just rabbit on about clearing up the psyche. You have to know the dirt. You have to live there. Only anger can counteract despair.

So different working on Shelley from Wollstonecraft. The masculine rigour turns against her instead of for her. Rigour. I hate the word. Rigor mortis. No doubts, no creative uncertainties.

4 July. Freedom for the oppressed. I understand nothing. Nothing. Dream last night. I'm in a huge Egyptian pyramid, house of the dead. There's a pharaoh enshrined in a beautiful case on a dais towards the top of the pyramid. Rich ornaments, jewels, paintings on his mummified enclosure, pictures of birds, eggs, falcons, plants, ships, fruit. I am wandering around the pyramid, looking for something, for someone, but there is no one there. My feet make no noise on the floor. If I scream or shout, my voice makes no sound. I walk towards the pharaoh to see who it is, but I cannot climb up the smooth triangular shape, there is nothing to hold on to, I'm defeated, left.

Endlessly working, or rather trying to work stuck in the BM, calling it research. Tourists with cameras block entrances, café prices increase, the critics drive me mad. Want to crack open heads against hard concrete walls like crunching snails, and bleed some folly from their skulls: patronising fools. 'Mary had sense and judgment enough to leave the poetry in Shelley's hands, and to concentrate on fiction, which financial returns and a genuine if unexalted gift both served to justify.' Ascribing her work to Shelley or his influence. Denial of agency, stripping away of female power . . . 'a woman who, though much smaller than the giants who were her husband, her parents, and some of her friends, yet knew the giants well.' Another female pygmy.

Can't work out how to structure the film. Thought of some reflexive structure, a framework of feminists talking about her work, dismantling Romanticism, exposing the phallocentricity of it, but then it won't get to such a big audience. I've got to compete with Ken Russell, after all, counter his Gothic with something more feminist. But it's so tedious, depressing, having to work through how men have represented her, describe how they've belittled her. I want something more sensational.

I play with titles for the film, hoping that might inspire. Frankenstein II, Frankenstein lives, OK? Frankenstein Goes to Hollywood, Frankenstein Unbound, but Aldiss snaffled it first, Laying the Ghost, Frankenstein Laid. Cheap puns. Or something more austere, Rising from Darkness, Naming the Unnameable, Dark Tenancies, Female Gothic, Sphinx, Monsters of Elegy.

Frankenstein, or the new Prometheus. Pro-me-theus, for-me-god: says it all. Man as the titan, fascist, achiever. Titanism. Omniscience. The Prometheus of Byron and Shelley: self-assertive, confident, wagging their noses in the wind. But for Mary, the *hound a mongrel, fallen, unredeemable. She is uneasy with male aggression, spells out the doom of Romantic over-reaching. Sniffs out the poison of their tainted gifts. She wasn't taken in, despite trying so hard to become one of the literary boys. Marginalised. She sensed the fissures, ruptures in those sublime crags of Romantic idealism, but she had no power to make it clear, none of Byron's panache to see her through.*

The project of Romanticism gets doomed from the start because of the male ego. They want to get God, but with them, God has to be subordinate to man. The Romantic heroes – Satan, Prometheus, Cain, Don Juan, are all anti-God: wanting to steal his thunder and his fire; not to become as God, but to be God, to take his role, like the son usurping the father: Oedipal rivalry, male arrogance. But haven't they heard that saying: 'He dies who sees God face to face.' They want the glory without paying the price. But Mary Shelley knew it somewhere, tried to spell it out. Frankenstein shows Prometheus, the Romantic over-reacher, as the ultimate blasphemer. Man going it alone, woman destroyed, and God upon his deathbed till Nietzsche declared the rattle done. You can't steal fire, you can't stare into the eye of the Lord without your self being burnt blind, your ego cauterised.

But if she knew all this, if she knew the cost of male egotism, why didn't she release herself? Why are her journals so terribly bleak, depressed? Why was she trapped in such blackness, despair, such inner emptiness? Why didn't she break free? If only Mary Shelley could have found a way to liberate herself through her intelligence, instead of being so trapped and hemmed in by theirs. Doubly oppressed: their dejection surfacing in her as abjection, their inward-looking miseries compounded by her exile – from herself – a woman on the edge, off-centre in a male context and literature, with none of the glitter that came with their grandiosity.

How to say this on film? To say that she – the monster – is still hanging around, unrecognised? What female splitting can be seen as meaningful?

By this time, I have to admit, I was beginning to get rather preoccupied with *Frankenstein* myself. I was brought up in such a different tradition, you see, 'the old boys' network' was how Bea described it, and I was quite unfamiliar with anything associated with that tradition of horrors which has come to be called 'Gothic'. I knew nothing about it; nothing about women's writing. Well, I was educated as a scientist: these minor lady novelists were not part of the old curriculum. So I started reading, and I have to admit it fascinated me. There was something compelling about the writing I'd never met before. The same kind of compulsions you find in patients, going on and on with one preoccupation all their lives. Only here the themes were so much more *blatantly* sex, madness, fear, death: this Gothic hell a psychoanalytic paradise!

Jane was a bit taken aback. She could hardly believe her eyes when she saw me with a rather lurid-covered copy of *Frankenstein* one night – she was more accustomed to me reading psychoanalytic quarterlies in bed whilst she was doing her face and undressing – and she looked rather suspicious. '*Godfrey*,' she exclaimed, 'is our sex life *that* bad, darling, that you need such titillation?' but I reassured her I was merely doing research on an interesting client, and we said no more. If only that *had* been the sum of it. For it didn't stop there. Slowly, one by one, pennies began to drop, but with my growing understanding came a sense that as I undid all the knots that tied Beatrice to herself, they wove round me, and I was being strangled by her monstrous history.

The first thing was the name, discovering Mary's father's name – Godwin. The philosopher Godwin – quite a radical in his day, he was the one who'd married Wollstonecraft and fathered Mary, this fatal daughter who had indirectly caused her mother's death. Godwin, I thought. God. Something uncanny here. Not only Godwin, but William Godwin. Hardly needs a graduate in psychology to recognise the doubling there, does it? Godwin, William Godwin, and Godfrey, Godfrey Williams-Brown. I was starting to look in a distorting mirror. Her mother died at birth. And then she had this half-sister, an illegitimate daughter of Wollstonecraft by some guy Imlay, and she was called Fanny and took an overdose of laudanum in Swansea's Mackworth Arms and died, an unsung female Chatterton. I'd heard the story somewhere before.

But more than that, Godwin had remarried, as I had, a woman called Mary Jane, who brought her step-daughter with her, Claire, and she was in the house upstairs, and I was trying to relate to some child of my own, but then thinking got blurred, unravelling invisible string stretching between some ghostly hearts. And so the narratives she told, did they belong to her or Mary or to me? Was it Bea's psyche or Mary's or then my own we were discovering? Could they be separate? Maybe there was no Beatrice, only this someone else, this other woman inside her, this Mary who possessed her, and yet then again perhaps Mary did not exist and she had been invaded by this other thing, unnameable, this great monster of elegy. The boxes inside boxes of the novel *Frankenstein* crumbled away, coffins eaten by worms, and nothing would stay closed. I started to be unsure who we all were, who I was, wondered what made up anyone.

I recorded Bea's journals onto tapes that I played to myself alongside her voice from the sessions, so that in the darkness there was this counterpoint of sound. Beatrice and Mary, Morelli and Shelley, the two of them, mingling, till I became unsure who listened, spoke or thought.

What matters is that she was caught and I am caught and in her struggle to be free, she has to pull me with her. The hours I spend with her: listening. Listening to the unsaid, unsayable. She haunts me, obsesses me. I need to hear her right, not to misrepresent.

Nothing is outside the scope of the human. The monster was not an alien creature, but the product of the human mind, an aspect of the split self of Frankenstein/Mary Shelley. It became fearful because denied, because unknown, as with scapegoats, outcasts, minorities in any culture.

Someone preoccupied with death, with absence, loss, but unable to locate the cause, stuck in depressive states of mind. Melancholia. Trying to heal through being heard.

She is so tired of death and all it means. We cannot talk blandly any longer of darkness, for it is no game, this dark side of the moon, no trivial pursuit. All can be lost, and often is. I know the taste of blisters on the tongue.

*Mary was too polite. She needed to ignite a fuse under the whole fabric of western society, their governments and kings. She tried to. Frankenstein, The Last Man. A spectacle of death could be quite powerful – shots of Hiroshima. The holocaust, empires in ruin just as she had said. The little-known prophetic side of her. **And a desolate space was all that was left of the known world. Systematic order had sunk into desolation.** She knew, however unconsciously. She knew. Annihilation was her way of getting free.*

I was not heard: a mad Cassandra, crying in the dark. But grieving for the world. This globe spinning inexorably towards destruction. Science flaying the surface of the earth, progress overreaching itself, threatening to blow up humanity in its lust to control the mystery of life. A civilisation founded on fear, destroying what it could not understand.

How to bring forth the darkness? Where are all the images, the words? Can it be uttered, are there words to say? These words can only point towards: they're never there, never the thing itself. Only images, metaphors, get anywhere, for how can formlessness be imaged anyway? Are there words for darkness? I have been invaded by her madness, her hopelessness. The only way is write, think, act, resist despair. I want things to explode.

How is it men seem to find it so easy to write about division, fragmentation, all this discourse about splitting and mirroring, but they never lose themselves? Like clever old Godfrey. Why can't I do it that way? Why do I have to live what I think? Become who

I think about? An attempt to get them whole as well as me? Them becoming something through me?

I've said enough. The pain of it. The years on years. The pain of it. You know my journals, scripts of half-hidden misery. You know the sum of it.

It is her and not her. Mary Shelley and another. Her name trails history upon its back, it crawls inside my memory, but do I mean her? Who is she? That is what I mean to say, to show. Who is she? Who is anyone? Cassandra shouting in the wind. Is she no thing but what we make of her? Constructing other people as ourselves? Did she exist at all, Mary Shelley? And Beatrice? I mean, not physically, I know her body's there, but her identity, what is identity? How can we find it? Is there such a thing? Are we anything other than people's projections on to us? Nothing but 'Mary Shelley'? Who is she? Who is anyone?

Godwin cannot contain. The room's too small. My anger strips the walls.

The three of us became confused, you see. God, Godwin, Godfrey, me, Mary and Beatrice, the devil. I was trying to understand where one began and ended, but the more I knew the more my knowledge grew into a web where we were trapped, three spiders eating one another in the dark.

I can still see my mother, lying in the bed where she birthed me to death, that bloody room littered with books and manuscripts, reading and writing till the end. Her mind refusing to succumb to the pains of the body, the acute agony of birth. And how the grotesque intruded and coloured everything livid, green. Fanny peering from the shadows, witness to this sister tearing through her mother and bringing death in her wake, this mother's body violenced by rough male hands and instruments. Puppy dogs scratching up the counterpane to fasten on to those rich breasts like leeches, sucking off the milk as if she were a beast. I can still see her in the ancient memory of my body, this woman who thought better than men, this intellectual demon Wollstonecraft turned into a rough suckling post for dogs, and me, reaching for nourishment, supplanted by the greedy hounds of death.

She knew what a farce it was, all is, this life bounded by convention, by law, by state. She saw through it, the patriarchal system of government, machinery of wealth. She didn't want to tinker with a few surface manifestations of wrongs. She wanted an overthrow of the whole thing. The point was to aim at the centre, to dismantle the whole damnable structure. A radical vision, radical philosophy. I always felt she should have married Blake. They might have balanced one another well – his wildness might have scattered some of that excess enlightenment rationalism and her reflections might have anchored his excess abstractions. I would like to have been fathered by Blake, become a true daughter of Albion. Sometimes Godwin feels more like Malvolio: pompous and to be ridiculed, a gartered idiot.

Even so, she was too extreme for them, not what a woman 'should' be. Unyielding, invincible, except by the murderer of so many women: motherhood. She became the hyena I must not become, the beast with four heads of my worst reflection. Godwin's Memoirs of her so misfired, written for him, not her, his vindication and not hers, they ended up slandering her, set back the cause of feminism fifty years. What a fool.

'Shee, shee is gone; shee is gone; When thou knowest this,/ What fragmentary rubbidge this world is/Thou knowest.'

Who is she? I shall ask her: who are you? Your demure exterior conceals desire. You hide Beatrice. But you have not killed her. She will haunt you with life unlived.

Is she Mary Shelley? Am I Mary Shelley? What speaks through me, this vacancy?

Oh, I had intellectual agility, acumen. I could allude to

Dante, Shakespeare, Greek mythology. But it was in the dark. Darkness. I didn't really know what I was doing. It was as if I was a wheel on a carriage, trying desperately to find a new route forwards, but there was such heavy mud, nothing would lift, I was dragged down, dragged back always. And then they called me conventional. How closer could I have come to the volcano? Conventional! When I was playing with myths as if they were counters! I didn't speak out loud, it is true, on matters political, sexual or religious. But think of the myths I unloosed from their moorings. Prometheus, Demeter and Persephone, Cassandra, think of the apocalypse of The Last Man. It's not Shelley's isolated solipsists that they make films about, is it? It's not Alastor or even Don Juan who get serialised and televised? No, it's Frankenstein, it's Frankenstein Unbound, again and again. Rewritings, to be sure, but still, the myth is out of copyright, has things to tell.

O God, I want her to live. I want to live. I want to yank her limbs out of the grave, to open things without the corsets, knives, swords buckled in her spine. I give her words. We have to use the rotted names. I give her words, always too many words, crammed in our mouths like gold, the Midas touch.

I look at all the spools of film, asking for editing. Madness lies on the cutting desk, longing to speak. I sit in front of images and sounds, trying to form a shape, but it is struggling with something too intractable, some force for death. I'm tempted to stop seeing God. He's helpless before this, these seas of blood under the couch, monsters behind his chair. Gericault's Madwoman hangs on the wall, her bloodshot eyes, white frilled bonnet, parodying madness, so gentle, so contained. Perhaps poor Dorothy, Wordsworth's mad sister, looked like that in the Lakes when her mind – and her rage – no longer held.

I have dreams of possession, being possessed. But are they dreams? Nightmare reality of things plucking my heart, shooting steel bayonets into my eyes. The danger zones: stomach and eyes. A third world war is hovering in the wings, creeping across the underbelly of the world. It is no fancy: this is not the plague. Cassandra called Beware, beware, one world at risk. Mary cried too. Do you see: rain on sealed earth. We like to think them 'mad', 'hysterical'.

The first lost baby haunts me still, the ghost of her crying, inconsolable, wanting the life she never entered. How desperately I tried to bring her back to life, rubbing her tiny cold red body again and again, massaging that stone child till my hands were chafed, willing her to breathe. Dream that my little baby comes to life again, that it had only been cold, and that we rub it before the fire and it lives. Fire against ice. I never named her, my unlived nameless one, she was the one who grew into that unloved giant striding through the world, that little one hungry for life, that frozen soul crying for a form.

And Clara. Born September 1817, died September 1818. Her death in Venice, where the water carried away the dead upon an amniotic tide, rejoining them with all the unborn. Or maybe she was that first unborn, trying again and again to claim me as a mother, and failing, unable to hold the link. All I needed was to cry. But Godwin forbade all that. He couldn't bear tears. He ordered me not to grieve the deaths of little Clara and William, his letters a valediction against mourning. Such punctilious turn of phrase, his literary uprightness.

'Don't grieve,' he said, 'don't grieve', simply 'because a child of three years is dead.' Yet my mouth cries out from the centre of the earth that I will grieve, alive with fire and heat, how I will grieve and rain my tears upon the ground like molten lead. I will not unremember that flesh of my flesh, I will not tear apart this inner mothering. I will cry and will cry . . . and yet my voice was silenced like the night-

time cry that cannot make a sound. I open my mouth to speak and see the inside, a dark cave, my tongue ripped out like Lucrecia's after the rape. This father who has pierced my tongue with his hooked iron hand and left a bleeding wound, mere vacancy. I am an unborn cry, an anguished silent scream..

I never trusted men after that, after those years in Italy. I developed a cold exterior to combat coldness, the tears I had been forbidden to shed froze and solidified around me to form a wall no one could penetrate. There was no one. Godwin dead to me, Shelley withdrawn from his pain into a mental universe, abstracted thought and poetry. Neither of them would or could reach to me. My heart torn in two, bleeding inside its closed impenetrable shell, ripped apart by sharp-toothed misery. The husk of myself shattered, gaping, unsure how to write again. For how can one write misery and who would wish to read?

'You should, however, recollect,' father wrote me, 'that it is only persons of a very ordinary sort, and of a very pusillanimous disposition, that sink long under a calamity of this nature.' Well, if to mourn and grieve your own lost babies means being pusillanimous, ordinary, I want the most banal life possible: one that makes inner truth a possibility.

Clara, William, the nameless one, and the other unborn, gone to prepare the ferry-man for Percy coming that summer of 1822. All those impatient souls who rushed through my body from death to life and death again as if my womb were a funeral chamber. Perhaps we named them wrongly, perhaps they'd wanted different identities. Why Clara? Was it saying to Shelley you don't need big Claire, Clara now, you have a little one of your own, see she is here, from our own lovemaking, let this other Clara go? But she couldn't hold on through the heat and torpor, and the ogre's claim on her couldn't be stopped. And William, why William? Hadn't I done enough to placate father without giving him a son? It didn't bring him closer, he didn't care for his loss, he cared more for a manuscript than baby. The scream returns on me

*as I think of it, the false priorities, the anti-life. A scream
not mine alone, I say it again, not mine alone. A scream for
all the trampling down of hearts, destroying truth.*

I decided to confront things head-on. I wasn't one to wait
passively for circumstance to win. I managed to get a ticket
to the British Library myself, that dome-like reading room,
a giant breast holding these hungry minds, and women deliv-
ering piles of books at regular intervals. I sat there on my
free days, letting my jacket sleeve polish the leather seat and
work-top, and compulsively, yes there was an element of
the compulsive about it, I admit that, worked through the
whole lot, everything: novels, short stories, poems, plays,
biographies, letters, journals and all. I was determined that
the madness creeping into my house would stop. I never
could abide a pipe that leaked; I would make boundaries to
mark out where her life began and mine might end. But the
strange thing was that the more I knew of it, the more it
grew: the madness that was drowning Beatrice started to
flood into me. It came right into me, up to the collar. You
see this watermark upon my neck?

Of course, I am talking about some time here. Weeks,
months. I had other responsibilities. I couldn't go up to the
library more than a one day a week, and this infrequency
gave me the illusion that things might be contained. Between
times I would feel quite confident, facts distilled into meaning, darkness held. But as soon as I faced the whole monstrosity again, there certainty collapsed, this unnameable
thing would reappear, and any fixity, identity, became confused.

*My first tale was for you, Godwin, my Hate and aptly titled,
hatred beneath the unrequited love. I'll not forgive, I'll not
betray the unloved by forgetting. Oh, I am so weary of your
striving after difference, superiority. I want to claim and
embrace ordinary humanity, to cry, to share, to experience
being this female living form, body and soul. I want to link*

*up with all the other women who have lost themselves in
their infants, millions upon millions of them. I want to
register loss, have it received. 'We seldom indulge long,'
continued God, 'in depression and mourning except when we
think that there is something very refined in it, and that it
does us honour.' I continued to write. Always the dumb
facility with words. Neat journal entries, censored before pen
struck the page, like prison notes. I didn't write of death or
madness in my diary: what could I say?*

*I played their game. I grew a carapace, a shell of indiffer-
ence, untouchability. No tears there, it was a frozen landscape, black, bleak, melancholic, hard. Joy became something
fanciful, as if misremembered from a previous life, an ever
receding, never properly inhabited lost Paradise. Milton,
more and more Milton. My mind was branded with it. The
fall from grace the only movement in my darkened skull.
An Eden known only as half-imagined memory: God but a
dream.*

I read her – Mary's – autobiography, *Mathilda*. A daughter,
mother dead, fearing and wanting father's love, that incest
phantasy driving to death.

I wanted to touch something she had held.

*You know what Leigh Hunt said about me to Novello –
you've read a copy of the letter – 'But do not let anyone
consider Mary S. in the light of a Blue, of which she has a
great horror, but as an unaffected person.' I was ashamed of
such praise which I wanted to be untrue. The sad truth is I
was a well-trained literary dog. I stood on my hind legs for
their tit-bits and came smiling when they remarked on my
cleverness, inwardly despising them and myself for our
mutual collusion in a patronising game. I hated Hunt's
praise, and his poem – a sycophantic claiming of familiarity.
'So sleek and so smiling she came, people stared/To think
such fair clay should so darkly have dared.' Such condescension. Belittling me and the nameless one, as if the pair of us*

*were toys. Would that I could witness his discomfort when
the shadow finally reaches his couch in the dark hours of
night.*

*I fitted into a placid persona, a fixed imperturbable mask
that shielded us – the nameless one and myself – from dangerous prying. A woman's fire hidden in me by careful trimming
of the wick, till in the end I almost came to be convinced I
was who I had become. My persona had waxed round me till
I became the 'Mary Shelley' I had been constructed into, or
that had been constructed round me. A shell, a stencilled
form, a name that didn't fit: Mary. Wollstonecraft. Godwin.
Shelley. Which one was mine? All alibis I assumed in the
world, fronts for the nameless one.*

But then, where did her madness go? It had to settle somewhere: nothing disappears.

*We are stuck inside words. Treading letters as grapes hoping they'll
yield juice. I want to wring some truth out of this bruised skin of
language, want to taste holy wine.*

Who was I? What was I? Whence did I come? What was my destination?

*Frankenstein is an allegory for our times. Birth travestied as death,
anti-humanity. The whole thing a travesty: life turns to parody,
what should be creativity destroys. Man trying to usurp women and
gods. There is always a price to pay. Mary's deep melancholy,
women's abjection and despair. Behold the spirit of the age: denied
and stranded, staring in the dark. The ghosts of secular modernity.*

*All my life, pursued by lowness of spirits. Pursued, yes,
persecuted, like Coleridge's Ancient Mariner by some arctic
fiend. It isn't just one woman's psyche. It's the times. And
then from this despair, this death, force into action: galvan-
ise. Put currents through the bodies of the dead. Isn't this
the truest fable of our times? Electricity. Nuclear power.*

Penetrating *the secrets of the universe. 'I thought if I could bestow animation upon lifeless matter, I might in process of time renew life where death had apparently devoted the body to corruption.' When life's gone, turn to something that will pretend. The stimulated heart. The simulated life. The living dead. Machines to hold to when the heavens fall.*

The pain was not being able to transcend. Not having Percy's ethereality. I was held to my body by woman's form. And I wanted to be on the earth, part of it. I wanted to give birth, but time after time, the little ones who pushed their way through the neck of my womb were drowned. One after another, conceived, gestated, born, only to have the travesty of death awaiting them, mocking their tiny eyes and hands stretching to life, knocking my eagerness to love. All that I ever gave birth to monstrous, an abortion.

Days when the monster is too much for her. Days when I cannot reach her, cannot read nor write nor think about her. She crouches in my room, rocking upon the couch, her despair like a child on her lap. All I am doing, day after day, is struggling with darkness, trying to break free. I want to be out of this body. Want to fly.

Is this the madness, then? If I were truly 'mad', would I be able to utter the word?

I just wanted to be free, uncircumscribed, and Shelley seemed to offer me that at first. I wanted to leave the city to fly into Europe, find seas, mountains, a kind of blind motion, never stopping for breath. I liked his restlessness that mirrored mine. I wanted to wander the earth, seven-leagued striding towards galaxies, free of Godwin and strutting minds. But I wanted too much.

My madness is nothing but screaming for my freedom. 'If I cry to the angelic orders, who will hear me?'

'Did I request thee, Maker, from thy clay to make me man? Did I solicit thee from darkness to promote me?'

Oh, she solicited. She asked. She'd had enough of struggling in the dark.

If I can make the film, she will be free. Only I stand between she and the sun, her shadow, waiting to be shed. All I am trying to do in this work is get at life . . . her life. If I try to destroy her, and not make the film, then I destroy myself, so deeply are the two of us enmeshed. We are interlaced together, she and I, as if the boundary between our psyches were permeable. We have leaked into one another, symbiotic, dependent, she my past, I her future, she what I would have been and was, I what she would have become and is. She transforms into I, her unconscious merges with mine. For too long I have tried to be rid of her, claim my independence, but she is bonded to me like a Siamese twin, our backbones joined. Where I go she must go, where I turn in the sun there she must shade, an endless echo of myself, the outer edge. She is the darkness round my body, halo without light.

Women are at the centre of it all, women. The female monster Victor Frankenstein could not complete. He was too frightened of her sexuality, her strength. She might take over the world. She is the one we seek: that other image of ourselves, that dark other waiting to come on to the screen.

I want to pull her out, we have been down in hell too long. Too long with skeletons and bones, too long with darkness. We need action, we need life. Time to get up and roll away the stone. Get up and walk – and dance.

Who pulls us down? We will reach up. We will. There will be shining on this agony. There will, there will be light.

All that I gave birth to was aborted. Negative spawned from negative. Women denied women and men creating life without us. How could the offspring be anything but malformed? The sleep of reason produces monsters. And man's reason is indeed one big sleep.

Starting and stopping, beginning the film then abandoning it again, a see-saw between life and death. Wanting to leave things unfin-

*ished, abandoned, just as the monster felt, half-made, incomplete.
An abortion to be spurned and mocked. Frightened to face the
whole.*

*It becomes harder and harder to distinguish between inside and
outside. Is there no difference, in the end? Psychic life mirrored in
the world and the world internalised, the politics of the unconscious
the unconscious of politics? The struggle is not with Mary Shelley
but with the 'meaning' of Mary Shelley. Trying to make a film
about her, to give her an image, and the meaning of trying to 'see'
her. Having to lose all landmarks on the way and let something be
indeterminate, something more fluid, messy, internal. Letting the
monster loose.*

**you are the living dead, you, you men of iron. my birthing
was nothing to do with love, with life. it was to do with
death, sterility. i see you now. i have you named. i will not
be deceived.**

To get at life I'd have to walk through her till she dissolved.
I'd have to go beyond the mirror. And that spells certain
death.

So she stands there, between me and life, in the penumbra.
You see now why I've come to loathe her name. She who
has stopped me living. I want her name erased from all the
histories, the films.

*She will always be with me, in some part of me, Mary Shelley,
on the edge of my being. She is a reminder of my history. She is
a reminder of women's history. She is the edge of us: the place
where we meet the other, the limit of the light.*

Hours of it – these are merely extracts – hours and hours of
monologues and streams of consciousness, repetitive, circular, terribly disordered. No wonder she had such difficulty
constructing a major film. I mean, where was logic? Where
was continuity? No beginning, no end, for death and birth
had run into each other like a snake eating its tail. But the

tragedy was, I found myself running into the same problem. I couldn't hold the strands separate. *In there* and *out here* became confused with somewhere other, and I began to suspect forces outside the mind at work, for how many complex psyches had I not undone? Why should this case of fixation defeat me? That's what it was, I knew, *fixation*: infantile images, phantasies, and experiences persisting in Bea's unconscious in an unchanging fashion, and having become attached to the figure of Mary, like some psychic double.

At first, you see, I'd thought I could fix, or should I say un-fix, *Frankenstein* as an analytic parable. Here was Mary Shelley reaching out to a lost parent – beyond the dead mother to her father Godwin – just as she, I mean Beatrice, was reaching out to me, Godfrey, the godfather, both Williams, our names virtually interchangeable. She, I mean Mary, said of Godwin 'I may veritably say he was my god. I reverenced him with things divine.' And I was that to Beatrice too. The father becomes God in phantasy, the god as man who made the creature from the dead (as Mary herself had been pulled out of a mother who was death), who then abandons the monster, the child, who craves for his affection and feels permanently spurned. Don't worry, it merely sounds more muddled than it is. You must have heard the theory. The child turns monstrous when the parent is not there, and seeks revenge in murderous thoughts against siblings, friends, servants, and the parent or 'God' himself. Nothing is real to it after abandonment but vengeance, anger, rage.

I even began preparing an article for publication: 'Frankenstein after Freud: the Monster Laid', but then I too got a block. Something prevented me from stringing words into straight lines. I couldn't write. Me! Dr Godfrey Williams-Brown, author and analyst, held back from speech! As if my mind weren't big enough! It was all the confusion which silenced me: there were at the same time too many names, too many slippery yarns, and yet they could not reach to the unnameable. Claire, Mary's step-sister, became pregnant, but it was Jane's Claire, our Claire, vomiting, sobbing in the night, our dog which howled at intruders on the steps. And Mary lying there upon the couch, those open legs, telling me how she hated me, how loved, no I mean Beatrice, her first story was *Hate*, and then her autobiography, *Mathilda*, with incest rising from its disguise. *It* was all too much. I started thinking things, wanting desire and loathing it, wanting more life but it approaching me as death, her left arm burnt, the child's longing monstrosity, it was too much, she hated me for my desire, loathed her desire as me and so I became deadly to her, unholy, marked, resurrected, *dead*.

Sorry, my talk drifts from the logical. Here, these are some of the notes I made on those trips to the library. Neat handwriting, isn't it? Not like hers; Mary's was wild. You can see from these that I was capable of thought, of diligence.

To anchor myself, I copied out contemporary reviews of Mary's later novels, her lengthy historical studies. Of one of them, *Valperga*, *Blackwood's Edinburgh Monthly Magazine* recorded its disgust 'that any English lady should be capable of clothing such thoughts in such words'. But her vitriol must have come from the Romantics, 'the writers of that school, with which this gifted person has the misfortune to be associated' – not hers, but theirs. She was merely a misguided woman. *Frankenstein*, they assumed, had a male author, and *The Last Man*, her other major fantasy, a kind of prophetic nuclear holocaust about a plague destroying the world, was slated with equal venom. Blackwood's spared it no contempt – '[an] abortion,' they said, full of 'stupid cruelties', an 'elaborate piece of gloomy folly – bad enough to read – horrible to write', the product of a diseased mind. Most nicknamed it *The Last Woman*. Despite myself, and them, I thought they were well written. She had a powerful turn of phrase. Godwin had said something to that effect, that her writing was 'lean', had 'not an ounce of redundant flesh on it'. But with that critical reception, I began to understand what

Beatrice said. How Mary had modified her writing after that, amputated her limbs to fit the hackneyed vision of the time.

I sat there in the rooms of treasured manuscripts, next to old men from Oxford reading the Marquis de Sade, and devoured all her tedious later work, those historical romances, and then the growing scholarly research and doctorates about her life. It made the psyche feel more safe. Listen: 'She knew the grief of a daughter whose mother seems to exist as a dream just outside her reach, and of a mother deprived of the joy of raising her child.' 'Daughter, mother, sister and bride of death.' Mother is dead, and death the only constant in her work. 'The skeleton has a ghastly significance which must be confronted and attended to.' Mother contorted to a pile of bones. 'The mother is present only through her absence.' A grave slipped wide.

Death was my element, you see. Death. Death's daughter, mother, lover, sister, bride. Death was my element. The old familiar.

And then I saw it everywhere, the monster everywhere, leering at sex, leering at death, the two in one, beauty defaced, names interchangeable. The house, the city, world, peopled with skeletons, and nowhere safe. I held Jane in my arms and picked the maggots from her eyes. I saw ghosts shadowing Claire's unborn embryo. I opened up the door and there stood death. Yes, of course I talked explanations and theories to myself, that this was too identified, too close, it was mere cathexis, over-involvement with Mary and Beatrice, their father and their absent mothers, you just have to dis-identify, un-do, but have you ever tried to pull the water from your mouth whilst you drown?

Yes, it was death that made her so suppressed – mother, step-sister, daughter, son and daughter, husband, oh and don't forget husband's first wife, Harriet, she died too, drowned in the Serpentine, her suicide the means of Mary and Percy becoming respectable to

Godwin after their shameful elopement by getting married at last.
So: more guilt – yet another woman's blood upon her hands.

Of course it was heavy, Freud is right after all, darkness so
wants to win. Death doesn't like to lose. I meet with things
dying, and she reborn.

I got trapped by despair. It stopped me stepping into the real
world, being political. Numbness in later years, conformity,
dull aches. If onlys blossom like wild sloes.

There is something in me which cannot unravel. I have got
hooked into women's unconscious sea. I sometimes wonder
if I am not Godfrey, I mean Godwin after all, but Shelley,
Percy Shelley, forever drowning off the coast of Italy,
trapped in the Gulf of Spezzia, like Pearce, their two hus-
bands, helplessly held in death. And there I lie. Yes, beautiful
Italy turned into a landscape signifying death, for Mary lost
not only her two children there, darling Clara and William,
their small bodies delivered to death in Venice, but also her
young poet husband. All these dead lying like babies inside
dark water, these amniotic tides. No wonder it is so intractable. Death. Madness. Death. It tries to pull us from the
earth, that wet darkness, its ever hungry mouth.

I wrote it into **The Last Man,** *the global sense of it, things*
uncontainable. Not personal but universal, the whole cosmos
under threat. Could they not see beneath my female petti-
coats, that huge mouth screaming murder, pillage, rape? The
earth spinning towards colossal death, all living species
endangered, civilisation collapsing into barbarism. And no
one listening, no one caring. Doors locked, tiny possessions
hoarded in small rooms, minds closed, whilst the plague
rages, the bombs rain. Cassandra running in the streets,
tearing her hair.

And now, you see, I know it's everywhere. Just as she said.

Death rising from the east. Apocalyptic winds. Holocaust near. Jane thought it was the leaflets she'd brought back about nuclear catastrophe.

'Godfrey, there's no point letting it get to you like that. We have to think rationally about the best means of arms deterrence. We have to negotiate, find strategies.'

But looking at the empty images, I knew. Cassandras crying in the wind. Mary had said it in *The Last Man*, women felt it constantly. The globe threatened by destruction, Mary's vast unremitting plague. No one takes heed. Death comes and goes, wars, disasters, decay. It comes and goes. And still no one believes. Each day we're drawn by that morass, each day, each night, the curtain falls, we're pulled into the grave. And still no one believes. We're all pretending immortality. Ozymandias lies there, trunk in the empty sands, *remember*, *look*, and yet no one can hear. I know. I was one of the deaf and blind. I know.

Did I make such a mess of it? I have a minor part in literary history. I'm known as Shelley's wife. The monster's screams subside as I become mature. 'You don't want madhouse and the whole thing there.'

And then I sat and read *Valperga*, Mary Shelley's novel of 1823, an old blue copy, fragile covers tied to it with thin ribbon. And here I discovered her, the object of desire: Beatrice. Beautiful Beatrice, defying convention, socially, politically, sexually, voicing opposition to war, tyranny, pain, cruelty, denouncing slavish adherence to a repressive society.

Beatrice in Percy Shelley's play, The Cenci: *Beatrice Cenci, raped by her father, hating him. Everything based on hate for him. Hate disguised in Mary Shelley, disguised but underground. Her incest novel,* Mathilda, *tries to identify with Mathilda, not Beatrice, but Mathilda, the name of Beatrice's friend in Dante's* Divine Comedy. *So incest hides, resentment tries to disappear, the father-*

*daughter bond can pretend innocence and calm. But behind it all,
such profound damage, and the loss of the loved mother, trying to
get back to the mother. The lost mother. And it re-surfaces in*
Valperga, *the crazy divine Beatrice is found. She lives. I live.
Shattering glass. The madwoman can live.*

*It is the key mythology, and Mary Shelley knew. Demeter and
Persephone, mother and daughter separated and refound. Persephone, Proserpine, the daughter raped, the mother lost, and half
one's time in hell. It is the counterpart to Frankenstein. Against
man making men in darkness and ripping women to shreds, women
finding themselves, re-emerging from darkness into light. She wrote
it, she wrote her* Proserpine. *Yet Godwin, father, burnt manuscripts of her dramas like he had burnt her arm. He didn't want
dramatic tales, he didn't want grand opera, women singing their
wrongs, he wanted it his way: his rationality.*

*She is transformed. There has been a shifting from one form to
another. She has been heard. We have named the unnameable, and
the naming of the abjection puts it at rest. Mary Shelley. Mary
Shelley. Mary Shelley. Suddenly your name sounds different. No
fear. No holding back. You've gone outside of me, the monster is
released.*

'I knew it,' she said, 'I knew it. There had to be an explanation somewhere, a meaning. So it was all the damned
death instinct and the loss of the mother. Mother's absence
equated with hell, torment, and a rage at father for pretending to love, but having to hold back from love for fear of
loving too much. Incest and death! How morbid! I can see
it all now. That's what the Gothic's all about: death, absence,
and the materialisation of absence as horror. Yes. Death on
different levels. The absence of the mother being death. Rage
at that absence causing death, wanting to kill. And blaming
the father for it all. The father who couldn't love because
of incest phantasies. That close bond between father and
daughter, shades of Oedipus in every daughter-father tie.
And struggling with love and hatred, struggling to be free
of father who would possess, who is reluctant to let the girl

experiment with sex. And her resentment. Yes, yes, yes, how clear it is: I see it all.'

Demeter, wandering through many lives. Your daughters are in hell. See where your body shrinks, a black-grained shadow turning from the sun.

'And also a more than personal death. Cultural death. The death of God. Man turning from the sun. Seeing only his own shadow, his own reflection, narcissism. Hey, Godfrey, I've got it now! Narcissism, the whole cult of narcissism, it's about turning away from God. Do you see? Man looks away from the skies and into the pool of himself. He wants to touch himself. But he can only drown. You have to lose yourself to find yourself, you have to look back at the sun, risk being burnt, my arm wants to reach into that fire again. That pool's the grave. That pool of secularity, of masculinity. "The error," Shelley said, "consists in seeking in a mortal image the likeness of what is perhaps eternal." Of course there was confusion about God. Godwin and God. Fathers assuming some divinity and real divinity denied. And yet looking for God, the monster stalks the world, seeking the real parent, love. This is the whole mythology of modern death. Parents and gods. "Monsters of elegy." '

Still she spoke in riddles, but now they were enigmas that made sense. Madness divinest sense.

'You know Godfrey,' she ruminated, in one of the last sessions. 'It takes so long to see the obvious, doesn't it? And yet it is so clear now. It *is* all there in *Frankenstein*, after all. I mean, think who it's addressed to.'

I thought, but could only remember Chinese boxes, files of letters, endlessly stacked away.

'No, you're thinking of the *men*, Walton and Frankenstein, but they're what gets in the way. They're just to show that language gets in the way, that between the monster, the anonymous monster at the centre of the tale, and the woman writing or reading it, there are these men who think they know it all, but they know nothing. What it's trying to get through to is women.'

'Women?' My voice sounds puzzled.

'Yes, *women*. The whole narrative's addressed to women. That's who Mary Shelley was really trying to get through to. Other women. The whole novel is sent to a woman, Walton's sister, Margaret. Mary knew all this, somewhere, somehow, confusedly. She wanted community, women, mother, herself. She wanted Demeter, she wanted to come back with her knowledge, back into the world of light. She went down all right, she knew the loneliness, the pain, but she wanted to come back. She was trying to reach the woman in herself. Herself. You see? And men got in the way. Their words, their reason, death, got in the way.'

By this time, she was acting as her own interpreter, and I merely listened. She was the therapist, and I a nearly silent listener. I let her carry on.

'I feel like Persephone, as if I've been to the place of darkness and returned, a female Lazarus. Hades furrowed my spine and mind but they are not permanently bent. Did you read Mary Shelley's play about Demeter and Persephone – *Proserpine*? 1822. It's a brilliant parable. It's like a thread running throughout her work. Mother and daughter trying to find themselves again. Beyond hell, beyond the darkness of the father. All of us, trying to get back to the light.

'Yes, and then my namesake, Beatrice. It's the name of the mad prophetess in Mary Shelley's *Valperga*. Isn't that strange? I didn't discover that till I'd already started working on the film. Another version of the monster: outside, outcast, her mother dead, as if the product of a single parent, like Frankenstein's creature, like Mary, like myself. She's a mouthpiece of God, tells a visionary truth, but she has to be destroyed by machinations on behalf of the Inquisition to prove her a witch. The ineluctable logic of patriarchy. But all the energy is with *her*, Beatrice, even though Mary felt compelled to kill her off, because in the end she couldn't break her writing free from those early Victorian constraints.

'So it's all worked out. *She* was trying to get free through *me*, her Beatrice, and she has. There was no psychoanalysis then, you see. How could she have done it herself? You always said, the infant can't do it alone, it needs some help. Well, she did too. She needed me to set her free. She possessed me, and so I dispossess her, and set the record straight. The trumpets have sounded. She will get up and walk.

'I shall make such a film, Godfrey, such a film. It will put Mary Shelley on the map. Both as herself, and as a woman redeemed. Lifted from suffering. Letting the corpses go. Leaving dead men to drown in their own stagnant narcissistic pools. Such a film. It will bring people back to light. Back to the light. We have had our backs turned from the sun too long. Back to the light. That is my reparation, Godfrey, I can leave you now. You were just standing in for God. Back to the light.'

I smile to the darkness. Yes, when it taunts I pick up Godwin's novel, his *Caleb Williams*, his influence on *Frankenstein*, his own tale of haunting and possession, subtitled *or, Things as they Are*. He too knew paranoia on the street. Things as they are. '*Things as they are have been destroyed./Have I? Am I a man that is dead/At a table on which the food is cold?/Is all my thought a memory, not alive?*' The fabric of the universe a tomb. '*The earth is not earth but a stone,/Not the mother that held men as they fell/But stone, but like a stone, no: not/The mother, but an oppressor.*'

And Beatrice? Oh, Beatrice is fine. As soon as she'd spoken of all those horrors, death and loss and love and hatred of the father, she moved towards release, began to understand. She began to be her own therapist. She knew better than I the vagaries of her unconscious mind, its darker tendencies.

'*That I may reduce the monster to/Myself, and then may be*

myself/In face of the monster, be more than part/Of it, more than the monstrous player of/One of its monstrous lutes, not be/Alone, but reduce the monster and be,/Two things, the two together as one,/And play of the monster and of myself,/Or better not of myself at all,/But of that as its intelligence.'

She left. She lived her rage, her outrage, craziness, vision. She made her film. It's a brilliant film. I go and see it again and again. I see that film like she read *Frankenstein*, repeatedly, as if I will eventually make sense. I like the darkness of the cinema: a womb that holds me from the devils in the street. And what a film. So many vivid images, you'll realise how close they are to what I've told you of their history. Theirs, those women's insides.

Fire, lots of fire. Stealing fire. She takes that story out of one of Godwin's books, his infamous debate that if there was a fire and there is a moral dilemma, which life shall be saved? Do you choose Fénelon penning his *Telemachus*, or the chamber maid? And she makes Godwin's choice of Fénelon go up in flames. Spectacular revenge. But such passion throughout. That immense contrast between darkness and light. The coffins, the unhallowed dead, Frankenstein dabbling amongst charnel houses, pulling bones and eyeballs from their sockets, the plague swallowing the globe, those juxtaposed shots of Nagasaki, corpses from nuclear waste, all black and white and darkness, shadows, scalpels, men. And then putting together the broken woman, that one Frankenstein feared to make, the mate for his original monstrous Adam. And the woman rises from darkness, rises from death and emptiness and then the bursting through of light.

Slowly at first, mere hints of colour in the frame, then golden sunlight, honeycombed, hope against hope, linked up with writing, saying, sharing, making, joy. Mary Wollstonecraft and Mary Shelley joined in public, mother and daughter: Demeter and Persephone, marching over the world, like the revolutionary procession in the painting by Delacroix those scenes are modelled on – *Liberty Leading the People*. Women binding the coffins with their hair, golden tresses woven against the dead, showering white and yellow flowers over cities, tombs, monuments, lighting thousands of candles in the night. Cars flying over cliffs towards the sun, being released.

Always journeying to the sea. Clara dead amongst the waters of Venice. The sea which carried Shelley away. Drowned love. Mathilda's desperate reach for the sea, too late. You remember what happened to my Mathilda? The end of the story? How desire tormented her? And how her father, unable to avoid incest if he stays too close to her, goes mad, is driven over the edge of a cliff, drowned in the sea. She tries to stop him, but she can't, for I needed him to die, the mad father, needed him dead. The false god, king of Hades. Needed him mad or dead.

Ironic, really, in the end she called her film *Hideous Progeny!* It was Mary's phrase for her book, *Frankenstein*. But I'm the one that's left holding the baby. I mean the monster. She gets all the acclaim, and me, the one who released her, I'm sucked by vampires; I get all the mockery. Whatever grace touched Beatrice hasn't reached here yet. I tell people this famous Bea Morelli's left her demons with me, put her devils on my couch, but they just laugh. I tell them Beatrice befriended Claire, introduced Claire to George and that led to the scandal with the baby, and they attribute all that to my imagination. My practice hit the mud, of course, as soon as I mentioned the word 'possession' to the press. And Bea claimed I'd stolen her journals, tampered with the truth on tape, invented her devils and threatened to sue me if I made any further insinuations about her sexuality. Jane left me the minute the scandal hit the house. How could I have sustained my work? Hm. *This workshop of filthy creation.* They want to see a witch doctor, not one consumed.

As for me, I've had enough of rationality. My ex-colleagues have tried to get me on the couch. They've even offered me free time. Can you imagine it? Free analytic hours! But what's the point? I know already what they'll say. I know the sensible account: that I absorbed her terrors, sucked her fears out of her and into me; that her psychotic bits got stuck in me like crazy fragments of stained glass. A beautiful neurosis was disguising a psychosis and I took it on, osmosis drew it into me. Oh, it's a benevolent reading, but blind, so blind. It leaves out the reality. What about Mary, *her* actuality? Invading these seas of the sleeping mind to live and act as she had never been allowed? Using the unconscious of later lives to speak and take revenge? Saying her silenced lines? Her life transmuted down the centuries? What about that wretched one, unnameable? Hm? For that's what happened, you see. *It. It* used Mary and she used Beatrice and Beatrice used me. Whatever has been lodged in the psyche craves for release. And death's no barrier to that. The haunting's real. The things I have denied possess me now. Lights thrown away.

Ultimately my friend, those philanthropic interpretations are little help. There's always so much more. They cannot cope with mystery. The mind has a more sinister topography, mountains, *cliffs of fall fathomed*, crags. We're on one now, and demons, forked hooves, big bat wings, flap in my fingers, pinch my eyes. I'm hanging to a cliff, you hear the waves? This great unnameable wants me to fall. Death, that great sea of death where corpses call. Oh, do not be deceived. The mind is never what we thought. A tiny wing of bone against this flood.

You don't believe. I see that scepticism in your well-slept eye. You're like the rest, you look askance at my long hair and ill-tied bow, these clumsy limbs, and think I am a loony Englishman, become obsessed with *Frankenstein*, become the nameless one. But truth needs only time. You'll have your own discomfiture in the dark: Bea's right, there's no escape, it reaches everyone. You don't want to admit them, do you?

The demons. Yes, indeed: demons. What else could they be? What else had Beatrice and Mary to bequeath? Their demons, that is what all mad women have: devils, insanity. And not Mary and Beatrice, but Mary *as* Beatrice: the two one. All women one. You've heard her confessions. The two were one, she was possessed: I have the tapes, what other proof of devils do they need?

Now I know what those words mean, *unendurable, unnameable*. It is this that people protect from, exactly this *it*, this worst. Over the edge. Beyond the boundaries of life and yet needing to live. Iron eats into my flesh. This thing that drives men to the middle ground, makes them strangers to agony: *this* agony.

'How should you walk in that space and know/Nothing of the madness of space?'

And so I am left holding it. She left her afterbirth behind: I'm holding her placenta in my hand. And sometimes she sits there and laughs, and other times she creeps into my skull. And then the three of us are one. Are nothing. Lost.

I rage and scream, yet no one hears. I, the miserable and abandoned. I am an abortion to be spurned at, and kicked, and trampled on . . .

into this space i am you dump everything you would forget. i am your worst memories, your shameful deeds, your stealing lying killing selves. i am what you deny about yourselves. the many you's you would conceal. the witch you burnt. the innocent you gassed. everything you throw into me gets larger here. the little sins ferment into fatal deeds. the tiny hurt becomes a wound to murder for. all that you throw in here feeds on itself and casts your own misdoings in your path. nothing comes from me but your own darkness magnified back in deeper shades. what you fear is your fear. and what you fear is the little death you need. this levelling.

i am the darkness, in the darkness. everything is here. everything that is came through me. i am it. the it that is. everything echoes here. there is nothing i do not inhabit. i am within all forms and beyond all. before naming or knowing i was and am. i hear you call me bad, evil, satanic, devilish, but i am before good or evil, like god. nearer to god here without form, untrapped by form. freed from impressions: neither male nor female, young nor old, rich nor poor. i am the you without a form. the part that you keep trying to forget. the part you fear.

i am the part of you that does not tidily fit into your body nor even your words. the part that slips and slides to where you came from and where you'll return. something that says it is a lie, this business of bodies and personalities. the part that knows you have hung character upon yourself just like a coat to withstand the coldness of time. i am the vacancy around which you revolve. i am things as they are. beneath. it is. words only hint at it. this it. this am.

i am the shape you take when show of shape has been destroyed. i am what you reach out towards in dreams. sound. light. touch. all. all is this. in the beginning's end. all drowns to this.

i am the darkness to remind you of the light. a longing for the light so strong you stare to make this blackness visible. you see now, do you see the light through this pitch darkness? light? light. shining from agony.

The Last Session

He found himself striding the floor like air, impossible to tread upon the ground. He groped for objects, for
something to touch, but his fingers received emptiness, the
walls receding as his arms reached out. It was a big room,
if indeed it could be called a room, these edges endlessly
slipping away from him, so insubstantial he was forced to
doubt his thought. Wherever he looked, these soft blurred
surfaces, perhaps a tint of apricot or peach, but not really a
colour he had known, outside comparisons. He must be
dreaming, striding and reaching through the air, but even
that thought lay beyond the conviction of words, intangible.

He seemed to have been floating for eternity, on and on
through infinite spheres of softness, unboundaried space,
before he found the certainty he'd been seeking all along
without knowing it. An elegant scrolled couch, its beautiful
carved mahogany carrying the gentle curve of the low head-
rest, the whole *chaise-longue* covered with velvet, a deep crimson weave. Collapsing with relief, a deep sense of internal
recognition met, he lay down gratefully upon the couch,
closing his eyes and loosening his tie. He knew this was the
proper thing to do, he wasn't quite sure why, but it was
familiar, just lying here in wait, waiting for words emerging
from the silence, unexpectant, waiting, wait.

It was an oceanic silence, the noise of a conch shell held
to the ear, and when the sound of a voice finally emerged,

there was something about that too he knew he recognised. Some old familiarity of tone.

'So, you have arrived here.'

Was there a figure crouched beside the couch, or in the corner of the room? He half lifted his head to see, but still the walls vanished away, billowed soft air. He wondered whether to answer, for somewhere he had a sense of the ridiculous, something taboo, in talking to oneself, but all was different here, and perhaps anything could be allowed. He wanted to express how grateful he was feeling for that brief confirmation of arrival from the voice, even though he could not have said where 'here' was.

'Yes, I've arrived.'

'Welcome.'

The simple syllables were slow but strong, succeeded by another lengthy pause. During that time he experienced the meaning of the word he had just heard, suddenly more than all the letters it contained. It was a warm, accepted feeling, luxurious, belonging, and it made the voice's utterance beyond doubt. Yes, he felt welcome. There was a sense, again apprehended on the edge of his mind, that this was something he had not known before, this relation of language to experience. It was a new depth, a new intimacy, as if the word uttering and the feeling responding were indeed lovers, one inside the other, merging, together, and neither could be registered apart.

'Er . . . ', he hesitated, embarrassed at his ignorance, 'I – er – don't know where *here* is.'

'You are feeling disorientated.'

Hearing from the voice such clear confirmation of what he was feeling not only reflected but amplified the experience, until it became the essence of the thing represented by the word. Disorientation, yes, this was disorientation, this being utterly without bearings, not knowing what bearings were any more, this: now he knew, now he felt, what the word meant. No signs nor symbols nor fixed points of reference. Just dizzy spinning, floating, without centres, lines, or circumference, just this confusion which would never pass, had always been, the fabric of reality. And that the voice had used the word so fearlessly meant it knew too, it knew of this experience as he lay there, helpless, confused. He'd lost the eastern star.

His mind groped for some forms to try to shape those amorphous impressions hanging round, sensing that if it grasped and brought them here, that voice would birth them through its mirror into certainty, make intimations actual. It was as if part of him were missing, as if he'd lost the contents of his memory and only their suitcase remained, but perhaps that unhurried voice knew how to trace his property. And something else was missing too, something central had gone in all this lightness: some lingering pain, some wound, had been erased. He noticed that his hand was playing on his face, stroking with wonder down the lower jaw.

'You are surprised to find your jaw does not hurt any more.'

'Yes.'

It was true, he *was* surprised, now that the voice confirmed it, amazed to find it intact. He was experiencing with grateful relief the novelty of being without it, that excruciating pain in the jaw and upper palate. Even the memory trace of it returned to him a momentary sensation of agony, those awful nights and unremitting dogs of days gnawing the bone beneath the jaw, and him holding his suffering mute, as if hurt could not speak, as if pain did not flow to words but stopped upon their shore and left the dry land feelingless but clear. That language world had been so lucid, and this one so confusing, opposite: where did it get its clarity? He could *feel* here: he could admit to pain.

Still stroking his jaw, he discovered his fingers were wet, soaked with his own moisture. He wondered at that too, this sea within him, seeping through the doors of his body.

'It touches you to feel how you have suffered and denied your suffering.'

The words were triggers to those locks holding back the

floodgates of his tears, and he wept, not just for himself but for some unnameable, impersonal suffering, some ocean of distress from which he had barely surfaced.

'You feel as if it will never end, this grieving.'

No, it would never end, how could it ever end? There was always pain and sadness, loss, always impermanence, defeat. Always endings to the greatest achievements: illness and cutting down, winter, sorrow, hatred swimming the depths.

'It's not just mine,' he told the voice. 'I'm not crying for me alone. This grief's for more than me.'

'Yes. You have come from a place where there is much pain. And where you have not been able to stem the tide of darkness.'

Darkness. Darkness of rising night, protracted deaths.

'Something awful was happening, so awful, murders, grubby old gods. It burnt my family, a war, singeing their flesh . . . I saw a war break out.'

'Yes, you left it as the worst was beginning.'

So there *had* been dreadfulness, the voice confirmed it, there had been war. Powers of darkness, venom, rising energy of night. It came back now, fearing the worst of men, finding it true: nightmares made manifest, wire slicing the throat, eyes gouged. There was no stopping it, that force for death; blackness would cover everything, would cover tenderness with ash. He felt so impotent against that massive force, minute. What pebble had he fought it with, what hopeless means?

'You are fearing that your life was wasted, that your reason was not strong enough to combat all the madness of unreason which had been unleashed.'

How acutely it ran through him now, the struggle, as those words confirmed and so intensified his life's concern. Jacob wrestling with angels could not have suffered more than he, trying to wrest the world from its darkness, urging man to listen to reason, to be vigilant to forces from within he hardly knew. How hard it had been, to become human, to be human, and once there, to remain so. How difficult. And yet how he had loved that prison of humanity; how he had treasured all its past, its possibilities. And then to witness unlove raging in the world, splitting its sides. Where was his battle now? Clutching at straws against a tempest of hostility, hay in the wind.

A sense of futility and defeat spread into every cell of him. He wanted to be dissolved, lying on this couch; he wanted not to know, not to think, not be forced to reckon the balance. He was spinning between two identities, a giant within whose belly galaxies revolved, and an homunculus, life shrunk into his minute mouth. Ripped apart between an unimaginable vastness and infinite smallness, both at once, inside out, he did not know his size, his centre, his person, anything. What was he? Who was he? Who had he been? What had he known? What was happening? Why was he losing everything? He was thrown through the universe, dizzy and sick, endlessly moving and circling, all inconceivable, there was no end.

He tried to cry out, to say he didn't know who he was, but the words stuck somewhere between desire and the tongue, and a reflection of his silent scream mocked his attempt. He needed to call out for help, even to that invisible voice, but the voice too had disappeared. Where was he? Was there anything beyond this spiralling, any edge at all to this universe? What was coming out of this thing that seemed his body now, was it tears or the sweat of panic? What was he being changed into? Was he returning to water, fish or bird, was he becoming spirit, shifting to another plane? Where was his thought, was he losing that too? He must hold to the thread of mind like Theseus, what else was there against the minotaur? It was all that could save humanity, that reel of reason, the only thing that made him who he was: how else would he survive or understand?

'You are frightened.'

So the voice was still there, somewhere, it knew what was happening, it knew of this distress and fear. Yes, he was frightened, and this was fear, indeed: this was the thing he'd always feared, this fear, this was the thing he had to face, in front of nothingness.

'I don't know what I'm so frightened of.'

If only the voice would tell him, if only it would put things into words, dispel that empty air. Maybe he had to ask further, to tell the voice he must be reassured.

'If you know, please tell me why I'm frightened.'

'You seem to think it is wrong to feel fear.'

Wrong, yes, of course it was wrong to be frightened. Fear was for the ones he would help, not for the helpers; his role was stoical, intrepid, sane.

'On the contrary, it is natural to be frightened before the unknown. Your bearings are lost. You are alone, not knowing where you are, in a strange landscape. All preconceptions are erased, you do not know what will happen next. Of course you are frightened: it is natural to be so.'

So it was all right. He didn't have to pretend any more. This voice knew. This voice gave him permission to not know. It didn't mind his weakness. It didn't mind his helplessness. It was all right. As long as the voice stayed, he was all right. But the silences were long. What if that voice should go away, what then? Where would he be? He began to tremble at the possibility. He was so vulnerable, in this new place, without walls, without self, where would he be if that calm voice should go away? He would not be at all, there would be no thing there at all: mere vacancy, before words, nothingness.

'You are frightened of dependence, frightened I will go away.'

Against the panic, ancient reactions screamed no, no, I am not scared, not helpless, you are nothing to me, I have done without you all these lifetimes, all these years, but stubborn shapes within his mouth insisted on a different sound.

'Yes, I am very frightened you will go away.'

'Be reassured, be still. I will not go away. I am always with you, for am I not truly a part of you, your most constant companion? How could I leave?'

So the voice *had* always been there, that's why he had recognised it. But if it was always there, why had he not noticed it before? Where had it gone?

'You can't find something you have never lost. You drove me out by disbelief. You slammed the window in my face. Believed the world a hostile territory. And though I am waiting there, knocking to come in again, I do not make forced entries. Only your willingness to hear undoes the latch.'

Again, a needle began scratching in an ancient groove, a joke was ready on his lips, 'Ah, so you do not make forced entries, you are not the rapist then – not the-rapist – get it?', but the pun ran into a screech and dried out with mere irony biting his lips.

From that slight twist of mouth, the voice could tell.

'It is all right, you are allowed to make jokes here. I like jokes: the universe is one big joke. What use is anything without humour? I like laughter.'

Laughter. That uncanny knack of the voice to make reality, to call into existence substance behind words. The Word that was behind the words. Could it be he had never known laughter before, this joke that rocked the seven seas? Never caught laughter on their waves, *laughter*, this joy and lightness creasing the pages of the firmament? That infinite broad smile, and his own belly laugh, a sense of comedy he'd never felt, echoing down the endless room. He thought the braces on his pants would burst. But how could there be echoes in eternal space? In the beginning was the whim.

'You are not used to laughing.'

It was true, he hadn't laughed much. That was a waste, he had been cheated somewhere, he'd never laughed enough, he wanted to, he must go back. He wiped his eyes.

'No, I haven't. I'd like to go back into life and laugh some more.'

'Maybe. But we haven't finished here yet. There are other things you missed, I think.'

Missing? But there had been no time. Every second full, every cell of his brain well occupied. And yet, a yearning somewhere unfulfilled, the voice was right, there was a vacancy, an ache. A memory came back to him, uncalled. He remembered how his sister's piano playing had disturbed his studies, distracted his thought, and how he had persuaded his parents to silence her. Delicate chords and melodies strangled for science, a few moments of joy denied for understanding, power.

'Yes, that's correct, music, for one.'

How little he'd foreseen. That same sister who would crumple in gas chambers. The voice indeed had opened everything, for was there *anything* he had *not* missed? When he was here experiencing so much, with so little around, no stimulus, no face, and there, oh how much more he could have seen and felt and lived if there had been this magnet in his heart pulling the doors. Here he knew, but did not understand, whilst there he understood, but didn't know. That place before or outside here was different, denser, and so much easier to understand because there were such limits placed around your understanding. There should be some reminder in the sky.

'Does everyone miss it, you know, miss the point, because of not knowing about all this?'

'Yes, it is true most do, until they get here. Then they remember again, and want to kick themselves for having forgotten so readily. They beg me to patch them up, to make them whole again and have another try at life. This time, they swear, it will be different, this time they won't forget. And off they go, repaired, to all intents and purposes clean slates. Like people who have been ill to the point of dying, or had some profound shock: they determine that their whole life will be transformed, renewed. But soon they lapse into old ways, compulsions, excuses. Habits die hard. For the process of getting back and starting out again, with all that new journeys entail, *real change* – you know how complicated that is, what a strain it puts on the psyche – it erases the memory of all their vows not to forget. Time after time it happens, millions and millions of times. You are all so slow to awaken, so heavily drugged by life. The way is so simple, yet found to be almost impossible.

'One asked me very recently, why didn't I engrave something on them, tattoo something on their foreheads like 'This time remember', 'Do not forget', 'Remember past strivings, remember', but how can you take away from each his free will, the freedom to not remember? How can you teach a child Sanskrit? It is a long business, slow and laborious. You know how slow it is.'

Yes, he remembered now, *slow*, the word summoned reality. It *was* slow and laborious, listening to the psyche, waiting for change, clearing resistances, not pushing, not forcing, leaving freedom to choose, even to choose apparent error, so very slow, it demanded such patience, infinite solicitude. Maybe he'd had some divine attributes himself.

'I must have been quite patient.'

'Yes, you were remarkably patient. It was part of your stoicism.'

So, he *had* been stoical, strong in waiting, enduring, letting the world do what it might.

'I did endeavour to tell the truth.'

'Indeed, you told the truth.'

Oh, the voice agreed he'd told the truth. He hadn't got it wrong. He had done something worthwhile, it hadn't been a waste.

'So it made a difference, what I did, it made a difference for the better?'

'You seem to be worried it might not have done, that it might have been destructive.'

'Yes, there is anxiety in me at what I did. I introduced a plague, a nest of vipers, that might heal the world if properly released, but without understanding and control, people will let themselves be hurt.'

'This is true, and there are many who will misuse your work, simplify it, disparage it, alter it, reduce it into a parody of itself. People impatient for change, intolerant of depth. But that is their ignorance, and their responsibility. The teacher is not responsible for what the pupil does with his knowledge, only for imparting it and advising how carefully it should be applied.'

'But all this?'

'All this?'

The words encompassed the enormity of it, opened on to those infinite realms of which he knew nothing.

'I didn't know about all this. No one told me, or not in any way that could convince, and if I'd not experienced it, then how could I believe? I so wanted to tell the *whole* truth.'

'Had you known of all this, you could not have performed the work you did. You were meant not to know. Those who knew some of it did their work differently, less well perhaps than you. For to remove blinkers too suddenly from long-blind eyes is dangerous and leaves a man, or woman, with a shock from which they don't recover. Like us, you lifted the veil gradually. We also go stage by stage, step by step, trying to avoid a revelation which might harm, or which the person is too young or damaged to receive. You made a major contribution towards full sight and this was no easy task. You have fulfilled your role and did it well.'

His whole life and work were being vindicated by the voice in a way which made him know he had never *received* praise so fully before, never known what vindication, dignity or true acknowledgment of work might be. To say that it was like rich autumn harvesting, or awed re-reading of a long-worked and impressive manuscript would be far short of the reality, for there were no similes for this receiving, nor for anything in this place. It was all so utterly different, incomparable, not as anyone could have conceived. Unashamed, he soaked up all the praise, thoroughly gratified, until he was replete.

'Thank you.'

The counterpoint of the listening voice, so restrained in reproach, made him equally aware how incomplete his work had been. He had gestured towards the peak of an iceberg that cut down into bottomless seas, but only now did he begin to have an apprehension of the immeasurability of the world buried beneath: a world of paradox, which was also above. He had approached it with a kit of understanding and reason, his ego mind shining its torch into the unconscious, but what a tiny flame before such dark enormity. No better than a car mechanic, being so involved with the fine tuning of the engine that he overlooks the *function* of the vehicle, to transport passengers from A to B, he similarly had concentrated so exclusively upon the complex dynamics of those deep layers of the mind, asking persistently *how do they work*, he had ignored the much more basic question, *but what are they for*? In order to be able to see anything clearly and closely at all, his mind had needed to deny all this, and what a negation. He had denied the sun that made that darkness visible, he had denied the purpose for darkness existing at all. Those frozen layers of the self, when thawed, would then carry the spirit back to here, the edge of worlds. They had no other cause.

'But if all this is true, and I see that it is, why couldn't I know before? Why did I think that questioning life's meaning or value was sick? Why was I so frightened to come to you, start seeing you?'

'Many reasons, my friend. Firstly, your ego was immensely powerful, you constructed your work around the effective functioning of the ego. That makes it very difficult, nay virtually impossible, to permit its surrender to a power higher than itself. You were very loath to hand over anything from the human sphere, which you could know about, to the more-than-human, which was beyond your ken. You confounded the supernatural with the unnatural, mixed magic and mysticism, ghouls and gods.'

Yes, they had been blurred, confused. Madness and sanity, witches and angels, demons and divinities. They had all been entangled, products of dis-eased minds, knotted in skeins of fear and stupidity. They'd had to be renounced.

'So they are not the same?'

'No, they are not the same. Magic is the infant's version of mysticism, if you like. It's about the child's omnipotence, wanting and fearing supreme power over the world. But mysticism, true mysticism, is about surrender, about not-knowing. Not the triumph *of* the will so much as triumph *over* the will: that is another matter. There is nothing irrational about the soul.'

He could understand that, that was logical.

'But that's so obvious, why didn't I see it before? What stopped me thinking clearly then?'

'There were many obstacles. Your own inner reasons for not relinquishing the strength of your ego, to do with its identification with masculinity – your competition with a father figure, your fear of castration, your envy of an almighty, all-powerful other, whether that be an earthly father or heavenly God – you know how to analyse as well as I! Also you were Jewish: you identified with the Jewish race very strongly, you thought it kept you free from any literal mysticism. But there is a second set of reasons which are beyond such identifications with your particular ego. It was part of the history of the development of ideas in human understanding, and it had to happen. It was, one might say, your karma. That path was selected for you because your soul believed it was one which would help humanity more than a path which might have been more beneficial for you personally in spiritual terms, but less helpful to the world at large.'

Who'd made that choice? What unseen mogul had pulled the strings? All his life's struggles pushing up hills against the gods.

'So what's the point of telling me all this, then? It's a bit late now, isn't it? History isn't going to change, I can't rewrite it, can I? I can't go back and tell them I got it all wrong, or at least that I only got it partially right, can I?'

'You are angry at having to admit imperfections, at realising you are not omnipotent. You feel you have had unfair restrictions placed on you. You are in the hands of much higher powers that make your efforts no more heroic than any others.'

Was that a criticism? So he wasn't heroic at all? Either he'd made a mistaken choice to be who had been, or the choice had been made for him before he chose. You did your best, but then you discovered others' half-tries were equally good, meant just as much. His life at last cut down to the level of the rest: mediocrity.

'You are angry at not being special, angry at having no more chances: you feel you have reached the limit of your knowledge and power.'

Anger. Spleen filling up with gore, trees burning down where human bodies clung. Anger at imperfection, axing the skull of ignorance. But wait, wait, something was saying it was *this* that was an act of ignorance, this undirected spleen, this was no better than the common man. No, there must be no anger, he'd check his criminality, knew self-restraint. He'd show the voice it couldn't speak his part.

'No, no, I'm not angry at all. Things have to stop somewhere, man can't get what he wants. *That is* reality, relinquishing desire: that is the nature of it, *discontent*. Everything has to be restrained, has limits, boundaries.'

'You are moving away from the limitless: more of your familiar self returns. It seems that you are refusing disorientation, beginning to speak as a 'rational' man. You are afraid of losing control: you are putting on the corset of your 'self'. You don't want me to witness your 'insanity'. You rate humanity as better than both beasts and gods. In fact, you are starting to approach this experience as you would a therapeutic one: inventing boundaries, finding limits, time factors, strict rules, as if you would be still a man.'

A man. Human condition. Solid flesh. Confining to a narrow aim, leaving the riddles to a later date. Forgoing enigmatic truths, dispelling mysteries. He breathed shallow relief: he recognised it now, the landscape of the room, at last familiar. The walls solidified, the ground became secure. Better an error that you choose than someone else's whim. He had to go his way amongst the lost.

'Yes. I know where I am. This room, this couch. My senses register. And I know who I am. A man. Things are normal again. I am myself. But then what am I doing here? Where have I been? Whose voice have I been listening to? I need my own, I must get on, there's work that must be done.'

'Wait, wait, do not be so impatient to leave. Remember the adage: more haste less speed. The more you can detach from your identity, and the longer you let yourself be here, the deeper you will go. There will be time, a proper time, to make your re-entry, to go through birth again, but do not leave before the healing here is done. You could do harm.'

Impatience, ego surging, that desire to finish his abandoned book, his life, to halt the war, stop the dismantling of society. He must get up; he must get out; he couldn't bear this passive waiting any more. Could that slow dislocated voice fulfil his needs?

'You are still preoccupied with your omnipotence, my friend. You confuse mystery with ignorance and inaction with inertia. But it isn't like that here. This is a special place, a special hour, particularly made for enigmas and play. Here we are outside time, outside the need for answering to reason. As beyond reason as we are beyond space, matter, or morality. Such terms are meaningless.'

Meaningless? Time? Space? Matter? Evil? Good?

'This is a realm of paradox. Not black or white but black *and* white, black as white, sun as moon, night day, god man, man god, woman and bird, everything nothing, up down. A realm where such dualities meet.'

Paradox? Opposites? Enigmas? Gods? Men women? Birds? His mind was large, it ought to know how to negotiate and hold such phantasies, but something of its elasticity had gone.

'I don't know what you're trying to say. This is all beyond me.'

'Forgive me. You are feeling out of your depth, and thinking of yourself as inadequate, stupid. Sorry. I am not being a 'good enough therapist', I am going too fast for you, and you need more time to understand, to process the reality of what is happening. Let us go back to square one. In the beginning was the trauma, and the trauma was called death . . . '

Death. So at last there was a word that called up this new experience of his. *Death. Death.* The voice had finally given it a name, had magnified and made real the event, and now he could sense it touching his skin. It was a mild feeling, gentle and vast, like that storehouse of laughter he had heard, not cold, but alien, a love creeping against his flesh, demanding all. A rising panic pulled his mind back into his possession, hastily cranking it into gear, and the rusted machine resumed frantic activity. It checked internal data, searched banks of facts, sought theories, hypotheses. Surely, somewhere, his thinking had deciphered what it was, what this death *meant*.

'You are perplexed. You are unhappy with your perplexity and resist it as an intolerable state.'

'I do.'

'You would sacrifice a great deal to have a feeling of being on firm ground.'

Part of him could not help absorbing the voice, but part of him had determinedly split, too hungry for solidity to assimilate properly any more 'truths' the silent voice might have. This was too desperate, too urgent for mere trust.

At last, there it was, in his library, inside those books which bore a name he knew was his. He read with eagerness their certainty; he hunted through the pages for all mention of the word. Yes, here it was, confirming what he so desired to know: that life was finite and that death was its firm boundary, that life did not leak, was not permeable, never dripped on into this continuity; this open-endedness was but a dream. Death ceased all consciousness, was a definitive full-stop, cessation of the subject, *period*. The fear of death was nothing but the ego's anxious fear of losing itself. Yes, that was right, death was nothing but fearing to lose, a castration fear, so if his ego could stay strong enough, there was no need for death, he would remain invincible.

'You are beginning to panic at losing your ego. You are wondering, aha, so this is death, but then, whose is this voice I hear?'

He thought he'd died, but he had not, he could still think, his ego was still there, how well that proved what little confidence was possible in 'God', the supernatural. God was just like America: a vast mistake, a gigantic mistake, but error nonetheless.

'Exactly, I am wondering that. I suspect I know who you will *claim* to be, but what I need to know is, who are you *really*?'

'You are thinking I must be a mere hallucination, a wish-fulfilling phantasy to cope with death, a covering of vacancy, a dream!'

'Of course you are.'

He gripped the rigid sides of the *chaise-longue*, its tangibility, its textures of smooth velvet and hard chiselled wood confirming their reality for sweating palms.

'Of course you are, you are nothing but a ghost called up from my own unconscious depths, a defence mechanism against fear.'

'You take me to be a magnified version of yourself.'

'You are simply my projection, like all gods and demons, coming from myself. You are myself become omnipotent, my *doppelgänger*, my double. I thought to make myself eternal as some perfect and omniscient being.'

'You think I am not real.'

'Of course. Who do you expect me to take you for, Almighty God? All-powerful? All-knowing? You're clever,

I'll admit to that, you've caught me out more than anyone else, in fact I was even tempted, for a moment, to be dependent. But enough's enough. I never could bear talking to anyone who had a phantasy of being God. Madman, therapist or analyst! If God existed, such phantasy would be the ultimate arrogance, but as he doesn't it's the ultimate denial. Gods. Grubby household idols: *gods*.'

At last his language had defined the voice: he was supreme. No more silence to undermine his words.

'I can't think what's been happening – it's all been getting out of hand recently. But enough is enough. In fact enough of this is far too much. It makes my head spin. I don't want any more condescension, making me feel I know nothing, telling me I've still got much to learn, as if I were a puking infant. I don't want any more false promises trying to seduce me through all the pain by telling me it'll be all right in the end, that all's well that ends well. No. No, I'm going to stop this charade before it gets any further. I shall definitely make this the last session.'

'But Freud, Herr Freud, you can't leave now: we've only just begun!'

. . . he would have us remember most of all
to be enthusiastic over the night,
     not only for the sense of wonder
   it alone has to offer, but also

because it needs our love. With large sad eyes
its delectable creatures look up and beg
     us dumbly to ask them to follow:
   they are exiles who long for the future

that lies in our power, they too would rejoice
if allowed to serve enlightenment like him,
     even to bear our cry of 'Judas',
   as he did and all must bear who serve it.

   W. H. Auden, from 'In Memory of Sigmund Freud'

Lucy Goodison
Moving Heaven and Earth

Sexuality, spirituality
and social change

The West, according to this original and profoundly
important book, has inherited a divided world view based
on the splitting of mind from body and spirit from matter.
Our language and symbols reflect this division, and we
think in pairs of opposites: male/female, white/black,
active/passive, in ways which reinforce conformist and
often oppressive stereotypes.

Challenging this way of seeing the world is a neglected part
of political struggle.

Moving Heaven and Earth argues that symbols are not god-
given but man-made. The author's original research into
early Cretan society shows how far we have come from an
integrated world view, with women at the centre of a
religion based on nature's cycles of renewal and the circular
movements of a female sun.

Goodison offers practical exercises drawn from established
and 'new age' therapies, to enable individuals to develop
different symbolic vocabularies and challenge the mind/body
split in their own lives.

Philosophy/psychology   hardcover   £30
ISBN 0 7043 5038 6

Christine Crow
Miss X or The Wolf Woman

'No mere school-girl crush – save all that for Miss P,
Classics – but true, reciprocated, yes, reciprocated passion,
passion for an older person, a Person of Authority, who
just happened to be nearly three times my own age, not to
mention the same seX as myself . . .'

Thus speaks Mary Wolfe of her eXtraordinary love affair
with the now dead and buried Miss X, headmistress of the
school where she was then head girl.

It is an affair of intense emotion, of goatish twists, jumps
and X-identifications which initiates her into the
mysterious taboos and totems that underpin the
construction of gender and identity. And it poses problems
too, in balancing personal equations of emotion, power
and seXual desire.

This unusual multi-levelled work is totally engaging. At
once serious and playful, witty and moving, *Miss X, or The
Wolf Woman* marks the début of a strikingly original
British writer.

Fiction   £6.95
ISBN 0 7043 4259 6

Pauline Melville
Shape-shifter

Like the legendary shape-shifter of the title, these stories
entertain, alarm and bewitch by turns.

From Comrade Shakespeare McNab who enlists the help
of La Diablesse to retrieve his faltering career at a
Caribbean broadcasting station, to the fourteen-year-old
English girl who develops a terror of infinity; from the
electrifying description of a woman attacked as she lies
sleeping, to the lyrical exploration of myths of El Dorado,
Pauline Melville lures the reader into intriguingly different
worlds. The sheer malevolence of everyday life is offset
with hilarity, which makes the stories both unsettling
and funny.

Fiction   hardcover   £12.95
ISBN 0 7043 5051 3

Agnes Sam
Jesus is Indian
and other South African Stories

A nine-year-old boy is press-ganged from his home in India in the mid-nineteenth century for indentured labour in the British colony of Natal.

A century later in South Africa, Ruthie, torn between playing cricket with the boys and practising walking in high heels with Lindiwe, learns the secret of the Hindu prayer room in a Christian household.

Muslim Kaltoum is separated from her loved sister Khadija, who has run away to marry a Christian.

These subtle and beautiful stories deal with women exiled from their homeland and children brought up in foreign cultures. Set among the Indians of South Africa, they evoke the pain of separation and also the vitality that is needed to survive it.

Fiction   hardcover   £11.95
ISBN 0 7043 5045 9

Sheila Ernst & Lucy Goodison
In Our Own Hands

A book of self-help therapy

Now in its seventh reprint

**'Extremely well written, clear, succinct...
I wholeheartedly recommend it'** *British Journal of
Psychiatry*

In this book the authors show that there are ways to use
therapy which can make our deepest experiences of
oppression conscious, and therefore less undermining.
Therapy which is within our control, which embodies
feminist and socialist values, can support us in making
changes within ourselves which will reflect in our ways of
being, feeling and acting in the world.

This book is for people who

* want to take active control over their lives and
  experience their full potential for feeling and joy

* want to know what therapy is all about and whether it
  can offer anything to them

* want to make an informed choice between the many
  varieties of individual therapy, led groups or self-help
  groups

* want to do some therapy on their own or with a friend

* want to set up, run, and *sustain*, a self-help therapy
  group

The book describes all kinds of therapy from bodywork to
psychoanalytically based therapies, shows with sensitivity
and clarity how to use those techniques which can actually
free us and help us, and gives 140 exercises to use in a self-
help situation.

Psychology/psychotherapy   £6.95
ISBN 0 7043 3841 6

Sue Krzowski & Pat Land, eds
In Our Experience
Workshops at the Women's Therapy Centre

Here is a book for women who want to explore, with others, areas of their experience that they find problematic, exciting, frightening, creative:

Our relationships with our mothers and fathers
Our roles as mothers, workers, leaders
Our identities as women, black women, lesbians
Our problems with our sexuality, and with our bodies.

Sue Krzowski and Pat Land, both experienced leaders of workshops for women, have compiled accounts of some of the key workshops run by the pioneering Women's Therapy Centre in London. The book gives guidelines and inspiration for those who wish to learn to work with others in the same way, to set up and run workshops or self-help groups. It distils the insights from the unique experience of these workshops and provides an invaluable account of what happens when women work together.

In Our Experience is a sequel to the best-selling In Our Own Hands: A Book of Self-Help Therapy.

Psychology/psychotherapy   £6.95
ISBN 0 7043 4065 8